The Scheme

MIA
KAYLA

Dedication

To my grandfather…

Papalo, there is not a single day I don't think of you.
I miss you.
I love you.
And I know we'll see each other again.

Prologue

"WELCOME TO EVANGELINE'S Psychic Readings. Come in young ones." Evangeline's tone was rough, like she was suffering from a sore throat, though her face was serious.

My voice barely squeaked a greeting. "H-hi, I'm Kendall and . . . this is Beth."

The psychic's eyes perused my cousin before intently locking on mine.

Beads of sweat formed on the back of my neck as anxiety rose within me. As I turned back to her, she reached out, took hold of my hand, and flipped it over, surprising me, then she glanced down at my palm.

With a light fingertip, she traced the lines before her knowing eyes met mine again. It was haunting, like she could see into my soul, which sent shivers down my spine. "Hmmm." She reached for my other hand, flipping it over and staring intently as though memorizing every moment in my life through my skin. "Hmmm."

That was all she said before a wicked smile popped up on her face and she turned toward a curtain of beads, which functioned as a door to another room. "Come on back."

I wrapped my arms around my stomach as nervousness bubbled in my chest.

Everyone knew of Evangeline. She was it, the psychic who knew all. People drove from all over the nation to have their fortune told by this one woman. Not to mention I had saved money from my last two birthdays for my turn with her.

She gestured for me to sit on the red cushioned stool in front of the wooden table for two. Well-worn tarot cards were perfectly placed on the circular table.

The build up to this moment was too much to take. I inhaled deeply taking in the scent of the strong incense coming from her candles that lit up the room. I peered back at Beth, who stood by the curtain as I sat down. She wasn't a believer, but I appreciated that she was here for moral support. Though this was about me and my future, I needed her here. I hoped her lack of faith didn't block any truth waiting for me in the stars.

Evangeline patted the top of my hand resting on the table. "Relax, child." Her gray eyes fixed me with a stare. "I know what you came here for." She said it with such certainty that, for the first time in a very long time, hope filled my veins and a lightness spread throughout my limbs. "You want to know what the immediate future holds for your mother."

I released a calming breath at her words, because that was only one of the reasons I'd come.

"More importantly," she continued, "you want to know your own future and I—" An eerie, knowing grin spread across her face. "—know exactly how it will unfold."

Chapter One

BRIAN

IT'S SAID THAT nice guys finish last. Sure, I believed it. At least, that had been my experience thus far. So if that was true, what was the point of being nice? It didn't get you anywhere. It didn't get me this job. It didn't pay the bills, and it sure as hell didn't get me the girl.

Six months ago, I had left Chicago. Six months. And yet I still thought of her. She had jolted me to the core when we didn't work out. Maybe because I thought she could've been the one.

Who the hell knew?

I guess this was what growing up with three sisters and watching Dad and Mom's perfect marriage did to you. I was bound to want the same things they had. But I was too young to be thinking of forever. What twenty-five-year-old guy thought of anything other than getting laid?

Me.

I had issues.

On another boring Friday night, I was sitting on my damn couch. My ass hurt from sitting at work all day, and now, here I was—sitting. My beer was on the table as my laptop rested on my lap. I shook my head, breaking myself from my random thoughts, and focused on the task at hand. I needed to get this proposal done.

"Let's go out, man. Get your ass off that damn couch." Trey, my high school buddy and now New York roommate, swaggered into the living room, buttoning up his blue striped shirt. His black leather shoes tapped against the hardwood floor.

Trey had moved to Manhattan for college. We'd been through a lot together through the years. I loved him like my own sibling, but at times he was a pain in my ass.

I gave him a cursory look, noticing he was ready to hit the club while I sat back, television on low as I sipped my beer and worked. Tonight, I'd needed to get away from the office. I'd been there the last three Fridays past eight, and I was tired of staring at the walls of my four-by-four cubical.

Being a banker at Financial State Bank was no joke. Since I'd moved from Chicago to Manhattan, I'd been working nonstop, trying to expand my portfolio by bringing on more clients. I wasn't a new banker by any means, but I was the rookie in this office. Starting over in Manhattan meant I had to prove myself to management all over again, when I'd already built a rapport in Chicago.

Checking himself in the living room mirror, Trey fixed the front of his dark brown hair and ran one hand down the front of his pressed cotton shirt. I fought the urge to laugh out loud. Trey was a preener. It was hilarious to watch, but I respected him for wanting to look nice, I guess.

"And here's a guy who's gonna have fun tonight." He rubbed his chin, glanced back at the mirror, and then threw a look my way. "Let's go!" He strolled toward the couch and shut my laptop. "Quit being so lame. What're you doing anyway that can't wait 'til Monday?"

I groaned. "Trust me; I'd much rather go out than do this shit all night, but I've got work to do." I flipped open the screen and moved the mouse so I could study the analysis of the Tiggins Corporation. "I have to finish this write-up for credit."

I felt Trey's eyes narrowing on me. "Isn't that shit your underwriter's job? You're such a sucker, man. You're too nice." He slammed my computer shut, harder this time, and almost right on my hands.

Sighing, I rested against the couch, picked up my beer, and chugged it back as the realization hit me that I had turned into an old man at the age of twenty-five.

I didn't answer, because Trey was right. If this underwriter's manager were to get hold of his lazy analysis, he'd be in deep water. A part of me believed I was completing his write-up to save his ass, which proved Trey's point—I was a sucker. I'd bet my next paycheck that twenty-two-year-old underwriter was out getting shit-faced tonight, while I was staying at home doing *his* job.

I cranked my neck from side to side to let loose some of the tension building in me.

Trey snapped his fingers in front of my face, impatient. "What the hell? Let's get going. Work's not gonna get you laid." He reached for my laptop and dropped it on the recliner. "Get your ass changed. I'm not taking no for an answer tonight."

The look on his face told me he'd drag me out by my balls if I didn't comply, so I stood. "Chill, I'm going, okay?"

I needed this anyway. For once, I didn't want to think about Beth, the girl who had left me brokenhearted. I didn't want to think of work, either. I needed to let loose.

I ran one hand down my face, releasing a heavy sigh, and headed to my room to get ready. Trey smirked as I walked past him, knowing he'd won.

Yeah, yeah.

KENDY

I RESTED AGAINST the counter, my arms crossed over my more than plentiful chest, and released a silent sigh as my eyes zoned and took in all of Dr. James Klein—tall, dark, and hot as mother freaking hell itself.

I swallowed my saliva down, preventing a drool pool from leaking out of the side of my mouth. If I didn't have any self-control, I would've been panting like a dog at his total hotness.

Oh, Dr. Hot Pants, I have the biggest crush on you.

I recited this little chant in my head often.

He was at the nurses' station, studying his clipboard, most likely for his next patient. Maybe I could break a bone, catch some sort of virus, anything to get him to notice me. Because I noticed him every second of our evening shift together. I practically dreamed about him in my sleep.

I worked the evening shift—seven p.m. to seven a.m. Lucky for me, I had seven more hours to ogle him.

Right now, I needed his white jacket off so I could check out his ass again. I'd coined him Dr. Hot Pants with the fine ass. And oh, was he super fine.

Since I'd moved to New York a month ago from my small town of Bowlesville, Illinois, I knew my life would be turning up with better opportunities. I was meant for more than the local hospital, where the most excitement that had happened was when our sheriff shot his own foot by accident.

I sighed heavily at the hunk of a man in front of me. As soon as I stepped onto the emergency room floor that first day as an employed nurse of New York Cornell Hospital, I knew, without a shadow of a doubt, that Dr. James Klein would belong to me, my husband-to-be.

He just didn't know it yet, but that didn't matter. I had a plan, and it included a house, marriage, and a baby carriage. At least, I hoped so.

When he started strolling my way, I straightened and adjusted my push-up bra. The way his wavy brown hair moved when he walked made my heart race in my chest. What I wouldn't give to run my fingers through his locks.

When he approached a few feet away, I pretended to look at my clipboard as I stood directly in his path. On purpose.

"How are you today, Kendall?" he asked, his tone smooth like silk.

I'd made it my point in life to turn his tone into hot, hoarse, and heavy, and more importantly, I wanted him screaming my name so even his neighbors knew who I was.

Patience, Kendy, patience.

"Good. Slow night tonight." I threw him my sweet smile and popped out my hip in a Kendy-like fashion, meeting his hot hazel eyes in the process. I tilted slightly to accentuate my curves, subtle, but not over-exaggerated. I wasn't normally this flirty, but I needed to step it up a notch if I wanted his attention.

He moved in closer, smiling his ever-charming smile,

which made my breath hitch in my throat. "Yeah, hopefully the slow night continues." He winked.

"I thought you loved all the excitement in the ER," I said kiddingly.

"Oh, Miss Kendall, I prefer my excitement outside the ER." The huskiness in his voice and his flirty stare increased my pulse rate.

Oh, my goodness gracious.

I bit down on the inside of my cheek to prevent my smile from widening.

He took a step back then peered down at his watch. "I'm going to make my rounds and hopefully cut out to the cafeteria for a snack."

"I'm an evening muncher myself," I joked, trying to give him a hint.

He smiled quickly, but then strode past me and down the hall.

Men.

I huffed out loud just when he was out of hearing range. Sometimes he was hot, yet other times he was ice cold.

Is he oblivious to the fact I'm crushing on him?

I frowned and crossed my arms, having my own little pity party. If I wasn't twenty-four, I'd drop to the ground and pound my feet on the floor like a three-year-old.

I had tried everything in my *Kendy Book of Tricks* to get him to notice me. I'd constantly showed up wherever he was, since I knew when his breaks were. He'd turn around and then *bam*, I'd be there. Did he think it was purely coincidental? He seemed genuinely happy to see me and chat, yet he'd never asked me out.

A woman could only smile so much in his presence. My cheeks hurt from my overly flirty grin. And to top it

all off, I had purposely bought smaller scrubs to accentuate my curves. You'd think I'd get some sort of reaction
out of him. Damn elastic made ridges against my stomach, but still . . .

Nada. Nothing. Zilch.

Maybe I'd have to change my approach, tone down
The Kendy. Be sweeter, more innocent? Maybe he had to
be the one to make the first move?

Yeah, that was probably it. He gave me the impres-
sion he didn't like the aggressive type. After all, a man
needed to feel like a man.

Luckily for him, I was sugary and sweet with a touch
of spice underneath to keep things exciting all day and all
night long.

With a hopeful grin, I watched him disappear down
the hall. As my confidence returned, I flipped my blonde
locks over my shoulder and stopped pouting. I knew
what had to be done.

BRIAN

I SURVEYED MY surroundings at the Clipper Night Club.
The laser lights blinded me as I strolled past security. We
had waited almost an hour to get in. Funny how women,
if in a group, were allowed easy access, but us guys had
to wait outside in line like kids waiting to enter Disney
World. No wonder they called this the Meatpacking District. Men swarmed like flies around the hot women here.

I stepped into the club and sighed heavily as I took in
the crowd. I realized the wait wasn't worth it. I should've
kept my ass at home and gotten that proposal for Tiggins

Corp done. Then I'd have less to worry about come Monday morning. If I intended on getting the promotion, I needed to land this deal.

I tipped my beer back, trying to drive out thoughts of work.

Well, you're already out. Let it go.

I loosened the collar of my button down. The amount of people jammed in the club made this place feel like a sweat lodge. The bass from the music echoed throughout the warehouse, thumping under my feet. That alone should have loosened me up, but it didn't. I let my eyes stray to the cluster of attractive women on the dance floor, swaying in a group.

The scene grew old quickly. I had done this life in college and post-college. I wasn't a saint by any means. A couple years ago, I would've strolled to the middle of the group, thrown the women some lines, bought them a bunch of drinks, and gotten my game on.

Tonight, I wasn't in the mood to *try* too hard. Maybe it was the deal I was trying to land at work, maybe it was getting older, or maybe I was just tired of the same shit, weekend after weekend.

I followed Trey to the bar, where he tried to squeeze through the mass to order us a round of drinks. The bartender, an attractive brunette, was serving the patrons in front of her. I moved in behind Trey, studying the intricate tattoo of a snake wrapped around her arm, which ended at the top of her wrist.

"I'm going to get your ass drunk tonight, loosen you up. We're gonna have a good time, you hear me?" He raised his hand to get the bartender's attention.

She ducked her head to take his order and proceeded to get our beverages. Trey threw some change on the bar and passed me my beer, then we headed to a less crowded area as the laser lights illuminated the space while the music blared in the background.

Trey's eyes roamed our vicinity. "BB, twelve o'clock. Dude, she's looking this way."

BB, meaning beautiful blonde. In high school we used to talk with abbreviations to get our game on. He pointed his beer bottle in her direction, and she smiled back at us.

"Blonde? Not my type." When pictures of a brunette with emerald eyes entered my mind, I rubbed the back of my neck and shook my head to bring me back to the present.

"Come on. You've been in town for months, and you haven't met any ladies. You're dick is gonna fall off from lack of use. Let's do this." He lifted his fist, waiting for me to fist-bump.

After a beat, I complied and connected my fist to his. "You go." I cocked my head in the girl's direction. "She's more your type."

Trey winced. "That was high school. I don't do blondes anymore."

I recognized the hint of hurt in his voice. Shit. I should've caught myself before I spoke.

Trey had dated my younger sister, Katelyn, for three years. Blonde, blue eyes, and beautiful. We'd gone to the same high school together in Wisconsin, but he'd up and moved to NYC to go to college and eventually work for his father.

I still didn't know what had happened between them, but from what I understood, he'd been the one left brokenhearted. If it had been the other way around and my sister had been heartbroken, he'd have gotten an ass-whipping. Being the older brother of three sisters, I'd always been overprotective.

But Trey didn't like to talk about that time in his life; therefore, I didn't force the issue.

He sat down on a stool next to me, his light and ready-to-party demeanor from a second ago now gone. This was turning into a sad night real fast. I tipped my beer all the way back, glancing back at the BB. It wasn't that I didn't have game. I was just tired of playing.

But for my boy, I'd do just about anything. I needed to lighten the atmosphere, so I zoned in on the blonde and took a deep breath. "All right then. Let me show you how it's done." I patted Trey's shoulder and stood.

Trey perked up immediately and slapped my back before I strode to the other side of the room.

The blonde was attractive, but in a slightly fake way. Thick makeup caked her face and bright crimson lipstick lined her lips. Up close, I could tell she was a bottle blonde. She reeked of wealth. I'd seen it many times before. The ladies of Manhattan liked to flaunt their belongings and their assets.

I focused automatically on the curvature of her breasts. Her V-neck halter made it known she wanted everyone to notice her body.

I debated turning back around since I didn't have time to think of a pick-up line, but she beat me to the punch. "Hey, handsome, you come over here to buy me a drink?" She touched my arm and angled forward so I could get a closer peek at her chest.

"What you having, beautiful?" I nodded in her direction.

She forced out a high-pitched laugh, and my eyes roamed up her slim, yet voluptuous figure. I knew what she'd come here for. Sitting at the bar, no girlfriends.

I didn't want to assume, but hell, her body language was spelling it all out. She'd come here to get laid.

Maybe I should've been upfront: *Let's go to the bathroom and get it done.* Still, the Midwestern boy in me knew there was a process to these things.

"I'll have a gin and tonic." The lilt in her voice sounded soft, cute, and somehow disconnected to her overdone appearance.

Part of me still wanted to walk away, but then Trey gave me a smirking nod from down the bar and I sucked it up once again.

After I ordered her a cocktail and another beer for myself, I leaned against the bar next to her. "Why are you here all by yourself? I know you women travel in packs." I forced a suave smile, my normal bravado lacking.

Her red manicured fingers inched up my chest. "I'm glad they're not here because I'm sure we would've had to draw straws for you." She laughed softly and batted her eyelashes. Her eyes held a sensual flame as they roamed up my body. "You're not from around here; I can tell. I've never seen you in here."

"I don't get out much." I tipped back my beer as I threw her my smooth smile, but when my eyes met hers, my stomach sank, because there was nothing—no spark—and I knew I'd already grown tired of a conversation that had only just begun. How was it possible to feel lonely when this woman was standing right in front of me?

"I just moved here from Chicago. Moved in with my best friend." I tilted my head in Trey's direction, who was already chatting up another woman, a brunette with a short bob. By the way she angled toward him, I could tell my boy was doing well. "How about you? You grow up here?"

"Born and raised in Manhattan. Most people here are transfers, but this is the place I call home." She crossed her legs, her skirt hitching up higher on her thighs. "I didn't catch your name. I'm Denise." A flirtatious smile crossed her face as she seductively bit her lower lip.

I gave her my name and downed the rest of my beer. I could tell this girl knew what she wanted, and I wasn't about to tell her no.

FOUR BEERS AND three cocktails later, Trey disappeared, nowhere to be seen. But Denise had just delved into her aspirations of becoming a model. She was on the hunt, currently scouting agents, and her mother served as her manager.

I'd found out that she was barely of drinking age, which had surprised me. She looked mid-twenties with all that caked on makeup. Too bad, because under all that grime I could see the attractiveness of her small features. It was unfortunate she felt the need to cover it up.

She angled into me for the millionth time, practically sitting in my lap. I got another whiff of her strong expensive perfume and barely stopped myself from coughing.

Her eyes glossed over, and I had to admit that I, too, was well into the hella-good zone. She giggled at everything I spilled out, and when she peered up at me with her dark-as-night pupils, I cupped the side of her face and kissed her.

Instantly, she opened her mouth to let me in and, within the next few seconds, her hand had moved down the front of my jeans. My cock stiffened on contact.

We made out for a couple minutes as she continued

to give me a hand job. I teased and suckled her lips as my cock strained against my pants, needing to break free.

And then she pulled back, breathless. "Wanna get out of here?" she slurred.

My eyes met hers then flickered to her lips. I felt nothing. Absolutely nothing when I kissed her. Maybe this was a good thing.

"My place is just down the street," she said sweetly as her hand brushed against the bulge in my jeans.

Shit. I wanted this, but I didn't.

I hadn't gotten laid in a while, and all of me needed this. But I didn't need complications, especially since my last relationship had failed. I wasn't ready for anything serious. I didn't have time for that with my responsibilities at work.

Judging from the smirk on her face, it didn't seem like she was looking for a relationship either. We were the perfect detached duo looking for a little excitement.

I nodded. "Yeah, let's get out of here." I reached for her hand and scanned the place for Trey. If I left, he'd know what happened. Hell, he'd probably wished this on me, since I'd been working like a dog. If anything, he had the same plan in mind for tonight.

We were about to exit, when I jerked to a stop. I glanced dazedly behind me to find a massive, tattooed male in a leather vest, gripping Denise's other hand and staring at me like he wanted to stuff my balls in my mouth.

Oh hell.

He shot daggers at Denise. "What're you doing here? I thought you were staying in tonight." His tone seethed with mounting rage.

I released her hand, unable to bite back the guilt.

'*Sorry, dude, you've just been played,*' didn't even need to be said. I'd been there.

I turned, about to leave them to handle their business, when he twisted her arm and her face registered pain. "You fucking whore! Is this the guy you're screwing?"

"Stop, Damon. You're hurting me," she yelped. "Let go!" She yanked her arm back, but couldn't budge as the man, I assumed to be her boyfriend, crushed her skinny arm in his grasp.

Watching him sobered me up real quick. Okay, so I wasn't the most standup guy out there, but I sure as hell wasn't going to witness this prick hurt her.

I stepped in between them, straightening my stance. "Listen, the lady said let her go." My voice was firm as I squared my shoulders, sizing him up.

He released her with a growl, and I tilted my head to take in his height. He had a few inches on me, but we had the same build. I'd taken down guys bigger than him before, but I wasn't expecting his aggression to escalate to a fight.

"Why the hell are you with my girl?" he growled, the veins on his neck bulging.

Before I even had a chance to respond—*POW!* In the face.

Surprised, I staggered back. My hand flew to my eye as pulsing pain rushed to the surface, the brass ring on his middle finger most likely leaving an indentation on my skin. The stickiness of blood gushed down my face.

Great, just fucking great.

I pulled back my arm, ready to fire back and beat the shit out of this bastard, but then Denise sheltered him with her body, saying to him in a panic, "I'm sorry, baby. I'm so sorry."

He narrowed his eyes at me until she threw herself at him and started kissing his face, running her hands up and down his shoulders.

I blinked and shook my head at the comedy of this scene, then let out a low, humorless laugh as the taste of iron hit my mouth.

When I felt someone behind me, I automatically brought up my fists, ready to spring into action in case his friends wanted to play 'beat the nice guy.'

"Whoa, dude, it's me." Trey was behind me with his hands up as if he was about to be the victim of my aggression. "You'll bleed dry if I don't get you to a hospital."

I groaned, knowing from the pain and the amount of blood oozing from above my eyebrow I'd probably need stitches. Having played football throughout high school and being the rambunctious kid that I'd been, I was familiar with the protocol. I unbuttoned my shirt, jumbled it into a ball, and applied pressure to the wound.

Shithead wasn't worth it. I could've taken him, but I needed to get fixed up and head home. Shit, I should've just stayed home, in front of my damn computer. Less drama.

"You'll need stitches," Trey said, following me out.

"Yeah, I know," I muttered.

Life was a bitch sometimes.

More recently, it seemed that bitch was intent on taking me down.

Chapter Two

KENDY

I ADJUSTED THE Michael Kors watch on my wrist. The larger than life gold dial told me I still had six more hours until my shift ended.

Coffee was calling my name and, as I advanced toward the nurses' station, I caught Sarah, my cute little friend, charging my way.

Her dark, pin-straight hair bounced as she rushed toward me. At five-four, half Hispanic and half German, she was a looker. When I'd met her on my first day, she'd slapped her ass and said that her big ole' booty had come from her Spanish side. She functioned as my daily dose of laughter, something I especially craved since I was the newbie and didn't know many people.

Sarah reached for my arm, catching her breath as though she'd just run a race. "What're you doing tomorrow?" The enthusiasm on her face and suffocated rasp in her voice from running had me smiling.

I noted her flushed cheeks and wondered if she was late to work. "Where are you coming from?"

She wheezed a short laugh. "I tried to chase down the late night burrito truck, but I couldn't catch up."

I couldn't control the fit of giggles that escaped my

lips. "That's totally something I'd do." I led us to the set of chairs against the wall. "What's going on?"

By the mischievous look in her eyes, I knew something was going down.

"I have gossip." She leaned in, her elbows resting on her knees, and I followed her lead. "So . . . I know where the hot doctors are going to be tomorrow."

"Even my man?" I asked, my heart fluttering against my ribcage. I crossed my fingers and toes, waiting for her reply.

I trusted Sarah. She had been good about keeping my secret about my big crush on Dr. Klein.

"Even your man," she cooed as she fluttered her lashes at me.

I didn't even try to hide my cheeky grin as I bounced on my toes and shook my shoulders in a shimmy motion. "Okay, details," I whispered to her, looking around to see if anyone could overhear.

Sarah always had the ins and outs of everyone's love life in the hospital, another reason why I loved her.

I knew we'd be best buds for life when she'd made it her secret mission to help me achieve my goals in landing him. In return, I had promised her a spot in our wedding.

"Well, you know that bar right down the street, The Bartlett?" Sarah's copper eyes widened with delight. "I know for a fact that your man and a bunch of other good-looking residents are meeting there tomorrow night."

She gripped my forearm a little harder than expected, startling me. "So are you going with me?"

"Uh, yeah, hello?" I absently rubbed at my arms, lifting an eyebrow at the silly question. "You did say my doctor would be going."

She chuckled and let out a hushed squeal.

Why hadn't I thought to track him down outside of work? I'm surprised I hadn't stalked him sooner. This would be the first time I'd see him out of the hospital.

Now what would I wear? My brain started going off on a tangent. I'd been working on getting him to ask me out on a date, purely by being my charming self, but now I had the chance to dress to impress. "Let me know the time and I'm there. I'll be bringing sexy back."

We gave each other a grinning high-five before discussing the plan.

My phone buzzed in my pocket interrupting our giddy session and indicating a new patient. "Hey, I'll check you later. Let me know a time tomorrow."

She reached over and gave me a hug, practically killing me with her squeeze. It was obvious she was excited to play cupid, a role she played often. "See you later," she sang, turning to head down the hall.

I picked up the phone, the nurse informing me that my next patient was a kid with a busted knee. "Room one-oh-three? Okay, I'm on it." I slipped the phone back into my pocket and rushed down the hall.

When I heard the high-pitched wails of a young child, I charged toward the room, ready to spring into action. "Hi, I'm Kendall Miller," I said in my professional but warm nurse tone.

I stuck out my hand, automatically introducing myself to the child's mother. But then I reeled back when I saw a familiar redhead—Clary Clensen, Bowlesville's biggest skank.

My blood pressure rose. Had I straight up died and gone to Hell? I searched frantically around the room. Maybe I could run out and get her another nurse before she recognized me.

"Oh my goodness, Kendy!" Clary clasped her hands together as her son, no more than four, continued to wail in front of her. An older woman was cradling the boy in her arms as Clary's protruding eyes scrutinized me.

She was wearing four-inch Louboutins designer shoes, and sitting at the edge of the bed was her Chanel purse, chilling like there was no tomorrow.

Funny how she acted with forced excitement, happy to see me, when we both knew we hated each other's guts.

"Kendall," I corrected her, adding under my breath, "Only my friends call me Kendy." Even though everyone in my small town called me Kendy, I refused to be called a beloved nickname by this hooch.

I would never forgive her for what she'd done. Never. Ever. Even when I was ten feet under dirt.

"You're a . . . nurse?" There it was—the condescending edge to her tone.

It took all my self-control to force a smile. "Yep." I moved past her to wash my hands and slip on gloves. Regardless of how much we despised each other, there was a hurt child in front of me, and I had a job to do.

I advanced toward the cute child with a full head of short brown curls. "Shhh. It's okay, buddy," I told the little boy. He cowered inward, now sobbing quietly, but I couldn't get a direct look at his knee. "I need to see your owie, bud. So I can make it better."

I gave him a small smile, though he paid no attention since the pain consumed him.

I turned to Clary. "What happened?"

"I'm not too sure. I wasn't there." She turned to the older woman. "Anne?"

"He slipped and fell against a glass table." Anne rocked the boy, held him against her chest and continually rubbed his arms to calm him.

My smile turned sympathetic. This was not going to be fun. Even being a nurse, I still hated watching people in pain, but seeing kids hurting tore at my insides. Each and every time, I'd wish it was me instead. Or even better—some other mean bitch, like Clary. Why couldn't she have fallen on the glass table?

"We're going to have him lay down," I said firmly.

The little boy started to scream, and Clary narrowed her eyes at him, propping one hand on her hip. "Billy Bob, you need to quiet it down."

My eyebrows shot to the ceiling.

Billy Bob? What the hell? We're not in Bowlesville anymore.

Sighing, I turned to Clary. "Can you hold him still? I'll need to examine his wound and get a better look to see if he'll need stitches."

Clary just stood stoic in her spot.

I quirked an eyebrow at her and waited for her to react. Do something. Anything. In the next second, I was about to cross the professional line and smack her on the side of her head.

"Anne will lay him down. She's his nanny."

I rolled my eyes as I moved toward the poor child.

Focus on the task at hand.

Billy Bob started to flail his arms as Anne tried to restrain him against the hospital bed. Blood trickled from his wound, spilling over to the white linen. The scent of iron, a familiar scent in my line of business, hit my nostrils.

I shot Clary an impatient look. "You'll need to hold his lower body."

Anne continued to kiss the boy's forehead while his own freaking mother stood there, fidgeting with her bracelet, looking like she was afraid to break a nail.

I shot daggers at her. Any moment now I was about to let her have it, but finally Clary removed her jacket, rolled up her sleeves in slow motion, and held his sides, as if her child wasn't wailing and his knee wasn't oozing blood.

I leaned in to get a better look. When I swiped the infected area with an alcohol swab, he flinched and his cries heightened.

"It's okay, buddy. We'll get you better."

I stepped back, reached into my pocket, and paged Dr. Klein. A few minutes later, he entered our room and Chlamydia Clary—as I had nicknamed her way back when—suddenly and mysteriously brightened up.

Surprise, surprise.

"Hi, I'm Dr. Klein." He gave Clary his professional smile before his eyes focused on the boy, assessing him from across the room. His voice softened as he approached the hospital bed. "It's okay. I'm here to fix you all up."

Clary straightened her shirt and displayed her winning smile as she stepped away from the child. I stood there, frozen, and gawked as they shook hands.

Oh, hell no.

I stood taller, my bones tensing like a cat ready to spring in between them.

"It's okay, Billy Bob," Clary cooed as she replaced Anne and held her son.

Unbelievable. A minute ago, she'd wanted nothing to do with him.

In my periphery, I saw Dr. Klein's mouth twitch at the boy's name. Though Clary's fakeness raked on my nerves, I released a dry cynical chuckle. Being fake was my biggest pet peeve. You should never be fake, unless a man was lying on top of you and you wanted to spare his feelings.

Dr. Klein continued with protocol, asking the questions he needed to ask before he continued with the stitches. The laceration stretched deep enough you could see the child's muscle. His wound spanned more than one-fourth of an inch deep, verifying the need for stitches. I assisted and held the boy down, watching Dr. Klein's hands administer a numbing shot and steadily mend the boy's wounds. His fingers moved slowly and deliberately, and my imagination went wild, visualizing how his hands would feel on me. With the same precision, I was sure.

"So, Billy, are you into any sports?" Dr. Klein's head peeked up as he continued to suture the cut. "Are you a Mets or Yankees fan?"

The diversion was working as the boy mouthed Mets through his tear-filled eyes.

"I root for the Mets as well." He smiled warmly at the boy.

A few minutes later, he finished and the boy seemed better, all patched up. His loud cries had turned into soft whimpers.

Dr. Klein patted Billy's shoulder. "All done, buddy."

Clary stepped away from the bed and, without warning, pulled my doctor into a half hug. He moved away, but not before she squeezed his big arms. "Thank you," she said in a tone that didn't match her real voice. "You saved my son."

His eyes widened as though he wasn't expecting such an overly affectionate gesture.

My fists bunched at my sides, annoyance rising within me.

Saved her son? He needed stitches on his damn knee.

I didn't know why this surprised me, though. Clary had always reigned as queen of melodrama in high school. I doubted things had changed.

"You're welcome," he replied, backing away, looking slightly uncomfortable.

I bit my tongue before a snippy comment fell out of my mouth, and I was turning to leave, when the bling on her ring finger caught my eye. It was massive and gaudy in a way that said 'I'm a gold-diggin' hoe'.

So she was married. And flirting with Dr. Klein. *Figures.*

"So, who's the lucky guy who brought you to New York?" I asked sweetly to disguise my disgust.

She seemed taken aback as Dr. Klein cleaned up, disposed of his gloves, and moved to the sink. "His name is Arthur Jennings the Third." Her tone oozed with arrogance as she turned her nose up. "He's into real estate."

Now that Dr. Klein was blatantly ignoring her, not interested in her trying-too-hard self, she felt the need to brag about the poor loser who'd won her.

I forced a smile as I gritted my teeth. "I'm so happy for you. You deserve to be happy after Tommy left you for your sister. How is Abigail, anyway?"

Clary blanched, and I tried my hardest not to laugh. If looks could kill, I'd be dead on the floor.

Dr. Klein moved into Clary's line of sight. "He'll be fine. The stitches should dissolve within a week or two."

"Thanks so much." And there it was, that annoying fake tone, which sounded like a squeaky irritating little mouse. The one that made me want to puke my dinner all over her Louboutins.

He offered her a small smile, one that usually made my heart swell, but not today, when Clary was all up in my face, dampening my mood.

I propped one hand on my hip. "I'm sure your husband will be so glad your son is okay," I called out as Dr. Klein waved to Anne and Billy Bob and then exited the room.

Clary's eyes turned murderous as she flipped toward me. "Oh, boy. I see Kendy has her sights on a certain doctor." She picked up her designer purse and glided it up to her slender shoulder. "I wonder if I should warn him about you. Does he know?" She flipped her long red locks off her shoulders. "That you can't keep a man?"

My muscles tensed as I fisted my hands at my sides, my nails digging into my palms. The next second, I charged toward her, mere inches from her face. I had a sudden urge to knock her cold on her ass. But that wouldn't have hurt her as much as she'd already hurt me.

She reeled back, but I moved even closer, just so she understood that she had messed with the wrong girl. "What did you say?" I tilted my head to egg her on.

She took a step back.

When she didn't speak, because she was a chicken shit, I narrowed my eyes as I threw words out at her like stones. "Expensive clothing, designer bags, and even a new city won't take the sleaze out of Bowlesville's biggest skank."

At that, I turned around and walked out the door, but not before she yelled out, "You know Cole was sleeping with me the whole time you two were together."

My fingers twitched as I stopped mid-step. Their indiscretion had hurt me, but the pain Cole had caused went above the cheating. Something only Beth knew . . . because she was the only one I'd told.

It took all my self-control not to lose it in front of her. I gritted my teeth, stomped down the hall, and tried to calm my breathing. I walked into the supply room, shut the door behind me, rested against the wall, and slid down to the floor. My chin trembled as I tried to calm the emotions brewing inside me.

Breathe. Just breathe.

I pulled my knees up, dropping my chin to my chest as painful memories paraded through my mind. A lump formed in my throat, and my body trembled as a glimmer of my past resurfaced. It was amazing how one experience with a man could alter your view on every man in your life.

Every relationship post-Cole had been short-lived. Though I didn't know if I could call my quick hook-ups real relationships.

My eyes fell shut. I couldn't do this now. Not at work. I couldn't let him affect me. He'd already taken too much.

My phone buzzed in my pocket again, thankfully breaking me from my thoughts and bringing me back to the present. Standing up, I swiped the budding tears from my eyes. I was bigger than this. I had my eyes set on someone new now, someone perfect for me. And tonight I'd drown myself in work and forget about Chlamydia Clary, Cole, and anything remotely related to my past.

BRIAN

THE CHEMICAL SMELL of the hospital wafted through

the room as I applied pressure to the cut.

"Are you sure you don't want me to stay here? Hold your hand or something?" Trey smirked, though his eyes narrowed in concern.

"Nah, go ahead. I wouldn't want you to cry or pass out from all the blood," I joked back, though my own sole focus was on not passing out. Once Trey left the room, I rested against the hospital bed, focusing on the ceiling.

When the door opened, I couldn't help but take in the attractive woman in the blue scrubs. The cotton fabric hugged her hips and accentuated her well- endowed chest. Even lightheaded, I could appreciate the curves. Then, when my eyes landed on a familiar pair of blue eyes, I couldn't help but sigh at my luck.

Fucking-A!

What were the chances that the nurse in front of me was the best friend of the girl who'd broken my heart?

"Kendy?" I had to make sure my luck hadn't just gotten worse.

At her name, her head flipped up from the clipboard, and her eyes flew to my chest then up to meet my eyes. I knew when she recognized me, because a swift shadow of shock swept across her features before she threw me a mean girl look.

I clenched my jaw and stifled a laugh. If I hadn't wanted to see her, the expression on her face indicated she wanted to see me even less.

"It's Kendall." Her tone was harsh, and the scowl on her face implied she was already in a foul mood. She lifted her head and started talking to the ceiling. "Seriously? What have I done? Is this some cruel joke? Am I getting punk'd here?" She scanned the room, looking for filming cameras, which clearly weren't there, then she fixed me with another glare. "I'm getting you another nurse."

A deep chuckle escaped my mouth. Too weird. What were the chances?

I found this situation unlikely, too coincidental, but even more humorous. I forced the smile off my face. Even annoyed, I had to admit she looked adorably cute. Her eyes wavered on what to do next as she bit down on her bottom lip.

The blood continued to drip down my face, onto my bare chest, as the sticky T-shirt I held soaked it up. "I'm bleeding here, Kendy."

"I. Am. Not. Kendy. My name is Kendall," she huffed and charged toward me, her temper rising with her words. "Forget it. The sooner I do this, the sooner you'll be out of my hair." She ripped my T-shirt from my hand and slanted toward me.

The sweet scent of peaches entered my nostrils. Shampoo or perfume? Whatever it was, I angled closer to get another whiff. The scent was intoxicating, or maybe it was the loss of blood causing my head to spin.

"How small is New York City?" she mumbled to herself. "To the point that I've seen two people from my past . . . well, sort of . . . and in my hospital?"

"Your hospital?" I raised an eyebrow, amused at her annoyance.

She threw me a nasty look, her eyes turning a darker shade of blue, as if they changed color with her moods. "Yes, sir. My freaking hospital." She pulled a pair of nitrile gloves from her pocket and slipped them on. The snap of the gloves against her skin echoed through the room.

When she opened up an alcohol swab and swiped at the open wound at my brow, I flinched as the cold stung against my skin.

"First, Chlamydia Clary, and now you. Everyone from freaking Bowlesville is creeping into my business." Her clipped curt tone was the complete opposite to her gentle professional touch, which had a calming effect, though the throbbing pain was still present.

"I'm not from Bowlesville," I corrected her. "I'm from Madison, and this is the main hospital in the metropolitan area." Anyone in the city who needed to be rushed to a hospital would end up at New York Cornell.

"So?!" She pressed the alcohol swab farther into my wound, and I winced at the burn. I wondered if she did it on purpose. A second later, her face softened. "Sorry," she mumbled, dropping the swab.

I reached for her free hand, my body acting on its own accord, and our eyes locked. A jolt of electricity surged between us. At five-five, an overall cuteness surrounded her. How had I never noticed it before? Her blonde hair was perfectly curled, and her makeup only highlighted her soft yet stunning features.

She smirked, catching me staring. "I'm not your type, boy." A moment later, her hand brushed against my chest. "I'm way out of your league." She leaned in closer, inches from my face, her breath tickling my skin as she whispered in my ear, "And I most definitely don't fuck good boys."

She drew her hand back as the blood from my wound immediately rushed south instead. Her naughty mouth was so out of her small town character, but so damn hot.

"Ouch," I said, placing a hand on my own heart, feigning pain. I was hurting all right, but the ache wasn't in my chest.

She flipped her hair over her shoulder, turned, and strode to the counter. I watched her perfectly sculpted ass move from side to side.

"It's not that you're not cute. I'm just not into your type." She threw the gloves and swab in the red trash can then moved toward the table.

My curiosity was piqued. "And what is your type?" My eyes zoned in on her apple ass as she turned to lay out her medical supplies on the metal table.

She shrugged casually. "Not the good boy, that's for sure."

"I was just in a bar fight. How am I a good boy?" I silenced another chuckle.

"Doesn't matter. I'm dating someone," she said.

My shoulders sunk at her words. They shouldn't have. I didn't need or have time for a girlfriend, so I didn't understand why I felt even an ounce of disappointment.

"Who beat you up?" She changed topics on me so fast I got whiplash.

I cringed as I remembered the whole stupid story. "Some random guy."

"What did you do to get this guy super pissed enough to draw blood?" She quirked an eyebrow, a sly smile on her face.

"Hit on his girl and tried to take her home."

Her gentle laughter rippled through the air, the change in her mood even more refreshing than her earlier annoyance. "No, you did not." Her eyes showed amusement, surprise even.

"Not a nice guy move, is it? Hitting on another guy's girl?"

"But you didn't know, did you? And I bet you didn't even get in a good hit." She crossed her arms over her chest and quirked an eyebrow.

I pushed my fist into my palm, playing the tough guy.

"You should've seen the other guy. He could barely even stand, let alone walk out of that club when I was done. Him and his friends."

Her eyes flickered to my biceps before landing back on my face. "Really?"

I shook my head as a deep chuckle escaped my lips. "No, the guy handed me my ass."

An irresistible devastating grin spread across her face. Her laughter was infectious, causing my lips to turn up wider in response. I noticed she had the cutest subtle dimple on her chin, and a sudden urge to run my tongue along her jawline came over me.

"Come on, did you even get a hit in? Surprise him with your fist against his jaw?"

I shrugged one shoulder. "I didn't want to deal with it. I just wanted to get home." Mentally cussing out Trey, I remembered I hadn't even wanted to go out in the first place.

She tilted her head, her blue eyes studying me. "See? You're too nice."

"Nope. I just have bad luck." Lately, that stroke of bad luck kept on stroking.

A knock on the door broke our conversation. When the doctor peered in, Kendy gave a nod, straightened, and popped her hip out, throwing a charming smile his way.

Her boyfriend?

I took him in, already sizing him up.

"Hi, I'm Dr. Klein." He strolled in, looking like he had a stick up his ass as he shook my hand. He had a weak handshake for someone of his stature and build. Being a little over six feet tall, I'd expected a firmer grip. He stood no taller than five-eight as his eyes assessed me.

"Brian Benson."

Kendy cleared her throat, and we turned our attention her way. "Hi, Dr. Klein." A forced sweetness, which hadn't been there a minute ago, flowed out of her. She fluttered her eyelashes, yet something kept them apart.

Maybe they're not together and she's just flirting with him.

I coughed to cover up my laugh, fixing her with a stare. It was funny to watch her turn professional all of a sudden when, a minute ago, she'd been reaming me out for bleeding at her hospital.

"Brian Benson, twenty-five-year-old male—"

"I gave the doctor my name already." I tried to hide the amusement in my tone, but failed.

She threw me the dirtiest look, but composed herself, covering it up with a smile when she realized that still had Dr. Stiff's attention. "A one-inch laceration by the eyebrow caused by a major impact to the face. Heavy bleeding for the last twenty minutes, indicated on his paperwork. No dizziness reported by the patient. He'll most likely need stitches."

Kendy handed the doctor some blue gloves, her hand lingering on his, but he seemed unaffected as he turned to me and proceeded to do his doctoral duties. I caught disappointment on her face, confirming her feelings were indeed one-way. That shouldn't have made me feel good, but it did.

Dr. Stiff numbed the area with a local anesthetic, threaded the needle, and then placed a hand on my shoulder, indicating I should lie down. I followed his lead.

"We're going to stitch you up. Just a couple to close this wound. They should dissolve in one to two weeks." His chipper tone irked me. Like he wasn't about to stick a damn needle through my skin. I was sure they'd seen more gruesome injuries in the ER.

Resting against the hospital bed, I closed my eyes, and then flinched when I felt the needle pierce my skin. As many times as I'd had stitches from playing football and being the rambunctious only boy in the family, I should've been used to the pain. But pain was pain. Before I had counted backward from ten, he'd completed his task.

"All right, we're done here."

I sat up, touching my brow as the roughness of the stitches brushed against my fingertips. He met me at eye level, forced a small smile, and shook my hand before quickly turning away. The gesture seemed practiced, like he'd learned it in medical school.

I pushed myself up to a sitting position. "Thanks, doc," I said as he reached into his pocket for his phone.

He barely acknowledged my presence before turning to Kendy. Where had this guy learned his bedside manner? "Kendall, can you clean up here? I've been paged to the front."

"Of course, Dr. Klein." There was that lilt in her voice again, and her eyes lit up like fireworks while he fumbled with his phone, then left the room.

She paid no attention to me as she tidied up the medical tools and my bloody mess.

"So, is that the lucky man?"

Her eyes finally met mine, sparkling as they did when Dr. Stiff had been in the room. "Yeah. Isn't he divine?"

I could hear the swoon in her voice.

Ugh.

My eyes flickered back at the door, where Stiff had walked out. Was she serious? I wanted to tell her straight up 'no'; he was far from divine.

"How long have you been together?" I knew they

weren't an item, but I wanted to entertain myself with her reply.

"Well . . ." My question had caught her by surprise, and her face faltered. "We're . . . we're not really together, just yet." Her cheeks flushed red, her self-confidence fading.

I lifted an eyebrow, waiting for some explanation as I barely bit back a shit-eating grin.

Before I could add to that, a short woman with dark hair walked in and handed Kendy some papers. Her eyes flew to mine before shooting back to Kendy. "He's going to be at Bartlett's tomorrow night. For sure. Just confirmed it." She threw Kendy a cheesy smile before saying, "You're welcome." And then she disappeared as fast as she'd come.

Kendall clasped her hands together like she'd won the lotto. She bounced on her toes, and a tinge of jealousy came over me. I hadn't had a girl excited about me in a while, and watching her made me realize how much I missed feeling wanted.

A moment later, she seemed to remember I was in the room. She narrowed her eyes and turned back to her medical supplies, disposing of the items in the red box on the counter. "Let's just say he'll be my boyfriend in the very near future. He doesn't know it yet, but he's going to fall madly in love with me." She grinned to herself.

I threw back my head, unable to control my laughter.

Her head flipped in my direction, and she stomped toward me until her pointed finger rested on my chest. "It's not funny. I'm taking it slow, but once he's fallen for me, it's going to be game over for him. He's my 'it' man."

"You're pretty confident," I quipped.

"Yes, well I have a lot of experience in the language

of love." She tilted toward me as if telling me a little secret then ducked her head until she was mere inches from me. "And I've got the power of the 'P'." Her eyes moved downward to between her legs. A small laugh escaped her lips. "Heaven on Earth down there," she whispered before winking.

Well, hell.

My cock hardened at her seductive tone, and my eyes traveled the length of her body. She had said it half-jokingly, but somehow I knew she meant it. I shifted to adjust myself, and it seemed as though she'd caught it, because the next second, she took a step back.

"You, my friend," she said, pointing a finger in my direction, "are never going to feel the power. I'm not trying to marry you." She raised her chin in indignation then turned around to grab the rest of the mess. "Good luck, Brian. There are papers on the counter with instructions. Refrain from getting the stitches wet. They should dissolve in a week or two, just like the doctor said."

She didn't bother to turn around, and all I could think was that she had some magical shit happening down there. Supernatural powers that could quite possibly change one man's world. I adjusted myself from the major erection I had going on, and once I deemed it safe, I went to look for Trey.

Chapter Three

KENDY

I RUBBED MY eyes open and looked at the digital clock on my mahogany dresser. The red numbers indicated three in the afternoon.

I stretched my arms, reaching toward the ceiling and released a satisfying sigh. My muscles were still tense, my body tired from my twelve-hour shift last night. More than that, my brain was mentally exhausted from all the run-ins with people from my former life.

The air conditioning in the background blasted on high. It was so comfortable I debated going back to sleep, but I remembered my meeting with a certain doctor, which jolted me from my half slumber and had an instant smile on my face.

My phone rang next to me, breaking me from my thoughts. A picture of my arm thrown around a beautiful brunette, my cousin, Beth, flashed on the screen. I picked up on the second ring.

"Kendy!" she squealed. Of course she had been up for hours already, since it was well into the afternoon.

"Hey," I replied, my voice still hoarse.

"Sorry I missed your call yesterday. Kent and I . . . well . . ."

I groaned. "I don't need to hear about your por-no-filled escapades."

She giggled, and I smiled as heaviness grew in my chest. I missed her. Our roles were reversed now. I had played the role of comforting her when she'd moved to Chicago, and now that she was all settled in and I had moved to New York, far away from family, I was the one who needed comforting.

I didn't want to seem needy, so I spewed out information I knew she'd find interesting. "You'll never guess who came strolling into my hospital with a busted eye."

"Who?"

"Brian-freaking-Benson."

"No way." Her pitch increased an octave. "Wow, what're the chances? What happened to his eye?"

"Well, he accidentally fell on someone's fist." I chuckled.

"Kendy, that's not funny." I could practically picture her frown.

"I know." I thought back to the night before, him bleeding all over his shirt and the six-pack he'd been rocking. I sighed. "Seriously though, he was the cutest thing. All bleeding and shirtless. Remind me again. You guys never got naked, did you?"

"No! We never went that far. And quiet yourself down, Kent is right beside me."

I laughed at her unease. "What? He's right inside you? Kinky. I like."

"Stop it, please," she whispered. "How's he doing, anyway?"

"He looked fine. I mean, whoa, that boy is fine, fine, fine. Are you sure you didn't pick the wrong guy?"

"Kendy," she scolded again. I heard her shift and

whisper to Kent. "There's only one for me."

I heard a smacking of lips and rolled my eyes. I needed a barf bag at how unbelievably cute they were.

"Hold on, I'm moving into the living room."

"Holding," I replied, shifting off the comforter. I swung my legs over the side of the bed, headed to the kitchen, then reached into the fridge for a jug of milk. I was probably the only adult in NYC who loved cold milk in the middle of the afternoon. Growing up, it was always hot cocoa in the evening before I went to sleep, and cold ass milk in the morning with my cereal and afternoon snack. Milk had done my body good.

I tipped my glass back, enjoying the cold drink, which awakened me further. As I set my glass down on the counter, I wondered if Beth had put me on hold to have a quickie with her man. "Girlfriend, you there?"

"Yeah. Sorry. Kent gets all loco jealous. You know him."

I would've spewed out some smartass remark, but I held my tongue. In their relationship, Beth wore the pants.

"I just wanted to check on you. I worry about you being there all alone."

"You worry about me? Pfft. I've got my big girl panties on. I've met a couple people at work. I'm all good in the neighborhood." I held the phone closer to my ear as my body slumped against the counter. I missed her voice, but I didn't want to be that needy friend. If I complained that these people I'd met were nice, but nothing compared to our eighteen years of friendship, she'd book the next flight to New York.

"Kendy?"

"Yeah?"

"Was Brian okay?"

"Is this your guilty conscience talking?" I tilted my head.

I knew she had no feelings for the boy. She was with the guy she was meant to be with, but still. Beth was no heartbreaker, and she probably still felt some sort of guilt from how things had ended.

"He looked great, Beth. Really," I said. "Plus, I didn't really talk to him. But guess who else I saw?" I paused for dramatic effect. "Chlamydia Clary." I bit back the bile creeping up my throat as thoughts of that fake witch resurfaced.

Now it was her turn to laugh at my misfortune. "Whoa, you have all the luck." She knew how much I hated that boyfriend-stealing hoe.

"I know! Go figure. As big as New York is, two people I knew from before walk into my hospital. What're the chances?"

"No kidding," she replied. "I wouldn't bank on winning the lotto anytime soon."

"Seriously." My eyes moved to the pile of bills I had to run to the post office, reminding me of all the things I needed to get done. "Hey, I gotta get this day going. I have a meeting with the doc tonight, but I've got some errands to run first." I stared at the clock, noting that I had more than enough time to run my errands, tidy up a bit, and get ready for tonight's mega meet up.

"Oh, you didn't tell me." Her voice hitched with excitement. "You guys are finally official?"

"No, but soon enough, babe. Don't you worry." I wasn't. It was going to happen. I could feel it in my bones. Sarah and I had a foolproof plan.

"I know," she said, sarcasm etching her tone. "The psychic's prediction . . . yeah, yeah."

My eyebrows pulled together as I focused on my glass of milk. I ran my finger against the condensation which had formed on the outside of the glass.

Evangeline's predictions were my only lifeline, my hope of any future for happiness. But Beth didn't take any of this seriously. Easy for her. Her life was perfect now.

I ignored her sarcasm and bit my lip as a shadow of disappointment filled me. "Well, I guess I should go. Love you. Tell your lover boy I said hi." I hung up before she could get another word in.

After I ended our call, I rushed to the shower. Tonight was going to be big, and I needed to clear my head of negative thoughts. Plus, I needed to shave—ahem, everything—and figure out what I was going to wear. Hopefully tonight would be Dr. Hot Pants' lucky night. And mine.

BRIAN

ESPN BLASTED IN the background as I sat in the same spot since I'd woken up, working on the proposal I had to present to the credit committee on Monday.

Trey strolled into the living room in boxers only. "My head is fucking killing me. Damn migraines." He stretched his arms over his head, making his already towering body even taller. It was his condo, so I didn't have much of a say if he walked around half naked or not. At least he wore boxers. I had to give him that.

"You look worse than me, and I'm the guy who got sucker punched." I smirked.

His eyes narrowed. "Shut up or you'll be sleeping in

the subway."

I threw my pen at his head, and he chuckled when it missed him by mere inches.

When I'd told him I was moving to New York, he'd offered me his spare bedroom. I had jumped at the opportunity. We were best buds in high school and had gone through some tough shit when we were younger. I knew we wouldn't have problems getting along plus rooming with him has saved me close to fifteen-hundred dollars a month in rent. I could've bought a house back home for what the landlords in Manhattan asked for a one-room closet they called an apartment.

With a sleepy nod at me, Trey strolled into the kitchen and pulled a carton of orange juice out of the fridge. He lifted the open spout to his mouth and guzzled it down.

Note to self: Pick up some OJ and label it.

Carton still in hand, he staggered toward me and plopped on the couch, staring at the TV in his zombie state. I ducked my head back into my computer as my fingers drummed against the keyboard.

"How's your eye?" he asked as he chugged back his drink. His expression held a note of mockery. "Someone took a beat down." He laughed.

Dick.

I touched the stitches at my brow, the puffiness evident and sensitive to the touch. When I brushed my teeth this morning, I noticed the swelling had gone down, but the blue tinge of a giant bruise had already appeared.

"What're you talking about? I fell down the stairs," I retorted.

Trey let out a carefree laugh, a glint of amusement in his eyes as he set down the orange juice on the center table. "Seriously, bro. What're the chances that the hottest girl at the bar, also trying to get laid, had a boyfriend?"

I grimaced, rubbing my hand along my chin. Newly formed stubble prickled my fingertips. "I'm just gonna turn gay, bro. No complications. Men are more upfront and direct." I wiggled my good eyebrow at Trey in a suggestive manner, clamping my lips shut so my expression stayed serious.

"Don't look at me like that," he chuckled, raising both hands. "I only swing one way. And you know how much I love me some ladies."

His words rang true. I thought of the revolving door of women I'd seen make their way into the apartment since I'd moved in. Trey was never without company. There was a time after my sister when he'd given up on women. I didn't know if it was because he was still holding onto the chance they'd get back together, or if whatever had happened between them had screwed up his view on the ladies.

He eyed my old half-eaten bagel, my poor excuse of a breakfast and lunch.

"Go ahead. I'm too busy to be hungry." For the first time since I'd gotten up this morning, I closed my laptop and let my head drop to my hands, rubbing my forehead. I let all the tension from my shoulders ooze out of me.

I needed to win this deal. I had expanded a couple of relationships at work, selling current clients different bank products, but this would be a brand new client I'd be bringing on. I needed the Tiggins Corporation to switch from their current bank to Financial State, where we could service their multi-million dollar portfolio. This new client would secure me the promotion I'd been working so hard to get.

"I need to land this deal," I sighed. "This would make

my quota for the year, so I won't be so stressed out."

Trey placed a light hand on my shoulder. "You'll land it, bro. I have the ultimate faith in you. First things first, let's get some real food, and then let's go *out*-out and try to find us some *single* ladies tonight." Trey eyed my bagel with a pinched expression.

I shook my head. "Did you not hear what I just said? I have to work."

"I heard you. I'm just not listening." He reached for my bagel with cream cheese, and made his way to the garbage. "You can't have bad luck two nights in a row. You're stressed out, and you need a little release that only a woman can give you."

This may be true, but I didn't want any more complications in my life. "Naw, man. I'm just not in the mood."

"I'm not asking," he said about as sternly as Trey can get. "Get your ass off that couch. I'll even let you pick the bar. And those stitches make you look badass. You'll be a huge chick magnet."

As if that was supposed to make the deal more appealing. But I knew, just like last night, he wasn't taking no for an answer.

I stood and stretched my legs, shaking off the cramp from sitting in the same position for so long.

Trey ran a hand over his hair then headed into his room. "Be ready in ten."

With all the time he spent on his hair, I knew Trey's ten minutes meant twenty, so I strolled at a normal pace into my room. My roommate had a love/hate relationship with his hair. Not like he had much to style anyway, and yet he had more hair products than all my sisters combined.

I shook my head. Maybe I had thirty minutes.

KENDY

I GAVE MYSELF one more onceover in my bathroom mirror. The overhead florescent lighting showcased the glimmer of my eye shadow. I had curled my hair to perfection to ensure it would bounce with my every step, and my white halter-top hugged and accentuated my perky breasts.

I also had to bump it up a notch tonight, so I had heels to fix my height problem. At only five-five, I needed to compete with the many models trying to make their break in New York. Tonight, I was wearing my four-inch-clubbing heels. If he hadn't noticed me before, there was no way I wouldn't get his attention tonight.

I texted Sarah, but no response. Her last text had given the address of The Bartlett's Night Club. Per our conversation last night, we had decided to meet there at nine, so I anxiously waited for her to get back to me.

Giving myself a satisfied grin, I strolled out of the bathroom. My heels clip-clopped against the hardwood floor as I sauntered into the kitchen. I opened the fridge for my boxed wine. Nobody was allowed to judge my love of *the box*. From the overhead cabinet, I reached for my pretty wine glass etched with a floral design, which Beth had given me for my twenty-first birthday, and poured myself a glass.

I rocked back and forth in my heels, just staring at my phone. My fingers twitched at my sides, causing the nervous jitters to jump up a notch as I waited for Sarah to call. Five minutes and an empty glass later, I texted Sarah

I'd just meet her at the club.

I didn't want it to seem like I had showed up to a place where Dr. Klein would be, so I had to get there before him. As if he would be showing up to *my* party.

I checked the mirror in the hallway one last time after grabbing my tiny silver purse from the counter. My gloss dazzled a perfect pink with added shimmer. I nodded once, satisfied with my ensemble, and then darted out the door.

BRIAN

WHEN TREY ASKED me where I wanted to go tonight, he'd mentioned a couple of bars, one being The Bartlett's Night Club. I knew it sounded familiar and, when I tried to recall if I'd been there, I suddenly remembered Kendy's friend had mentioned it last night.

Ironically enough, Trey knew the owner's son. There really wasn't anyone Trey didn't know. He was part of the *'in'* crowd of Manhattan.

After moving to New York after high school, he'd gone out and lived it up, partied with the elite. His father had money and, as long as Trey worked for him, he kept those funds coming.

As soon as I stepped into the establishment, Trey spotted his friend while my eyes zoned in on Kendy, already sitting at the bar and looking so smoking hot I couldn't tear my eyes away. Not like she hadn't looked good in scrubs, but she was dressed to perfection tonight, and I hadn't realized how hot her body was under her plain blue scrubs.

Before I could even figure out what I was doing, I was walking toward her, my feet moving against my own free will. Apparently, not talking to her tonight wasn't even an option.

KENDY

THE CLUB BOUNCED with the hip-hop music playing in the background. If Dr. Klein had chosen this place on a Saturday night, I had picked the right man. Because Kendy-Mendy loved her some hip-hop-hooray.

I pulled down my white scoop-neck halter and bobbed my head to the beat. I'd had to leave the panties at home since my dress wrapped my body in a tight vise and I didn't want any panty lines. I was convinced tonight was my night, and he'd be mine for the taking.

My knees bounced as nervous butterflies stirred in the pit of my stomach. To say I was excited was an understatement, as evidenced by my overly large grin, but my stomach was in knots. The center of my palms began to sweat as I tried to keep the bouncing to a minimum.

I hadn't had my sights on a guy in a long time. My pain was too great and it was easier to hide behind men who wanted nothing more than a quick lay. But now, I was done hiding my pain in one-night stands. I'd been looking for certain qualities in my forever male, and Dr. Klein possessed them all.

The truth was, he made me nervous. I wanted him so bad that the confident Kendy transformed into a school girl with a big crush when I was anywhere in his vicinity.

I'd been sitting here for so long, the ice in my Long

Island ice tea had already melted. The only thing that was keeping my mind occupied were the three attractive males eyeing me from across the bar. A couple of them had offered to buy me drinks, but I didn't want to do small talk, so I'd been upfront and told them I was waiting for someone.

When my phone vibrated in my pocket, I knew before I took a glance that it was Sarah. Suddenly, my smile vanished and worry seeped into my skin. She hadn't responded to my last four texts, and I hoped she was okay.

My face fell as I saw the text.

> Sarah: Sorry, babe. I'm not feeling well. I have this major stomach virus and everything I put in is coming out.

I lowered my head, hunching over to type her back, and released a heavy sigh of disappointment.

> Me: It's okay. I hope you feel better.

I leaned against the bar as my excited mood from earlier quickly faded. Why hadn't she messaged sooner, preferably before I'd left the house?

My selfish side wanted to tell her to take some medicine and get her ass over to Bartlett's ASAP. How the hell would I do this without my partner in crime?

We had rehearsed our lines and everything, and now my wing woman was unavailable. This blew.

I felt my full-on Kendy pout coming to the surface. I looked around, but I didn't see the entourage of doctors that Dr. Klein was usually with, so I knew they hadn't shown up yet. I didn't even have a game plan, because Sarah was supposed to start the night cracking her random corny jokes. My job was to sit back and relax until he noticed me. I gritted my teeth as a shadow of disappointment crossed my face.

Now, what was I going to do?

I bit my pinky nail and tried to formulate a plan. Maybe a, "Fancy seeing you here"?

I shook my head and cursed at my lame, cliché line. Maybe I should just go home.

All talk . . . no action. I realized my bravado only surfaced when Sarah was around, especially when it came to Dr. Klein.

Before I could let my negativity take over, I heard a familiar voice behind me.

"Well, well, well. Look who I found."

I cringed. My night had just turned from bad to worse. Slowly, I spun around and locked eyes with the blue-eyed culprit staring back at me, sporting a cocky smirk.

Brian.

I didn't even try to hide my scowl. "Great, just great. I hate my life."

He sighed dramatically, resting against the bar right next to me. "We're running into each other way too much lately. It must be a sign," he said, his voice tinged with humor.

I shot him a look and he laughed, which only piqued my annoyance. "Not a sign—luck," I said, angling toward him. "Bad luck," I quipped, using the line he'd used at the hospital.

His eyes raked my body, landed back on my face, and then he beamed with approval, which shifted my mood.

With a small sly smile, I rested my hand on his bicep and noted the well-defined muscles straining against his fitted white button down. My eyes focused on his face, pretending I wasn't even remotely affected as I squeezed his arm, not noticeably hard, but just so I could feel how firm his muscles were.

Any woman had to admire a man who took care of his body and it looked like Brian did that well. I came closer until we were inches apart. Suddenly, his smile faltered and his look started changing. His eyes raked me in with a lust I was all too familiar with.

My chest was almost touching his, and I knew I had his undivided attention. It was as if he wanted to eat me for dinner, and then for dessert, too. Heat rushed my insides at our closeness. My breath caught in my throat as electricity zinged between us. The air shifted and there was an unexpected and abrupt attraction so strong that I forced my eyes shut and pulled back to find my bearings and give myself room to breathe.

I blinked a couple of times, still admiring the view in front of me. I wasn't totally immune. No doubt, he was one attractive male. *Just not the one I'd come for*, I silently reminded myself.

I threw him a seductive smile. "Listen, I'm saving you the trouble. I'm too much *woman* for a good boy like you to handle." I waved my hand to motion him to the other side of the room.

After a beat, he composed himself. "I think you have me pegged all wrong, Kendy. Who says I'm a good boy?" A mischievous grin crept up his face, the kind of smile little boys used when they were hiding something.

I laughed, because only good boys would say that sort of thing. "Because I've done boys like you. I know your kind. Plus, I certainly don't take second servings." I scrunched my nose as soon as the words left my mouth, my face flushing pink. I had no filter. I should come with a muzzle to keep me from saying things I shouldn't be saying.

He just laughed, but I bit my lip. I hadn't meant to

sound so crude, or for it to come out like that. I knew he'd been heartbroken when Beth had chosen Kent.

I softened and tried to recover. "I'm sorry."

"No big deal." He shrugged, seeming unaffected. Maybe he was over her.

But what I said had been rude—honest, but still rude.

He seemed like a good catch. He just needed some coaching.

I straightened on the stool, ready to do him a favor. "Listen, Brian. Let me give you a word of advice. Quit being so nice." I shifted so my leg brushed against his side, shooting a tingling sensation up my thigh. "Most women want either a bad boy or a rich boy, neither of which you are."

There was a glint of amusement in his eyes as I spoke, which urged me to continue. "You can't change the rich thing, but you most definitely can change the good thing. So if you want to find a good girl, be a bad boy, because women want to change that bad boy and will stay put. We get bored too easily with the good ones. It's not that much fun. Trust me on this."

I flipped my hair to the side, exposing my neck. His eyes flickered to my bare skin and I smirked, loving how I'd grabbed his attention. "I know how to play the game, so you'd be good to take my advice." I patted his arm and nodded twice.

He gave me a disarming smile and my breath caught. I couldn't help but smile back, the reaction automatic.

He angled into me, so close I could smell his aftershave, which was intoxicating. I could pretty much recognize all the colognes at the department store, but the one he was wearing, I didn't. "You think I'm a good boy, and maybe I am." He inched toward me, his warm breath on my face, making my nipples pebble. "But let me tell *you*, this good boy," he smirked, pulling at his shirt, "can be," he angled in even closer, "a very bad boy. In bed."

I gulped, and my insides turned to liquid. I wondered if there was some truth to his words. I shook my head to get his perfectly sculpted, naked body out of my head.

Peering up into his baby blues, I pushed out my chest, being the tease I truly was. His eyes fell to my bust before landing back on my face.

Ah ha! The tables had turned. "It's too bad . . ." I breathed as my eyes flickered to his lips. "That I'm never going to find out about this bad boy." I ran a fingernail lightly down the inside of his arm, angling toward me. "I screw you . . ."

He licked his lips, his eyes focusing on my mouth.

" . . . and you won't be able to help yourself," I said, breathlessly.

His eyes went half-mast as he leaned into me, so close I could smell the mint on his breath, could taste him, quite possibly kiss him.

It took all my self-control to push at his chest with my pointer finger. "You'll fall in love with me, and that's something I cannot have on my conscience."

Then I swallowed hard, averting my gaze, and pretended his proximity did not affect me, while my heartbeat raced in overdrive.

Before he garnered a response, I recognized one of the attendees I worked with. Dan or Sam or something like that. Dr. Hot Pants would be making an appearance shortly. I knew it.

I straightened my skirt and pressed my lips together, evening out my gloss. "You need to leave. My date is coming any minute." I practically tugged on Brian's arm and motioned with my head for him to make an exit.

"Isn't your date supposed to pick you up, not meet you at the bar?" he asked, with a shake of his head. "Seems like you've got a real keeper there." His curious eyes followed my line of sight.

"Well, he doesn't know he's my date, just yet."

Brian lifted an eyebrow and, as I fixed my gaze back at the door, my stomach dropped to the floor. Dr. Klein strolled in . . . with a tall, skinny blonde on his arm. The skin-tight black tube dress and four-inch heels made her mile-long legs look even longer.

No . . .

An onset of nausea spread throughout my body, and my lips pulled downward as the realization that all the effort I'd put into tonight had turned to crap. I closed my eyes, took a big deep breath, and forced myself to shake it off. Shake it to make it. I had to, or it would break my mood for the whole evening and into the morning.

I smirked and sat straighter on the stool, again dusting off this hopeless feeling. Maybe she was his sister. Or maybe not. But either way, she was a tad bit skinnier and taller, but I knew I had all the right curves in all the right places, and the difference was my shit was real.

I pulled at my dress and adjusted my ta-tas. It was time to step up my game.

Brian watched as I fixed myself then his eyes flickered back to the bar. I had to give him credit, though. He was trying to be discrete about it.

I paused as a bright idea came to me. Narrowing my eyes, I pulled him by the collar and wrapped my arms around his neck. He didn't resist and, like a puppet master controlling their puppet, he molded against me and wrapped his hands along my lower back. A small smile played on his lips as though he was wondering what this psycho girl was up to.

I threw him my winning smile as I said, "I'm going to make you a deal, blue-eyed boy. You help me out tonight, and I'll help you out in return." My lips smacked together once more. "You can thank me later."

Chapter Four

BRIAN

THIS WOMAN HAD me pegged all wrong. I wondered if she thought I was a virginal good boy. I silently laughed at the thought, but I decided to humor her. If anything, I enjoyed her misconception about me.

"Go ahead," I said, wondering what her plan entailed. My hand rested against her back. The silkiness of her top brushed against my fingers.

"See that man with the blonde on his arm." With a tip of her head, she motioned toward someone who looked very familiar. "That's my date."

It took all my self-control not to laugh out loud. Her so-called date was Stiff, the doctor from the hospital. "So you're into threesomes? I'll join, but we have to lose the dude."

"No!" She laughed, and there was something about the way she laughed that got to me. It lightened my insides.

"That's the guy I'm going to *marry*," she said with all the confidence in the world. There was this glint in her eye when she uttered the word 'marry', and my curiosity spiked.

How well did she really know this guy? Judging

by the fact he was here with another woman, a sexy but fake-looking one at that, I'd say not so well.

And where had the sex kitten from a minute ago gone? Now she was bouncing on the bar stool, her arms still wrapped around my neck like we were at the high school prom.

"Are you sure he isn't already married?" I raised an eyebrow at her.

Not only was Dr. Stiff with another girl, but he was trying way too hard. His shirt was undone, showing off a bit too much chest. His dark hair was gelled to perfection. He was a player for sure, but he was terrible at not showing it.

Amateur.

I shook my head then glanced back at Kendy. Being a doctor must've been his only appeal.

"No, he's not married." Kendy jutted out her pouty lip. I had a sudden urge to bite it. "He can't be."

I'd hit a nerve; I could tell. That uncrackable confidence was suddenly breaking beneath her gorgeous surface. I wanted to say more, add that maybe he had children she didn't know about so she could push out that lip in my direction and I could run my tongue along the seam, but I thought better of it.

I set my beer on the bar as her eyes zoned in on the group of guys congregated by Stiff. "Let me give you the four-one-one. That is one of the ER doctors I work with. I've been stalking him since I got here a month ago. He's going to be mine. I feel it in my bones."

I laughed at her comment as she continued, "I'm serious. All I need to do is get him to notice me, give me a chance, and he'll fall in love. Hello?" She released me when my laughter continued. Her face pinched with

56

annoyance.

"Okay, I want to see how this is done."

She raised her chin, determination in her eyes. "Okay." She pointed her manicured finger in his direction and didn't blink as he talked up the blonde in front of him. "Once he gets to know me, fall in love, and I screw him, he's going to be mine forever."

"You're a hooker?" I teased.

Now it was her turn to laugh as an irresistibly devastating grin emerged on her face. "No, dummy." She slapped my arm and giggled, her eyes lighting up. But when she focused back on Stiff, she pursed her lips as her mood turned sour again.

He angled toward the woman he walked in with, chatting her up. A part of me wanted to bring Kendy to her senses. If he didn't notice Kendy and her beautiful spunky self, it was his loss.

As I watched her, it was in that brief moment that I saw the unshielded vulnerability in her eyes. But a second later, the insecurity vanished as a veil of toughness came down. I sensed she didn't let anyone see that side of her often.

She lifted her index finger and tapped her chin. "This night is not going as planned. My wingman backed out on me. I also wasn't anticipating any competition so early in the evening."

My eyebrows pulled together, trying to make sense of her thoughts.

She flipped her hair over her shoulder, the scent of peaches wafting my way. Maybe it was her lotion that smelled like peaches.

"I've conditioned myself for my forever man and he's 'it'." She shrugged. "So this little blip is no big deal." Her words said one thing, but her body language said another.

When her lips turned downward, I knew I had to change the subject. Quick. "Okay, so what's my part?"

She angled so we were facing directly, knees touching as we sat on the barstools. "Well, you're going to be my boy toy for tonight. He's going to get jealous, dump the fake, and get with me. Easy peasy, lemon squeezy." She licked her lips as she turned to take another look at Stiff. Her lips were hot and full, and my cock twitched as I wondered if those lips had been conditioned, too.

"And what do I get in return?" My dick jumped to attention, and I tried to think of fairies and sugarplums and people dying to get him to calm the hell down.

"I'll think of something. I'm just trying to land Dr. Klein so he can put a ring on it, and I can have his babies. One night is all I need." She said it like she knew it was going to be true, and I couldn't help but laugh at her ability to tell the future.

My eyebrows jumped into my hairline as I comprehended her last few words. "You're going to sleep with him on the first date?"

"Well, I'm definitely not against it." Her eyes flickered back in his direction as she twisted her hands together in her lap. "I know what I want and how to get it." Her voice softened as she chewed on her bottom lip, her earlier bravado fading. I wondered if she was as sure as she came off to be, but more than that, my curiosity spiked wondering if she believed that sex was all she was worth.

Somewhere in all this confidence and strange ease with all things sexual, this woman was a small town girl at heart. I knew this, because I had come from a small town, too. Was she putting up a front, but truly rattled with insecurity? Though I didn't know her, the protective side of me emerged.

"How well do you know this guy?" My eyes followed Stiff at the corner of the room. He definitely had a way with the ladies. Whatever he was spewing was working. Blondie laughed uncontrollably, practically hanging all over him. There was no doubt he was getting laid tonight.

"I've been studying him," Kendy explained. "Besides being a doctor, he's really sweet. Do you know his grandma calls him all the time? He loves his nana. Just look at him. That wavy dark brown hair, that body." She swooned and got this girly excitement in her eyes. I wanted to tell her I was looking at him, and I just didn't see what she saw.

She went on dreamily, "I know this because I'm the one who talks to his grandmother, and she leaves messages." She held her hand to her heart as a goofy smile crept up her face. "And he's obviously über intelligent and super loaded."

My face contorted as I wondered why someone as hot and educated as she was, would be interested in someone like him.

"Sorry, did I offend you?" she asked, concern etched on her face.

Amused, I shrugged.

"I mean, with the whole rich thing and you not being—" She stopped mid-sentence and wrinkled her nose.

I chuckled at her as she dug herself deeper in the hole with every word.

"No, not at all."

Money didn't matter to me. Recognition and advancing my career did; money was just an added bonus which came with it. I didn't mention I made close to six figures at the bank. I didn't know what Stiff was making, but it wasn't like I made chump change.

I suppressed a laugh. This woman had pegged me all wrong on so many levels.

KENDY

THE BASS OF the music thumped in the background as the heat index of the room increased. More and more people had entered the bar, making an already crowded area now overly packed.

I ran my finger along the top of my drink and glanced back at Brian. He probably thought I was on the prowl for a sugar daddy, so I needed to set him straight. "I know what you're thinking, but you're dead wrong. I'm not a gold digger."

He looked at me with feigned disbelief, which pissed me off even more because it couldn't have been further from the truth.

"A gold digger is looking for a man to support her, because she doesn't work," I argued. "I'm an educated college graduate. Bachelors of Science in nursing. That's right, BS, baby. Straight A's to boot." I tucked an escaping strand of hair behind my ear. "I'm not looking for a man to support me. I'm looking for a man to give me what I deserve, and Tiffany's is it."

He held up his hands in self-defense. "I never called you a gold digger."

"Well, you thought it, and I'm just setting you straight." I uncrossed and crossed my legs, and Brian's eyes flashed. I wondered if he saw I wasn't wearing any panties. I pulled at my skirt, making sure he didn't get another glimpse if he did see.

And maybe I'd had one too many drinks, or maybe it was my honest nature, but I ended up telling him anyway. "Yes, it's true I like to go commando. Why try to play games if I know what I want? And who knows? It might be his lucky night." *If I could only get his damn attention.*

"You want to practice first before you go on your date with him?" A small smirk played on his lips.

I laughed. There was no seriousness in his tone when he said it. "I've had much practice in the sex department, and if you think my shit is loose, I guarantee you it's tight as a knot down there." I pointed my fingers between my legs. "I do kegels regularly. Actually, right now as we speak." From the look on his face, he had no clue what kegels were. "Forget it," I said, shaking my head.

"It looks like you need to step up your game sooner than later." Brian nodded in Dr. Klein's direction.

I bit back the disgust forming at the back of my throat as his hands moved to the blonde's ass and his tongue darted into her mouth.

I narrowed my eyes and sighed, hiding my emotions. "She's got nothing on me. She's way too fake. Hers boobs are bought, hard, and stored in a plastic bag. Mine are au naturel. Here, cop a feel." I angled my boobs toward Brian.

His eyes widened, and he let out a low laugh, but then his face turned serious. He lifted an eyebrow as though he'd heard me incorrectly. A second later, his face broke out in a boyish grin. I could tell he thought I was kidding when I was being dead serious.

"Feel my tits." I angled the ladies toward him. "I know they look fake, but feel them. This is the problem with good boys." I reached for his hand and pressed them on my breast. "Touch them, squeeze them, feel them. I'm giving you full reign, so you know I'm not lying."

He bit his lip as if touching me pained him then he cupped my breast and flicked his thumb over my nipple. It stood at attention, fully erect. My pussy clenched at the contact, and I shifted in my seat as wetness dampened my skirt. Briefly, I closed my eyes at the sensation, and my breath hitched as he teased my nipple with his fingertips.

When he angled closer, I opened my eyes, aware of his proximity. "I can tell they're real. Real . . . nice," he said softly, giving me goose bumps. There was huskiness in his voice, making me think that maybe, just maybe, there was some truth to his words. Maybe Brian was a real bad boy in bed.

BRIAN

I PULLED BACK and shifted on the stool, hard as a rock. There was a mid-western cuteness to her overall appearance, but her honesty and her foul mouth made her jump on the hot scale from pepper hot to volcano hot. She was sweet innocence with a dirty mouth, a walking contradiction. God, was she damn sexy.

But as she continued to watch Stiff, annoyance prickled my skin. Maybe it was protectiveness, but I had no idea what she saw in the guy who had his hands all over some other girl.

Her eyebrows scrunched together, and all I wanted to do was smooth out the ridges with my fingers. To my utter happy glee, I watched Stiff stroll to the door and leave with the blonde. But then I saw the look on Kendy's face.

I had a sudden urge to make her forget about him, to make her laugh again as she had been earlier.

"He's leaving with her, and he hasn't even had a chance to look at my outfit." She crossed her arms over her chest. The very chest I'd been touching a moment ago.

I couldn't help but laugh silently. I should've felt bad that her purpose of the night was walking out the door with another woman, but her reaction amused me. More than that, I knew she deserved better than that loser.

"Hey, if it helps, I think your outfit is hot, and not to mention . . . you look absolutely beautiful tonight," I said, trying to break her mood.

It was the truth. She had been so focused on Stiff that she hadn't noticed she had the attention of most men in our vicinity. Stiff was the minority.

I garnered a small smile, but her eyes moved to the door and she frowned again, jutting out her lip even further.

I wrapped my arm around her shoulders and pulled her in. "Let's go, pretty girl. I'm taking you for a late night snack. You don't want to waste a good outfit, and I don't want you to think your night was all for nothing."

She peered up at me through her sad blue eyes and hesitated. Her look alone tightened my chest.

Knowing I had to see that smile again, I tucked an escaping strand of her blonde hair behind her ear and gave her a grin. "This is what good boys do; we take damsels in distress to dinner. And I figure, since the man you're going to marry just walked out with that blonde, you're in distress."

She sighed heavily, but linked her arm through mine. "I want some wine with my food because, just so you know . . . there is going to be a lot of whining tonight."

I pulled her hand tighter around my bicep. "Sounds good. Let me say goodbye to Trey and we'll get you that wine," I said, leading us out the door. "Wine makes everything better."

KENDY

WE WALKED INTO the first grease pit we saw. Greektown Gyros in neon pink letters was written on the auburn awning. My stomach grumbled, even though I'd had dinner before I hit the club.

A waitress led us to a table for two in the back and, as soon as we sat down, I plucked the menu stuck between the wall and the napkin holder. It was printed on the back of a brown bag. Real classy.

I scanned my choices of beverages. "I hope you don't mind, but I'm about to get really wasted." I was already tipsy, but I planned to drink even more to forget my ruined night.

He chuckled and eyed me over his menu. "Not at all. Shit, it's the weekend. I might join you."

The waitress wrote down our order. I got a Miller Lite, and so did Brian. Thankfully, she was quick to hop on it and bring us our bottles.

I chugged that baby down like it was water and slammed it against the table, causing the salt and pepper shakers to teeter back and forth.

Brian smirked. "Slow down. We haven't even eaten yet." He reached over and placed his hand on top of mine. Warmth spread through our connection, and I grudgingly pulled away.

I jutted out my chin, the image of Dr. Klein leaving with little Miss Blondie playing in my mind, dampening my mood. "I don't understand. He's all prim and proper at work. I know he has to be, but then he goes out and takes the first chick he meets home?"

"How do you know he just met her?" He reached for his bottle and took a big gulp.

"Well, he just left with that . . . that girl." *Good comeback.*

"But he walked in with her. How do you know that's not his girlfriend?"

I widened my eyes at him. "Because I stalk him relentlessly, and not once has a girl called him at work. No one visits him, and everyone who has worked with him for a while has never, ever, *ever* mentioned a girlfriend." I reached for the little bit of beer I had left, watching the copper-colored liquid swish against the glass. Placing the bottle under my lips, I closed my eyes and tipped it all the way back. Then, I placed the empty bottle on the table. "I don't understand him. I'm cute, right?"

He studied me, messing with the fork in his hand.

When I didn't get a response, I threw him my big puppy dog face.

"Of course, you're cute, Kendy." He laughed.

"You're very convincing." I rolled my eyes. "Then what's his problem? I've tried everything, all the tricks in my Kendy dating book, and nothing. I didn't even have a chance to show him my hot-to-trot outfit. Today was my chance, but he blew it out of that club faster than a marathon runner. It didn't help that my wingman called in sick on me . . . but still."

I picked up the fork on the table and, in an unladylike fashion, pounded it against the fake wood, causing the water glasses to shake. "Quick, change the subject." I didn't want to think about how this Saturday night turned into a total waste of time.

"Good. I don't want to hear any more about Dr. Stick-up-his-ass or whatever you call him," he replied, the pinched expression leaving his face.

"Stick-up-his-ass?" I asked, laughing.

"Yeah, I'd say that nickname is appropriate."

A waiter brought our gyros, breaking our conversation. I watched his eyes drift to my cleavage before placing the food in front of us, and I pulled up my halter-top, a little self-conscious now that we were in a fully lit diner.

"What is it about this guy?" Brian tilted his head, a tinge of concern in his voice.

"What do you mean?"

"I mean, how did he get so lucky to win your attention?"

Lucky?

He thought Dr. Klein was the lucky one? I couldn't help but soften, a small smile built at his thoughtfulness.

"You're sweet." A flush crept up my cheeks as the story only a few people knew wanted to roll out of my mouth. "Promise you won't laugh if I tell you something?"

"Promise," he said, but I knew just looking at his big boyish smile that he'd fail.

"Forget it." I reached for my gyro and took a big bite. Some of the cucumber sauce missed my mouth and slipped down my chin. Picking up my napkin, I dabbed at my face to wipe it off.

"No. Promise." He raised up his hand as if swearing on the Bible. "And when a Boy Scout swears, he means it."

I studied his face, which turned serious, giving me the

courage to continue. "So . . ." I swallowed the food down, looked toward the plate of French fries next to my gyro, and noted the pita overflowing with onions. "I believe in astrology, the alignment of the stars, fortune telling, and all that jazz."

His mouth twitched, and I debated stopping, but he motioned with his hands for me to continue. "Go on."

"I'm a Pisces and—practically everything they say about Pisces is true." I peered up at him through my lashes. "We're generous and emotional souls. Kind. Compassionate. I think that's why my calling truly was to become a nurse." I picked up my fork and poked it through the meat, which had fallen out of my sandwich. "Well, one summer when I was in high school, Beth and I went to track down this popular psychic in Leon, a couple towns south of our hometown."

I noted that he hadn't touched his food. He seemed engrossed in our conversation, which urged me to continue. "Beth didn't want to get her cards read, but I kind of coerced her to come with me. There was something I needed to ask the psychic."

I reclined against the chair as I recalled the day. I'd specifically gone to find Evangeline because I'd heard of her and needed to know things—things for my mama, for our family, and mostly for myself. She'd been known to be exceptional with fortune telling.

That hot summer day, one I remembered so vividly, Evangeline told me about my father and foretold my future.

Brian didn't need to know the specific details, and I didn't know him well enough to share, but I did tell him one piece of information she'd foretold that day. "She predicted everything about Dr. Hot Pants, and that's how I know he's the one." I nodded once, confirming the prediction.

Brian rubbed at his eyebrow. His lip quivered as if he was holding in laughter. When he composed himself, he turned in my direction, but I could already feel myself warming with irritation. I hardly knew this guy, and I didn't appreciate him thinking my life was some sort of joke.

"Never mind." I stuffed my mouth with a couple of fries and started to chew.

"No, go on. I find this interesting. Just because I don't believe in fortune tellers or astrology doesn't necessarily mean it's not true."

"Whatever," I mumbled, my mouth full of food.

"Enlighten me, please," he said sweetly. "I want to know what she said." His face turned serious again, his eyes no longer amused.

When had I ever cared what other people thought of me anyway?

I dropped my fork, ducked my head toward him, and continued, "This girl was good. No crystal ball or anything. She only read our palms and had Tarot Cards. She predicted I would move to a big city." His lip twitched again, but I just ignored it. "She predicted I'd major in something that would help people, and that my mama would remarry. She's not remarried just yet, but I don't doubt that her relationship with Hank is headed in that direction." I angled closer to whisper my next revelation. "And she predicted I would marry my soul mate, Dr. Klein. She said, 'He'll be the one that makes you smile every day for the rest of your life. Give you the happily-ever-after you deserve.' As silly as it sounds, I believe her."

"What did she say exactly?" he asked, seeming truly

interested as he leaned in farther. "Did she say, 'I predict you are going to marry a doctor, his name is Dr. Klein, and he works at New York Cornell Hospital'?"

"Of course not." I frowned at him. "I mean, when she said I'd move out of Bowlesville to a big city, she didn't say New York."

He rested his elbows on the table, steepling his fingers together. "Well, then how do you know she meant him?"

"Because she said I'd really meet my soul mate at work. And she saw papers and moons in my future. She was vague and precise all at once." I shook my head, knowing that I made no sense. But I'd been there, and I knew with such clarity she'd seen my future. "She specifically said that I'd marry the man who'd give me the moon," I whispered.

His face broke out into a sudden smile. "Oh, yeah?"

I could feel my mouth turning up to match his smile. "Yeah, and on my very first day of work, I was already attracted to him. I mean, look at his fine ass. Even being the alpha male that you are, you have to appreciate a fine specimen when you see it."

"So he reached up in the sky and grabbed the moon and handed it to you, and that's how you know?" He started to laugh, which made me want to hit him in the face.

"Of course not, dummy. A couple days after I started working, I was looking for something to take notes on when we were at the nurses' station, and Dr. Klein handed me a kid's notepad to take notes and on it . . ." I felt my eyes widening, like I was admitting a conspiracy. "Get this . . ." I gazed left and then right. "On the right upper hand corner of the notebook was a moon. A *paper* notebook. I didn't understand her prediction until that moment."

Brian grinned and nodded with understanding then coughed to cover his laugh, eventually breaking into full-blown, uncontrollable laughter. The sound of it rippled through the diner and had everyone turning in our direction.

I narrowed my eyes at him, thoroughly annoyed. "It's called a sign. Ever heard of it? Look it up in the dictionary."

He continued to laugh, holding his stomach as my body temperature rose, the heat reaching the tips of my ears. I'd had enough. I pushed my chair back and stood to leave. I didn't have to sit here and take this—him laughing at my life, thinking I was some sort of joke. I reached in my purse, grabbed a twenty, and threw it on the table.

Brian instantly calmed down and grabbed my hand. "Hey, where are you going?"

I ripped my hand from his grasp. "Home. Jerk!" I stomped out of the restaurant, never looking back. When the warm summer air hit my skin, sweat beads formed against my forehead.

I hated him for making me feel embarrassed about this. Evangeline's predictions had come true in succession. Her prophecies were the only hope I had in my own future. It's the thread that kept me together. I lived with the comfort of knowing how my life would play out.

Swallowing down my emotions, I raised my hand to hail a cab, but the stupid cab traveled past me. I dropped my head and closed my eyes. I couldn't believe how awful this night had been. Sarah had fallen sick and ditched me. I had wasted all my effort to gain Dr. Klein's attention but instead he'd left the bar with another girl. The last straw was Brian mocking me.

My lip quivered, followed by tiny tears prickling my eyes, and I wrapped my arms around myself, feeling small and insignificant. After a second, I lifted my head to search for another cab.

I hated that all I wanted to do was go back to my normal town of boring Bowlesville. I'd give anything at this moment to watch movies with my mama and sit in the kitchen, drinking the hot cocoa that she made me every night. I'd thought I wanted the big city lights, but not anymore. I wanted my old life back. I should've stayed at that hospital and continued helping old people pee.

As I waited for another damn cab, the first tear fell down my cheek, and I angrily swiped it away. I'd never felt so alone.

Who was I kidding? I wasn't this big bad girl moving to the big city. I was one big wannabe fake.

Chapter Five

BRIAN

WELL, SHIT.

I felt like a total douche. I was a douche. She'd told me not to laugh, and that was exactly what I'd done, but I couldn't help it. Her total belief in what the psychic had said was ridiculous. Sure, I didn't believe in shit like that, but still, I didn't have to be rude.

I picked up her cash, dug into my wallet, and threw my own cash on the table, well over the check and tip amount, and darted out the door, hoping to catch her. Thankfully, she was standing at the corner, by the stoplight. She was slumped over, holding her stomach. When I jogged closer, I noticed her cheeks glistening, wet from fresh tears.

I'd made her cry. *Way to go, shithead.* My stomach clenched as though I'd been punched in the gut. "Kendy!" I called out before I came closer.

She might give off this tough girl appearance, but I had a feeling she'd be embarrassed if I caught her crying.

She gave me a once over and crossed her arms over her chest, then spun in the other direction. From the side, though, I could still see her smeared eyeliner. She was obviously pissed, but she looked like a kitten playing mad.

And it was cute as hell.

"I'm not talking to you," she mumbled, blinking up at the sky and swiping at her cheeks. "There's so much pollution here . . . Something's in my eye."

I was right—kitten playing tiger.

I bit my lip to keep the smile off my face. If I lost it, there would be no way I could redeem myself.

"I'm sorry," I apologized right away before she could get a word in. I truly meant it, and I hoped she heard it in my voice. "Even though I don't believe in that sort of thing, that doesn't give me a right to put you down because you do."

She turned in my direction, her eyebrows still furrowed, but I continued, "I'm sorry I laughed at your story."

A cab pulled up, and she had every right to step right in and not look back, given the way I behaved.

When she reached for the door handle, my stomach plummeted. Guilt ate at my insides. I took a step forward. "Let me make it up to you by buying you some dessert. I was a total ass, and I'm really sorry."

I didn't want us parting on bad terms given the way I'd behaved, but there was something else. I couldn't put my finger on it. All I knew was I didn't want her to go.

She pulled the door open and slid into the cab. It took all my energy to stay in my spot, when my first instinct was to go after her. "I'm sorry," I called back again, hoping she heard the sincerity in my voice.

Her face showed no expression as she placed her hand on the car door. I was about to turn away, when she peered up at me through her lashes. "So are you going to just stand there, or buy me dessert?"

I gave her a small smile, approaching the cab. As she

scooted over, I hopped in next to her. Hell, yes. I'd just redeemed myself, and the night.

* * *

KENDY

WHY DID I let him in the cab? Free dessert, maybe? Or maybe it was that he looked genuinely apologetic.

We ended up at Serendipity. I hadn't been to the staple landmark since I'd move to New York, though it was on my checklist of things to do.

When he asked where I wanted to go, I told him I wanted to drink hot cocoa. I'd been thinking of my mama and, even though I was miles and miles away, I wanted a part of her with me tonight, especially since I was having such a shitty evening. There was a direct correlation between hot cocoa and home.

Brian held the door open and, as soon as I stepped into Serendipity, the scent of chocolate wafted through the air, already releasing my happy endorphins.

The cute waitress sat us down at a round wooden table for two at the very back. I pulled out the white wooden chair and plopped down on the seat. The high ceilings made me feel shorter than I already was. Charming colorful lights above us brightened the room.

Brian had said very little on our ride here. Maybe he was afraid I'd chew his head off, or maybe he didn't want to interrupt my deep train of thought as I stared out the window.

"So, what're you having?" he asked, finally breaking the awkward silence. He seemed apprehensive, careful even. I knew he'd seen the waterworks earlier. Maybe he was worried he'd break the dam open again?

"The famous frozen hot cocoa." I pointed at the picture of the chocolate frozen drink topped with whipped cream and chocolate shavings. Serendipity was known for their frozen hot chocolate. From looking it up on the internet, I knew the drink was served cold. The reference to 'hot' was because of the restaurant's secret dry mix that one would put in regular hot cocoa made at home. I had no doubt, judging from how busy the place was at eleven in the evening, that there would be one big party in my mouth from drinking it. I couldn't help my knees from bouncing from my anticipation.

"Is that it?" he asked, his face softening.

"Yes, thank you." I smiled up at him, giving him the indication that nice-girl Kendall was out and he didn't need to worry.

When the waitress approached our table and asked for our order, he turned toward her. "One frozen hot cocoa and a coffee please."

I shot him a bemused look. "You're going to order coffee at Serendipity? You can order coffee at McDonald's."

He shook his head and peered up at the waitress. "Coffee is fine."

The short brunette waitress threw Brian a seductive smile, wrote down our orders, and took our menus. She lingered for a few seconds, leaning toward him before sashaying away, most likely hoping he was paying attention.

He seemed unaware, his eyes never straying from mine.

"You can have her if you want," I said, gauging his reaction to see if he was interested. He gave none. "She's into you; I can tell."

He glanced back at the woman then shrugged. "I don't know. She's not my type."

I frowned. Not the normal reaction I would've expected. I usually had a good gauge on guys. "What's wrong with you? She's attractive. Did you switch to the other side?"

"No, I'm good." His eyes dropped to the table. "I'm not really looking for anything right now. I figure when it happens, it happens." He reached for his glass of water. "I got loads of things going on at work. I'm way too busy for anything serious right now." As soon as the word 'work' left his mouth, his shoulders sagged, as though he was fatigued by the thought. He rested back and took a sip of water.

Hmm. Interesting. I filed that away in the recesses of my brain. "You liking New York so far?" I asked.

"Yeah. So far, so good." His fingertips tapped against his water glass. "I haven't been out much lately." I sensed wariness as his tone dropped.

"You're not dating anybody?" I was, not discreetly, pressing him for more information.

He squinted, trying to see where my questions were leading. "No, I've been so involved with work it's all I can think about. In Chicago, I was established. Here, it's like I'm working from the ground up."

"Being a workaholic is boring, Brian." I groaned. "Borderline alcoholic sounds way better."

He chuckled. "I came here for work."

"I thought you came here to run away from a certain girl." It slipped out before I could stop it. Damn me and my inability to be tactful. "Sorry." I grimaced.

He just laughed, not an ounce of sadness in his eyes, which made me feel a tinge better. "I always wanted to be in New York. I landed in Chicago by default, but . . . I would've stayed for the right girl."

I bit my cheek, not knowing what to say to that. I couldn't exactly tell him the truth—that Beth was having her happily ever after with Kent. Still, my insides were swooning at his words, and instantly, I felt a little bad for him.

"It wasn't meant to be." He shrugged, seeming unaffected, yet I sensed a tiny ounce of disappointment.

I sat straighter. "You know what? You'll find a girl that's just perfect for you. I know." I added, "But you have to be a little more aggressive, or other guys are going to snatch up what you have your sights on." I knew firsthand—if you had your sights on something, you had to take control and take action.

"You're giving me girl advice?" He pointed to himself and let out a carefree laugh, as though it was absurd for me to even suggest I could help him out with his dating life.

"Yes, I am." I flipped my hair over my shoulder and leaned into the table. "I know a thing or two about the opposite sex."

"Oh, you do, do you?" He rested his elbows on the table, his eyes holding interest.

Before I could continue, the waitress placed his coffee in front of him. Her eyes flickered to his chest, his face, and then back at me. I gave her a sweet smile, and she flushed pink. I wondered if she thought we were together. If we were together, I wouldn't be smiling if she was checking out my man. I would have scooted closer, practically sitting on Brian's lap.

She set the cup of frozen chocolate in front of me. My mouth watered at the fluffy cloud of whipped cream on top, sprinkled with flakes of chocolate shavings.

When she left, I widened my eyes at the concoction of heaven as the aroma of sweet chocolate filled my nose. I rubbed my hands together like a small child about to open a toy. "I'm like super excited."

"Yeah, I can tell. And all for a cup of cocoa." I caught him eyeing my cup like he wanted to take a sip.

No way, buddy. Not before I get a taste.

"I love hot cocoa; it's a long story." I closed my eyes and inhaled deeply, the scent bringing me back to my kitchen table, sitting by Mama while our old school Nat King Cole music played in the background.

I pictured her by the stove, and the yellow, faded, flowery wallpaper a stark contrast to her red apron. My breathing slowed as calmness washed over me.

I opened my eyes to find Brian studying me. He hadn't taken a sip of his coffee yet. I shrugged, bringing both hands to the oversized mug. It felt strange, sipping with a straw, so I pulled the straw out and brought the delicious drink to my lips. Taking a deep swallow of the cold liquid, I frowned. It was good, but nowhere near as good as my mama's.

Brian laughed at my reaction. I'm sure everyone else would've loved it, but as the cold cocoa hit my tongue, all I could think about was Mama's sweet hot chocolate, fresh from the stove.

"That bad?" he asked.

"No, not at all. It's my issue." I picked up a chocolate shaving and popped it in my mouth. "It's good, but it's nothing like my mama's. Hers is made from scratch. Real milk chocolate morsels melted in a pan, two percent milk, and topped with marshmallows." My breathing slowed as I recalled the memory. I peered up at him through my lashes as a soreness spread in the back of my throat at the thoughts of home.

He ducked his head, sympathy leaking through his eyes. "Do you miss home?"

I hated how transparent I was when I tried my hardest not to be. I averted my gaze, focusing on my oversized mug. "Sometimes." My voice turned quiet as a flood of emotions rushed to the surface. "But it was time to leave."

I picked at the pink straw, flicking my fingernail against the edge. "It's always been Mama and me . . . especially when my dad left us." I narrowed my eyes, zoning in on a chocolate shaving which had fallen on the table. I didn't want to see the look of pity in his eyes that I knew was clearly there. "It's why I originally went to see that psychic . . . I needed to know if Dad had left us for good." My voice was barely above a whisper as familiar pain shot straight to my chest. You'd think the blow would've lessened over the years, but it hadn't.

Evangeline had predicted that my father was never coming back. He'd left us when I was eleven, moved in with another woman, and never looked back. I had kind of sensed it in my gut that he was never coming back, but I'd tried to deny it. After Evangeline's prediction, I could finally stop wishing for it and help my mother move on.

"But then she met Hank." I exhaled heavily, finally raising my head to meet his eyes. "She never fully got over my father, but I'm happy for her," I said, smiling. "It's just . . . sometimes I miss when it was just Mama and me." I reached behind me, pulling my hair to the front, using it as some sort of curtain. I was suddenly shy for letting my vulnerability shine through.

I'd known it was time to leave the comfort of my home when Hank had stepped in and I'd started to feel like the third wheel. I'd always thought my mother was a crutch, keeping me in Bowlesville. In reality, I had been the one using her as an excuse to never leave.

I shook my head to break me from my mood. "It's exactly as the psychic predicted. Even though it hasn't happened yet, he's going to marry her. Hank's told me his plans. It's just a matter of time." At that, I felt the despair lighten a little. "I'm so silly, right? Big girl missing her mama."

I chuckled at my own patheticness. His gaze upon me didn't falter. If anything, his eyes softened as he placed his hand on mine, shooting a tingling sensation up my arm.

"It's okay to miss home. Nothing wrong with that."

Warmth spread throughout my fingers. When I pulled my hand back, Brian brought the coffee to his lips as I stirred the chocolate drink with my pinky.

"So, Brian, is coffee your beverage of choice?" I changed the topic quickly to take the focus off me. My voice shook as I spoke. I shouldn't have revealed such intimate details to someone I barely knew.

"When I'm at work, yeah. But out of work, beer it is." He smirked, reclining in his chair. "I'm a workaholic, alcoholic all at once."

That garnered a laugh from me. "So, how about you? When did you move here?"

"Six months or so ago. You?" He cocked his head in my direction.

"A month ago, but it feels longer. It's kind of weird moving from a place where you know everyone to a place where you know no one." I perked up, remembering the nervous jitters I'd felt that first day of work. I could've sworn Nana, my late grandmother, had been watching me from above, because Sarah had introduced herself as soon as I saw her.

"It's okay, though. I've made friends. As you can see, I'm very likable." I grinned wide, but I felt like I was hiding. Because it had been hard making friends, becoming part of this chaotic society. It was a different world out here, and I sensed my normal confidence fading. "So, no girlfriend? Where's the boyfriend?" I teased.

The laugh lines were evident on his face. "You're funny. You know that?"

"Funny, beautiful, smart. Yeah, I know." I lifted my eyes to the ceiling for an exaggerated effect. "So you live by yourself?"

"With Trey. He's a really good friend from where I grew up. His parents are divorced. His mother still lives in Madison, but he moved to NYC to work with his father, who's a big real estate mogul. He's a transfer, just like me."

"How do you know each other?"

"From high school and . . . he dated my sister for years."

I blinked at him with fake shock. "They're not together anymore, and his balls are still intact?"

He winced. "Well, my sister dumped him. If it had been the other way around, let's just say we wouldn't have been friends anymore."

I clicked my tongue. "Two brokenhearted transfers from Madison move to New York City to mend their wounds by scouring the city for women to ease their pain." I felt a wide grin spread across my face. "You can sell the movie rights to Paramount."

He shook his head slightly. "None of that is happening over here. No time for the ladies. Not now, at least."

I shrugged. "Yeah, well, my story is much more

interesting than yours. Beautiful nurse and her quest to land the doctor of her dreams, versus banker Brian and his addiction to work. My story sounds like a sitcom."

His lips curled up into a smile as a deep chuckle escaped him. Brian reached for the sugar to pour more into his coffee. And I thought I was a sugar fiend. I should've asked him if he wanted coffee with his sugar.

"So . . . what're you going to do about Stiff?" he asked.

"Stiff?" I scrunched my eyebrows in confusion.

"The doctor."

I gave him an 'ah ha' face. "Oh, you nicknamed him that because he gets stiff every time he sees me?" I cracked up at my own joke, and he just shook his head again, that now familiar amusement crossing his features.

"No, really. What're we doing about him? I thought we had some sort of deal." His smile widened, and I wondered what he had in mind.

"What's in this for you?" I asked, my curious smile matching his.

He tipped his head back and then winked. "That's what I'm sticking around to find out."

I let out a carefree laugh as my eyes assessed him. "It's not what you think."

His lips turned downward in a pout that could almost rival mine.

"Give me time to think this through." I stuck my pinky into the whipped cream then into my mouth, and then I swirled my pinky and repeated the motion. Maybe the hot cocoa wasn't the same, but this whipped cream had to have been homemade or something. It was hella good.

I sighed. What was I going to do with him? Sarah was supposed to be my wingman. I glanced up again and repeated the process of swirling my finger in the whipped cream and sticking it in my mouth. How would it even work if Brian were to help me land my doctor?

I guess I could get Dr. Hot Pants all jealous, use two wingmen. Yeah, maybe that would work. "I'll have to mull it over. I'll sleep on it and get back to you."

Pursing my lips, I put the straw in my mug and started to slurp it down. When the drink was finished, I rested the oversized cup on the table. "What're you doing on Friday? Wanna meet me at Central Park? I'm off next weekend. I can think of the logistics, and we can go over it then."

This seemed so cliché, me getting the man of my dreams by using another guy. Still, I'd seen it work before. "Of course we have to keep things platonic, but you'll have to pretend to like me."

He reached over and surprised me by running his finger over my upper lip. I widened my eyes as he brought the whipped cream he'd wiped off me between his lips, making my pulse quicken.

"I do like you. You taste sweet." He winked. And I swallowed. Hard.

This platonic thing may be more difficult than I had planned.

Chapter Six

BRIAN

RUBBING THE BACK of my neck, I tilted my head side to side, trying to release the tension from a long week at work. I rested my elbows against the table as I steepled my fingers against my lips and glared at the computer screen in front of me, analyzing the write-up that I had spent the whole week pondering over. I ducked closer, squinting, hoping the numbers would change.

Sensing his presence behind me, I turned and lifted an eyebrow at Conner Clinton, the Third, another banker who'd been at One Financial as long as I had. He loomed above me, his eyes flickering to my computer screen.

Nosy ass.

"Did I tell you?" His grin was cocky, the kind that made me want to fire back with an 'I don't care'.

I could almost predict what he was going to tell me. "No, what?" I said with fake enthusiasm. That's how I had to play in the game of sales. My face said 'Sure, buddy, what's going on?' while my head was screaming, 'I don't give a shit!'

"I landed the Rosedell deal." He sat at the edge of my desk, crossing his ankles like he was staying for a while.

I straightened in my seat, throwing him a

congratulatory smile. "Good job, bro." I forced gusto in my voice, just for his benefit. I didn't care what deals he landed. I didn't care what he was currently working on. Why he was so concerned with what I was doing, I had no idea.

He sighed happily. "That'll make one new deal and two expansions of current clients. And all in this quarter. I'm sure I'll be on management's radar for that promotion. Perfect timing with Joe's retirement and that vacated spot."

My muscles tensed.

Over my dead body.

Work brought out my competitive nature. I never deemed myself a competitive guy, but now that I was thinking of it, when I was younger, I had always excelled when it came to sports and academics, consistently topping my previous quarter grades or motivating my football team to make the championships.

I nodded in fake approval. Maybe if I remained mute, he'd get the hint and move the hell on.

"Yeah, man. I'm crushing my goals." He pushed his glasses farther up his face.

I'd had enough of Cocky Conner and his designer clothes, which his trust fund had paid for. "Good for you," I said, flipping back around to my computer.

I wanted to yell, 'Show a little modesty, dude'. I didn't go around letting everyone know when I had landed new deals in my portfolio. I didn't broadcast every little accomplishment.

My manager's voice had me raising my head again. "My two favorite boys." Jason stepped into my cubicle with a file folder in his hand. "Good job on Rosedell, Conner."

Conner nodded, pleased with himself. "Yeah, it was a tough win boss, but you know I'm always up for the challenge." He pushed out his chest, all proud and shit, and I coughed to cover my laugh.

Jason smiled, but it didn't meet his eyes. It was one of the many gestures which gave me tiny hints that Jason didn't like Conner as much as Conner thought he did, which made me appreciate my manager that much more.

Jason was a no-bullshit kind of guy. He worked hard and had climbed to the top by pure determination. We had one quality in common, which was one needed to excel in sales—Jason and I were good people readers. We knew when to speak and when to shut our trap, and we knew exactly what to say to reel clients in and close the deal.

Conner talked out of his ass too much. He never listened, and a part of me believed a lot of his current deals were won by his well-connected father.

Jason pushed the file folder into Conner's hands. "These are the additional files for Rosedell. You should contact our operations team to get them on board."

With a slight nudge, Conner stood, like a doggy receiving an order. "On it, boss." He nodded once then swaggered out of my cubicle.

"And Conner," Jason called out.

Conner swiveled, coming to heel on Jason's command.

"Don't forget our eight a.m. call on Monday."

"I'll be there," he said a little too cheerfully.

With a slight shake of his head, Jason chuckled. "That's Conner for you." I assumed his comment wasn't a positive thing. "So, how's that Tiggins deal you're working on?"

"Pretty good. I'm typing up the proposal and getting

ready for my spiel next week in front of their CEO. I've got this in my back pocket."

He slapped my shoulder, his eyes filling with pride. "I don't doubt it, son." He sat at the edge of my desk, crossing his arms against his chest. "You remind me of myself twenty years ago. You'll make it far here, Brian. You're good at your job and, above all else, you work hard." He stood and straightened his pant leg, turning to walk away. "Don't stay past five tonight. Remember, work is work. It'll be here next week."

I smiled up at him. He knew I was a bit of a workaholic. And I would've stayed all night if I hadn't already promised I'd meet Kendy at Central Park. The tenseness in my shoulders eased up as I thought of our meeting later that evening. My curiosity spiked as I wondered what she had planned. Whatever it was, I would soon find out.

KENDY

AFTER TIDYING UP my apartment all day, I was ecstatic to get outside and enjoy my walk to Central Park. I spotted Brian on a bench at the corner of 5th Avenue and 85th. As I'd expected, he was punctual and exactly where I'd told him to meet me. I smiled big as the warm breeze brushed against my face, the warmth of summer soaking into my skin.

When he spotted me, the corner of his mouth lifted, as though I'd amused him in some way. He was business casual, in a button down and slacks, looking professional and boyishly cute all at once.

In a chipper mood, I plopped down next to him as the

warm summer sunlight beat down on my face, forming little beads of sweat on my forehead. I pulled my tube top a little lower, as I didn't want any tan lines while I let the sunlight wash over me.

"Hiya," I said as I opened a bag of chips. "No suit or tie?"

"No client calls today, plus Fridays are usually our laid back days at the office," he said smoothly, eyeing me as I chomped away. "Are you going for a run or something?" He eyed my short workout shorts and gym shoes.

I looked at him like he was crazy. "Kendy does not run unless she is being chased by a wild animal." I pulled at my tube top. "And run in this? My boobs would be bouncing everywhere."

A flash of humor crossed his face. "I'd like to see that."

"You and the rest of the males at Central Park. Chip?" I pushed the small bag in his direction, chewing animatedly.

He squinted against the sun and shook his head.

"More for me." I shrugged. My bag was dwindling down to crumbs anyway.

I had come here on a mission, not to shoot the shit, so I angled toward him, getting down to business. "Okie dokie, so let's talk about this deal."

He was still smirking at me, and I had no idea why.

"What's so funny?"

"You." He grinned, but he motioned for me to continue.

"So I narrowed down my proposition, and you're going to love, love, love this one." I laughed, because he was still smiling at me. I guess he must've been in a good mood, too. "So, as you already know, I've been secretly stalking Dr. Klein." I popped a half chip in my mouth.

"And so far I'm having a little difficulty." I scrunched my nose, because, seriously, I had no idea why I was having a tough time with this guy. They must be built different here in New York.

"Anywho," I continued, "I've tried every play in my playbook. I've flirted sweetly. I've worn fitted scrubs, which are very uncomfortable, by the way. And outside of the hospital, I've kind of secretly stalked him at that one bar. I've done everything shy of stripping naked and asking him out." I raised my pointer finger for emphasis. "But . . . now I have a plan."

Brian displayed a wide grin, most likely at my enthusiasm. I placed my bag of chips on the bench and shifted to tuck one foot under my butt. "Men like competition, right?" When he didn't respond, I continued, "I think we should pretend to date. I mean, you have to pretend to be interested in me. And also, we have to formulate a plan where he sees the both of us together. We have to make him believe you want to get with me."

I extracted the crinkled piece of paper in my back pocket. "This is a rough draft. The key is to show up wherever he's going to be. Maybe you can come to the hospital a couple times? You know . . . pretend to court me?" I peered up to gauge his reaction. Judging by his happy-go-lucky smile, I went on. "Maybe come with flowers or presents, like you want me bad."

I folded the piece of paper within my fingertips. "I mean, of course I wouldn't want you to buy me things. I'd be buying them and signing the card with your name." When I locked eyes with him, my insides soared knowing that he was on board.

He laughed when I was finally done. "Why can't you just ask him out?"

He made it seem so simple.

I shook my head, my cheery mood slipping. He obviously didn't know how the chase worked. "Guys like him want to feel like they're in charge. No one likes an aggressive girl. You bang those types of girls; you don't marry them."

He raised a curious eyebrow. "Didn't you say you weren't against sleeping with him on the first date?"

"That's different!" I sighed heavily, my face pinching together. I didn't want to go into details on how Evangeline's prediction had foretold that our relationship would be purely physical at first, but would blossom into more than anything I could ever imagine. This was what I had, so this was what I was going with.

His eyes lit with curiosity. "When do we start?"

I let out a squeal and threw my arms around his neck. "So you'll help me?"

He faked a longsuffering sigh. "I guess. If good boy me is your only option, how can I say no?"

I knew he was joking, but I couldn't be happier. "Ahh, thank you, thank you, thank you!"

At that, I pulled away and got down to business again. "Well, I have the inside scoop that he's going to Bartlett's again tomorrow. Sarah, my former wing-woman, says so." I looked to the crowd of people as I spilled the plan in my head. "You can go to the bar, too. Be there before me. This time, our meeting will be planned. After I show up, flirt with me like you normally would, but this time it would be staged. We can go over your exact pickup lines. This'll get him jealous and badda-bam, badda-boom, he'll ask me out, and then it'll be happily ever after from there." I raised both shoulders to my ears and pointed to my cheeks where dimples would be if I had any.

This was so going to work. I just had the best feeling.

BRIAN

THERE WAS A carefree lightness in this girl, but most of all, she was just plain funny. Her idea was humorous, and the funnier fact was her certainty that her foolproof plan was going to work.

I still didn't like that it was Stiff she was going after, but the overprotective side of me was agreeing to her deal just to prove he wasn't who she thought he was.

"What is it about him?" I felt like I'd asked this question a million times. "How are you so sure he's the one?"

She softened like he was already her world, and a sudden but fierce pang of jealousy coursed through me, making me uneasy. There was absolutely no reason why I should be jealous.

"He's obviously good looking and smart." She stared into empty space, falling into a dream-like state. "And he's sweet and charming." She turned to me then. "The way he cares for his patients. I especially swoon every time he handles children." She slumped against the bench and sighed. "Let's reiterate again; he's a doctor. Plus, I think I just love him."

I wanted to tell her, 'To be nice to people and fix them up is his job.' I still didn't understand her obsession with this guy. I probably never would.

"Like I said before, I'm not a gold digger." She sat straighter in her seat and jutted out her chin. "I'm like the song; I work hard for my money. If I'm in search of a guy who does the same, what's wrong with that? If he wants me to retire so I can raise his babies, what's wrong with that, too? So quit trying to make me feel like I'm a gold digging hoe like Chlamydia Clary."

I blinked at her, trying not to laugh. "Who?"

"Never mind," she muttered, but clearly I'd struck a nerve.

"I never said that, Kendy, and I don't think that of you." Moving on. "So . . . what's in it for me?"

Her eyebrows pulled into a V as she placed her fingers on her lips, in deep concentration. "Hmm." She let out a carefree laugh that lightened my insides. "And here I was thinking all about me."

Just like that, her smile stretched across her face, and if I could have bet my last paycheck, it's as if she found another great idea. Her eyes gleamed with excitement. "I'm going to find you a girl."

"Go on," I prodded.

"I'm going to teach you a little about how to play the game, which in turn will land you that forever girl." Her face brightened.

Did this girl only think in forevers? "Okay," I said hesitantly.

"Don't be like that." She gave my shoulder a light-hearted punch. "Nice boys always finish last, right? So, say we make you not so good. I can show you pointers or something. Maybe we can even head to the bar and find your 'it' girl."

I cocked my head. It didn't sound like much, but if it revealed what an asshole this guy was, it'd totally be worth it. Besides, I had been so work focused I could use a change in my day-to-day. Maybe I needed this.

Trey was right. I deserved to have a little fun.

I gave her a light shoulder punch back, ready to commit to this. "Tonight it is. I'll see you then."

Chapter Seven

BRIAN

SHOWERED AND CLEAN, I tugged up my jeans. The tightness in my muscles told me that maybe I overdid it at the gym today. After slipping on my button down, I applied a little of Trey's hair product to the tips of my hair and stepped out of my bedroom.

"Whoa, hot date?" Trey was slouched against the couch, beer in hand, while the TV blasted in the background. I was surprised he was chilling tonight, staying in. By this time, he'd be ready to hit the clubs. Maybe he had a lady friend joining him.

"No, just going out," I said, fixing the buttons on my sleeves.

He lifted an eyebrow. "Going out alone looking like that? Someone's on a mission," he said, tipping his beer back.

"I'm just going out with a friend." Glancing at the Miller Lite in his hand made me want one for myself.

"Do I know this friend?" Trey asked, prodding for more information.

I squinted at the clock on the wall. I still had time to chill, so I strolled to the fridge and grabbed a beer. "Yeah, remember I was telling you about that nurse I met at the hospital?"

"Nice," he said, nodding in approval. "Finally. I like seeing you putting yourself out there."

Sure. Putting myself out there. He had no idea what Kendy had planned tonight, and I wasn't about to clue him in on her crazy scheme. I didn't want him to read more into it.

I plopped next to him and zeroed in on the soccer game he was watching. "So, where's Jenny today?" I wondered how serious this latest girl was, but I didn't want to pry.

In the six months I'd been here, I'd seen a revolving door of women come in and out. Most were models. Trey had high standards, and I swore every girl he dated had been as tall as him, with legs that went on forever. Jenny was the most recent constant.

"She's hanging out with her girlfriends or going out or something," he said, his eyes absent of any emotion.

"You guys serious?"

His tone hardened, getting touchy for a reason I couldn't place. "I don't know, bro. I'm trying . . . but something's off. She's a sweet girl, but . . . I just don't know."

My phone vibrated on the table, and I saw my little sister's face pop up. Trey stiffened as his eyes moved from my phone and then back to the TV.

I debated answering.

"Hey, man, it's cool," he said, but I could read the hurt behind his eyes.

I picked up on the third ring. "Hey, Katelynn," I answered warmly, well aware that Trey was right next to me. It'd been years since they'd broken up, and although he never talked to me about it, I knew there were still some unsettled issues between them.

"Hey, Bry. Ah! I miss you. I haven't talked to you in weeks." Her sweet voice automatically had me thinking of home, instantly relaxing me, and it got me wondering about my other siblings.

"Sorry. This new deal is kicking my ass." I rubbed the back of my neck, a habit I noticed I'd formed whenever I thought of work.

"It's fine." I could hear the enthusiasm in her voice. "Guess what?"

"What?" A smile crept up my face to match hers I sensed over the phone.

"I got the job!"

I could picture her blonde hair in a high ponytail as she bounced on her toes. At twenty-three, she still acted like a little girl. Then again, being the youngest of four kids, that's all I saw her as.

"I'm so excited," she continued. "I just went on my last interview a couple days ago. I had my phone glued to my hip. Mom kept asking me daily, and I didn't want to let her down, so I'm so glad I got the position. Program associate at the NOD, the National Organization of the Deaf."

I chuckled, picturing the goofy smile on her face. Katelynn had been top of her class at Champaign University, majoring in Early Childhood Education and earning her masters in American Sign Language. She knew what she wanted, and had always worked hard to get it.

NAD was the top non-profit organization assisting and educating others about the deaf. The company was headquartered in NYC, but they also had offices in many other prominent cities across the nation.

My sister was sweet as pie, and the most patient

person to boot. She had the biggest heart and believed she was put on Earth to change the world. I knew she'd be perfect for them and kick that job's ass. I loved her drive. At times, I believed we were two peas in the same pod.

"And guess what?"

"What?"

She let out another light squeal. "I'm going to be in NYC for a month for training." She paused, and then added, "They're putting me up in a hotel in Manhattan." Her voice lowered, which was a large contrast to her mood just a second ago. "I told them you live in New York, but I insisted I stay in a hotel. I just don't want it to be weird, you know . . . with him there."

I was beginning to wonder when things between her and Trey would go back to normal, or at least be somewhat civil. Like, when would she be able to say his name out loud, instead of calling him 'your roommate' or 'your friend'?

"Katelynn, don't worry about that. Everything will work out."

Trey seemed to be focused on the TV, but a part of me believed he was eavesdropping. I was certain he could hear Katelynn squealing over the phone.

"Just let me know, okay? Whatever you're comfortable with." My stare flickered in Trey's direction. "Anyways, sounds great, sis. I'm so proud of you. Was there any doubt?"

"I don't know. You can never be so sure, but once I know the details, I'll tell you," she said excitedly.

Trey's eyes were trained on a gym shoe commercial, the remote too tightly gripped in his hands.

"Sure thing," I replied.

"Love you, Bry. I'm so, so, so happy."

"I'm happy for you, too. You deserve it. Tell Mom and Dad I said hi." I hung up the phone and resisted the urge to probe Trey with questions.

His eyes flickered to mine and back to the TV. "So . . . how's Katelynn?" His voice shook as he uttered her name as though it pained him to say it out loud. His shoulders tensed like it was taking every ounce of energy to ask me that one question.

"She's good," I answered. All of me wondered what had happened years ago. One minute, they had been happy and in love, and the next minute, they were broken up. "She got a job at NOD, that huge organization for the deaf."

"That's good. I'm happy for her." He let out a jagged breath. "I'm happy that she's happy. Is she . . . How is she doing with Kyle?"

Awkwardness leaked into the air. I didn't want to talk about the douche, who wasn't anywhere near good enough for my baby sis, to the guy who I thought was. It wasn't my decision to make. I'd already told her how I felt.

"I don't ask about him when we talk."

Pain filtered through his eyes as he guzzled back his beer. "That's good," he said, somewhat sadly.

"She's going to be in New York in a month," I said, gauging his reaction.

He straightened, his eyes flying to mine. "She is?" His voice hitched up a notch, but in the next second, he reclined against the couch as though faking it was no big deal and shrugged. "I mean, that's good," he said. "That's good."

He'd said it twice, like he needed to convince himself.

This was getting awkward.

"Don't worry; she's staying at a hotel. She didn't want it to be weird between you guys."

He rubbed the back of his neck, his cool and calm facade fading. "Does she hate me that much?" He stood and stomped sulkily over to the garbage. "I'm fine with her here. It's ridiculous that she's staying at a hotel, when you hardly see each other as it is." The skin around his eyes bunched in a pained stare. "I'm fine. She's the one—" He cleared his throat. "—the one who left me."

Even though I knew he wouldn't divulge any information, I felt the need to ask again. "What happened between you guys? I thought you were it for each other."

He looked at me with a wounded gaze. "I thought so too, but . . . shit happens." He chugged his beer back, tossed it in the trash, and walked out of the room. "Have fun, whatever you do tonight."

I watched his retreat, knowing full well my sister would not give me any more info, either. She couldn't even mention his name.

For the thousandth time, I decided to let it go. I had to keep my head in the game. Literally.

I grabbed my keys from the counter and headed out to meet Kendy. I needed a good laugh tonight. I was going to be a fake boyfriend, and I needed to make sure I was a damn good one.

KENDY

I TUGGED MY black silk fitted halter dress just a little lower. It'd been a while since I'd worn it, and it was shorter than I remembered. Maybe because I was in my four-inch eff-me heels. I usually wore my three-inch gold ones.

I wanted to get noticed this time around. I wasn't going home without a second glance. No way, Jose. That was not happening tonight. I was dressed to impress, and tonight, less meant more. Especially in this dress.

I checked my makeup one last time and touched the draping, shimmery, gold triangular necklace that hung directly in my cleavage. It was as if the necklace was directing traffic to one of my best assets.

I wasn't expecting Sarah tonight. Brian and I had a plan, part one being I wouldn't be sharing a cab home with him, because I'd be leaving with Dr. Hot Pants. When my phone rang, I dug into my purse for it and saw Brian's name. My heart rate increased as I picked up on the first ring.

"Hey, I'm coming right down." I checked myself one more time in my floor-length mirror, pursing then smacking my lips together before I jetted out the door. I was hoping, wishing, and praying that tonight would not be another waste of time.

BRIAN

I RESTED AGAINST the brick, checking out the group in front of me. Saturday nights were bumping in Kendy's area. The amount of people out and about, all dressed up and ready go out, seemed electrified tonight. It would be tough to get a cab.

I was debating trying to get one while I waited, when saw a drop-dead bombshell stroll out the door. She was so damn gorgeous I had to do a double take. My eyes raked in all of her ensemble. Her black skintight dress accentuated every curve, and she must've been five-eight in her heels, which made her look like a runway model. Her hair was half up, blonde curls draping down her back.

Holy shit. Kendy had transformed from short and cute small town girl to bombshell babe.

I wasn't the only one who noticed. Every guy's head slowly turned, their eyes following her as she made her way toward me.

"Hey," she said, going up on her tiptoes to give me a half hug.

As I hugged her back, I took in the intoxicating smell of her shampoo and breathed in deeper, hoping she didn't notice. She released me too quickly, and I took a slight step back to admire the view once again.

"You look great," I said, embarrassingly breathless.

"I know, don't I?" She fluttered her eyelashes in an exaggerated way. "Just kidding. But seriously, we gotta go." She reached for my hand, lacing our fingers, and led us through the crowd.

I flexed my fingers and rewrapped them, tightening my hand around hers as I pulled us in the other direction. There was no way we were going to catch a cab in this herd of people.

"This way," I commanded.

She complied and smiled as we walked half a block and stopped in front of an apartment building, where another couple was waiting for a cab.

I couldn't stop staring. She was strikingly beautiful, her makeup not overdone, but perfect. Her pouty lip shined with whatever lipstick she had on, almost tempting me to bite it.

She fidgeted in her dress, tapping her heels against the sidewalk. "I'm so glad you picked me up."

"Of course." I smirked. "Good boy and all," I said, pulling at my shirt. "Would you expect any less?"

"Of course not." Her laughter floated toward me.

When a cab pulled up, I opened the door to let her in and scooted in beside her, our knees touching. I leaned in as an overwhelming need to be even closer took over, like a magnet, forcing me toward her.

"The Bartlett," I called out to the driver.

She looked my way, her turn to take in my ensemble. She cast an appreciative glance, her focus moving from my button down shirt, then to my dark jeans. "I never commented on how good you look."

"I know, don't I?" I repeated the line she'd thrown my way, and we both laughed.

"Brian, you start hanging out with me and you'll turn funny."

Was I not already?

I was about to give her a comeback for that when the cab swerved left and she fell into me. I caught her with both arms, our eyes locking. A dizzying current raced through me, a tingling sensation traveling up my arm.

She peered up at me, glanced down at my lips, and then her eyes flickered back to mine. Her breathing slowed as my fingers caressed her skin.

She shifted from my hold and released a nervous laugh. "Getting frisky already? We haven't even hit the club."

Car horns blaring outside redirected our focus to the back-to-back traffic ahead of us, and she angled her knees away from me. "I just wanted to go over our game plan one more time." She clasped her hands together as her eyes danced with excitement.

"We've been through your 'game plan' five times already." Little did she know I had a plan of my own, which included exposing this guy for the loser he truly was.

Her laughter was marvelous, catching. "Well, I just want to make sure you know what you're doing." When she pulled down her skirt, my gaze traveled down the length of her legs. Hell, she looked so edible.

With a painted fingernail, she lifted my chin to meet her eyes, blatantly catching me gawking. Now it was my turn to laugh.

"Up here, lover boy," she commanded good-naturedly. "We're going to walk in separately. First you, and then five minutes later, I'm going to stroll in and you're going to hit on me. You're going to come on to me so strong. Everyone in the whole entire bar will know you only want me. It'll be dark, so we'll need an over exaggeration of normal body language, okay?"

"Don't worry. I got this." My voice was totally calm, but I sensed a little nervousness in her as she wrung her hands together in her lap. A strong urge to calm her came over me. "Don't worry," I repeated, placing one hand on top of hers to keep her fidgeting to a minimum.

When her stiff posture didn't let up, I scooted over and threw one hand to her other side, by the window, caging her in.

Her breath caught in her throat, and I whispered, "What's your name, beautiful?" I meant it as a joke, to break her from her mood, but my pulse was spiking from being so close to her.

Her lips parted as her eyes flickered to my mouth again. Her scent was making my head spin.

"Your name?" I commanded, my tone husky.

Goose bumps spread on her neck. "Kendall." Her voice was barely audible as her breathing turned shallow, her hands falling to my waist.

She bit down on her lower lip seductively, and I had an undeniable urge to claim her, to crash my mouth against hers. The air between us was charged, a gravitational pull tugging me closer, so strong that I couldn't resist as I dropped my arms and aligned my lips with hers.

"What're you drinking?" I asked, playing the part. I knew what I wanted to drink—her . . . all of her, take her mouth and suckle the tender part of her bottom lip.

She tilted her head back, the light from the moon catching the blue in her irises. As her eyes turned lustful, giving me permission, I closed the gap between us, about to quench the desire inside of me.

Then the car jerked to a stop, and I flew backward against the seat, which broke the tension between us. Moment gone.

I blinked a couple of times like I'd been shocked by the impact. She let out a nervous laugh.

"Is that enough body language for you?" I rubbed my neck and took a huge breath and blew it out slowly.

She nodded as she averted her eyes and stared out her window. "Perfect."

"We're here," I said, observing our surroundings.

I paid our cab driver, stepped out, and extended my hand to assist her.

When she placed her hand in mine, heat spread through my fingers, but she pulled away and glanced at her watch, the round gold dial spanning her whole wrist.

"He'll be there now. I just hope to God this isn't another waste of a Saturday night."

I felt a sudden sourness in the back of my throat as I

remembered our arrangement.

She extended her fist and gave me the cutest smile ever. "We got this, right?"

"Yeah, we got this." My fist connected with hers in some sort of pact.

It was funny, because I had no idea how I'd gotten pulled into this, when I really wasn't getting anything in return. I could get my own women just fine. But I sensed Kendy always had a way of getting people to agree with her plans. This girl entertained me, for sure. Before I knew it, I was saying yes to her crazy ideas.

The next second, she surprised me again by reaching for my hand. Her eyes danced with excitement as she squeezed it. "I'm so excited. I just have this feeling, like tonight is my night."

I smiled at her, all the while thinking, *This guy—this Stiff—better not be a dick.*

THE THUNDEROUS MUSIC played on the speakers as the bass pounded in my ears. I walked straight past Stiff and his friends and sat down right where we'd be seen. After I ordered a beer, my eyes focused on the group of guys in front of me laughing. Stiff already had a blonde practically sitting on his lap. She was wearing a black fitted tee with 'The Bartlett' across her chest. My jaw tightened at the sight. Immediately, I wanted to rush outside and intercept Kendy before she saw this scene, to protect her in some way.

When the blonde stood, he slapped her ass. "I want your fine self back here when you're done with your shift," Stiff yelled at her as she threw him a flirty smile before turning to walk away.

His friends gawked at a group of ladies next to them. Then Stiff, the bravest of them all, strolled over and chatted up his next victim, the most attractive of the three. Tonight, he was in blue jeans and a fitted, striped button down. It looked multi-colored under the dim lights of the club.

Whatever he said to the woman was working as she placed her hand in his, most likely introducing herself. My insides heated with irritation. Last weekend, he'd been with another woman, and tonight, here he was. Again.

Screw. This.

This shithead.

There must be some sort of appeal with the unattainable. I could see Kendy always being up for a challenge. He was nowhere near settling down material. I had no clue why she thought he was.

The redhead stood and followed him to the bar, and I fisted my hands at my sides. I was about to walk outside and snap some sense into Kendy, but she strolled through the double doors.

Kendy stood tall, her head high with an air of confidence that everyone took note of. All of Stiff's friends turned to check her out as she sashayed across the room and sat two stools away from me.

Even though tonight I was playing a part, if she were a stranger to me, I'd be checking her out as soon as she stepped into this bar.

She crossed her legs, which hitched up her skirt, revealing more of her perfect thigh. When her eyes caught mine, she threw me a flirty smile, one she was used to throwing. But then I watched her eyes skitter across the room in search of Stiff. I knew when she found him, because her smile faltered. She blinked a couple times, unable to hide her disappointment.

I got up and charged her way. I no longer gave a shit that I was supposed to wait five minutes. I needed to see that smile again. "Hey, gorgeous. Someone sitting here?" Those had been the exact words we'd practiced at the park.

It was comical, because we'd had to rehearse it multiple times until she stopped laughing. I had used every accent I knew just to hear her crack up.

Kendy's laughter was like an epidemic. It could spread across a room, or over a crowd like wildfire. It was high-pitched, cute, and irresistible. Kind of like a child giggling. And whenever she got into her fits, she looked younger, lighter, and I let her energy wash over me.

"Hey, gorgeous," I repeated when she didn't respond. Her eyes were still on Stiff.

My chest tightened at the look in her eyes. Her smile was fake, forced, but I didn't even give her a chance to respond as I plopped down next to her. "You're the hottest girl in here, and I'd like to buy you a drink."

"Sure. I'll just have a gin and tonic." Her voice was resigned, sad even.

I got the bartender's attention and ordered her beverage when her eyes flickered back to Stiff, watching as he sweet-talked the redhead, who was obviously taking the bait.

I placed my hand on Kendy's forearm, trying to break her from her trance.

"Hey, so let's cut to the chase. Do you want to go to my place, or would you rather go to yours?" I joked, winking at her.

I was rewarded with a small smile, which kept me

going. "Or we can just go to the back, the bathroom maybe? You're just so damn hot I might not be able to make it home."

"You're too funny," she droned, her small smile widening just a tad.

The bartender set her drink on the counter, and I threw my money on the bar and a couple dollars for the tip.

I handed her the glass and angled toward her. "Don't let Stiff ruin your night. We're still going to have fun."

I wished I hadn't mentioned his nickname, because her eyes flipped back to him. Now, he was making his way back to his group of friends with the redhead.

They were closer to us, but Stiff's eyes didn't make it our way, because he was preoccupied with the woman I was sure he was trying to bed.

"Hey, is your dad a terrorist?" I teased, pumping out my cheesy one-liners.

Her eyebrows pulled in. "What?" She finally gave me her attention.

"Because he made the bomb." I tried to maintain composure and keep my voice level.

A flash of humor crossed her face, making this man desperate for another dose. "Is that a space dress?" I paused for dramatic effect. "Because your body is out of this world."

Her laughter was contagious, which had me grinning like a crazy person. Still, I kept going. "My love for you is like diarrhea. I just can't keep it in."

"Stop," she wheezed, slapping the bar. "Aren't you the comedian?" Her laughter was a full-hearted sound, rippling through the room.

I chuckled along with her. "Are you a library book?

Because I'd like to check you out."

She pinched my arm playfully and brought her hand up to stifle her giggles. "Please, I can't take anymore," she cracked up, but then her body stiffened. Her hand flew to my forearm as her eyes widened. "Shit, he's looking our way."

When I peered over her head, the group of girls had disappeared and Stiff had indeed zoned in on Kendy.

"Stop staring," she squealed. "Quick, lean into me; say something in my ear."

I did as I was told, though her proximity was unnerving. Being this close to her, I had a sudden urge to lick the sensitive spot right below her ear. "What do you want me to say?"

Her eyes flickered to him then back to mine.

God, she was so close I just wanted to run my tongue along the seam of her ear. She smelled like peaches, and I wanted to see if she tasted like them, too.

She blinked twice as her demeanor turned serious, and I would've never guessed what was going to come out of her mouth next.

"Kiss me," she demanded frantically. "Full on. Right now."

KENDY

MY STATEMENT MUST'VE baffled him, because he got this dazed and confused look in his eye. "Kiss me, just do it." My eyes moved slowly in Dr. Klein's direction, just subtle enough so I knew he was still staring at me, but where he didn't know I was staring back. "It's part of the game."

Brian angled in but pulled back, hesitating.

"Come on. Give it to me, your best kiss ever."

And then he cupped the side of my face, grazing my cheek gently with his thumb. I shouldn't have felt anything, but I felt everything. His light hold sent a tingling sensation from my cheek, down my neck, making my nipples pebble.

He licked his lips as our eyes caught. The lust in his gaze was intense and, as he leaned into me, I found myself closing my eyes and letting him capture my lips with his.

When we touched, I jolted from the electricity that coursed between us. I hadn't expected that. At. All.

His kiss was soft and sweet, but urgent, and I melted into his hold. My God, was he a good kisser. He sucked on my bottom lip, and alternated between teasing my top and then back to the bottom. After a few seconds, he flicked his tongue for me to open, and I let him in. I felt myself become wet with desire as his tongue slicked against mine. My breathing hitched, and my heartbeat continued to beat hard in my chest, until I felt the thud in my ears.

When I'd told him to kiss me full on, I hadn't expected his kiss to be like this—all-consuming, overwhelming my whole body.

Then, abruptly, he pulled back, leaving me bereft and cold. My eyes locked on his, and my rapid pulse drummed against my wrist as though it was playing "Little Drummer Boy" on super speed. He left me breathless, but I could tell he was, too.

"Good enough?" he said with a small smile.

I couldn't do anything but nod. I was like an animal in heat, wanting his lips on me again.

Then I blinked, snapping back to the present, and glanced back at Dr. Klein. Well, damn. I had his full attention now. "Perfect," I replied, but I was feeling oddly torn, as my body was still preoccupied with that kiss.

I'd kissed a lot of men in my life, but I'd have to rate Brian's the best kiss ever. If he ever entered some sort of kissing contest, he'd win the trophy by a landslide.

When I finally caught my breath, I flipped around and noticed I'd lost Dr. Klein's attention. A new group of girls was now congregating in front of him.

Seriously?

My stomach dropped to my toes as my disappointment from earlier turned into pure annoyance. He was one tough guy to decipher. I couldn't figure him out at all. The nurses at work said he was always saying he was looking for serious material, yet he came to this bar and flirted with everyone wearing a skirt. Well, everyone except me.

Why?

He was a walking contradiction.

I huffed, crossing my arms over my chest.

But the psychic had predicted he was *it* for me. And she'd been right about everything else so far, so I had to believe her. If I wanted any semblance of a normal life, her prediction had to come true.

Maybe I needed to give this more time.

Dr. Klein stood with his entourage of guy friends and headed out of the bar with the group of girls. I didn't know if they had known those girls from before, waited for them, or had just met them. Either way, they strolled out together before I could even bat an eye.

I peered up at Brian, who had 'I told you so' written all over his face. I spun around, not wanting to hear him gloat about how stupid I was.

"I hate him," I muttered, but there was no bite in my voice.

I stared at the door where Dr. Klein and his friends had just left, huffing in frustration at another wasted outfit and ruined Saturday night.

I just didn't get it. Evangeline had said it as clear as day that I would get over my past relationship and the guy who gave me the moon was the one I was meant to be with. We'd end up happy. Together.

I should've asked her how to win the man of my dreams and how long it would take. I wished she had an eight-hundred number that I could put on speed dial. I hated how this was her last unresolved prediction about my life. It made me feel unsettled, unfinished somehow.

"Hey," Brian said. "Are you religious?"

I glared at him, already in a foul mood. "What?"

He angled closer, a glint of humor in his eyes. "Because I think you're the answer to all my prayers." He wiggled his eyebrows at me, trying to get me to laugh, which worked.

I decided I could let this whole failed night depress me, or I could start anew tomorrow. And my happiness was worth fighting for, even if it had just walked out the door with another woman.

I shook my head to break me from my sour mood. Tomorrow would be another day, and tonight was not to be wasted. "Let's get out of this joint and have some fun. I've got my dancing outfit on." I shimmied and gave Brian a hopeful smile.

Brian flipped up his collar. "Dancing? Do you know

how crazy awesome a dancer I am? I'll have you pulling me into the alley after one song."

His goofy face had me cracking up again. The man definitely made me laugh. That was a quality worth marrying. For someone else, of course.

The bartender placed my gin and tonic on the table.

"After this drink," I said, tipping back the glass to chug it. I felt the burn at the back of my throat and welcomed it. Maybe it would dull the rejection. "I plan to get butt-ass wasted tonight and shake my tail feathers."

At that, we clinked our beverages, my glass to his beer bottle. I probably wouldn't remember what happened tomorrow morning anyway. Maybe that was a good thing.

Chapter Eight

BRIAN

WE ENDED UP in the Meatpacking District at Enclave Night Club. The line stretched out the door and down the block, but Kendy used her ever-charming voice and hot body to get us in, totally bypassing the line.

She knew how to work it. She oozed sex appeal, but it was subtle, not annoying. One look from the tattooed bouncer had him practically drooling at her feet. She had a way with words, I was coming to find out.

We rushed straight to the bar, me leading her through the crowd to a spot where we could both fit against the masses. An hour later, we had downed multiple drinks. I'd lost count of the exact number. She kept ordering, and I kept buying. We laughed, chugging back and repeating. I didn't mind, as long as I kept seeing that smile on her face and her mind far away from Stiff.

I tossed out my one-liner jokes, her laughter fueling me to keep them coming. I didn't even know where I was coming up with half of this shit, but it was working, and that was all that mattered.

After a couple of hours, her eyes were glossed over. "I'm going to get my dance on," she said, downing her drink and moving through the crowd.

She ended up on the raised box by the DJ, dancing next to another woman. Without a doubt, Kendy outdid this woman in looks, stature, and with her moves. I watched a group of guys congregate below her, their tongues practically hanging out of their mouths as the strobe lights hit her face and showcased her alluring body. My jaw tensed as an overpowering jealousy surged through me.

Her eyes fell shut as she swayed and moved to the music. The men were like moths to a flame, and slowly, she had her own fan club of dudes vying for her attention.

The music was bumping, and I leaned against the bar. The black skirt she was wearing clung to her body like saran wrap, inching up her thighs with each bounce.

I tipped back my beer and ordered another. When I turned around, a guy had made his way behind her, forcing the other woman down from the small box. They were grinding to the music as their bodies meshed together. I watched the strobe lights flicker across her face. The glow made her look like she was the star of a show. My jaw locked when she molded her ass against the man behind her. He seemed to enjoy it. Who wouldn't?

But when his hands made their way around her ass and to her inner thigh, I slammed my beer bottle on the counter. Screw this.

Suddenly, Kendy froze and her eyes popped open in shock. She shifted toward him, looking like she was spitting words at him as I barreled through the crowd. I could read her face as the strobe lights flashed on her angry features.

When she hopped off the box, he jumped behind her and grabbed her wrist. She jerked her hand away, and I was a foot away and about to step in between them when I saw something I'd never seen before.

I widened my eyes when Kendy reached down, grabbed him by the balls, and twisted.

His face registered pain.

"Bitch!" he yelped.

"Pinky dick!" she yelled back. "I can't even cop a feel down there."

Just before he took a step toward her, I blocked his path. "Get the fuck away from her, asshole."

I gestured for him to leave, but he stood there for a moment, looking indecisive. I fisted my hands at my sides, ready for action if he decided to try to take me down. No way in hell was there going to be a repeat of the stitches incident.

His eyes met mine, sizing me up. A second later, he must've thought better of it, because he cast her a glare and turned to walk away.

Pussy.

I shook my head and glanced back at her. "Get a good feel there?" I was trying to make light of the situation, but I hated to think what would've happened had I not been here.

I doubted Kendy's reaction would've been any different.

"Yeah, fucker thought he could touch what wasn't his. I was going to rip his dick off and feed it to him." Her angry eyes narrowed and flickered toward the guy who was now making his way to a new target.

I didn't want to lecture her, but the words flew out anyway. "I know you can take care of yourself, but don't be too brave when you're alone." Maybe it was the big brother in me, or maybe it was the adrenaline spike. I couldn't tell. All I knew was I didn't want anything to happen to her.

She shrugged one shoulder, unbothered. "Okay." And then a small smile appeared as she grabbed my hand. "Let's dance." She moved us through the mass of bodies on the dance floor. "I'm not letting that guy or Dr. Hot Pants ruin my night. I'm still determined to have a good time."

When she found us a perfect spot, she placed her hands on my shoulders and crushed her breasts against my chest. The room was already warm, but our sexual magnetism turned up the heat level to scorching hot.

My hands slowly fell to her waist as her hips moved and dipped to the music. When the beat changed, she turned around and ground her ass against me. I followed her lead, our bodies in sync, and instantly I hardened. God, this girl was going to be the death of me.

I pulled her flush against me, and she turned back around and wrapped her hands around my neck. Her skirt hitched up a tad as my hands drifted to her stomach, inching to the bareness of her back, kneading her silky skin.

This woman was intoxicating, and I was powerless to resist her.

When she lifted her head as an invitation to kiss her, I did, different than before, with more urgency as my mouth covered hers hungrily.

She gripped my hair as our bodies meshed together. She tasted like peaches. Sweet, succulent peaches. I tilted her head to go deeper, sliding my tongue against hers, and she moaned into my mouth as her breaths deepened.

She was riding me on the dance floor, her core against my dick, which throbbed and begged to break free. I couldn't think clearly. I wanted to take her somewhere secluded to satisfy my need. Doing this girl would be a

complication, but hell, I wanted her bad.

KENDY

OH, GOD.

His kiss was overwhelming, addicting, and making my body tingle. From the goose bumps on my neck, to the shivers up my spine and the wetness in my panties. It had been a seven-month dry spell, and I needed water to quench this thirst, if only for a night.

Brian wasn't just a warm body; he was flipping hotter than the devil himself.

Somewhere, a little tiny voice reminded me why we were here—to get the doctor jealous—but my brain was mush. His lips against mine and his hands roaming over my body were making me lose focus. Any semblance of an earlier plan vanished in my drunken state. My body turned liquid beneath his hold. My raging hormones rushed to the surface as I molded against him.

His arousal pressed against my stomach, which only fueled the hungry fiend inside me. I needed release. Bad.

All I heard was the beat of the music, saw the flash of the strobe lights, and felt the heat of his lips, his tongue moving against mine. I reached down and rubbed against his jeans. He was at full attention, ready for me, and, God, was I ready for him.

I didn't care there was a massive amount of people in the club, watching me give this guy a hand job. Shoot, they all probably wanted one, too. Besides, the place was dark. I doubted anyone knew what we were doing.

"Damn, you're sexy," he said huskily.

His words raised the heat inside me. I didn't think that was remotely possible. My body was already on fire.

I wanted him to touch me, too. As if reading my mind, his hand trailed slowly from my waist to my hip to my bare outer thighs, pulling at the fabric. My ass cheeks were almost hanging out. It was the cutest but hottest thing, like he didn't want me exposed for everyone to see, though I didn't care.

He pulled my skirt down and gripped my ass through my clothes, pulling me flush against his length. My breath hitched and my pulse went haywire.

He ground himself against me, and I could tell he was well endowed, even with his pants on. I pulled back, bit my lip, and locked eyes with his as my breathing turned shallow. It was game over, because this man was going to feel the 'Power of the P' tonight.

"Let's get out of here." I dragged him through the crowd and into the fresh outdoors. My insides tingled with anticipation as my thighs rubbed together, ready for him to take me.

The horns of the cabs blared in the background, but I still knew nothing but his hand in mine.

My lips parted as he pulled me to the corner and raised his hand. "My place." His voice was strong with urgency as he hugged me close. I rubbed my aching breasts against his chest, needing the friction. No other words were spoken as he hailed us a cab.

We jumped in the back seat and, as soon as he sat down, I straddled him, rubbing against his length as my skirt inched up my thighs, making my panties even wetter.

After he recited his address to the cab driver, my lips connected with the pulsing hollow of his throat and then trailed to outline his ear with my tongue.

I fisted his hair as our lips collided, my tongue tasting, flicking, and exploring the recesses of his mouth. My breathing was labored as I dry humped him in the back of the car, making out like we were teenagers at a drive-in.

The cabbie didn't even try to stop us. This was probably common in Manhattan at two a.m.

I tugged at his hair, pulled his head back, and saw pure lust in his eyes. "F-T-F-ing," I said breathlessly, riding him as though we were at the rodeo.

He tried to kiss me, but I pulled him back, tugging harder at the ends of his hair. I needed him to agree. I didn't need complications. Not when he wasn't part of my ultimate plan.

I couldn't afford to hurt him, so we could only do this if he knew this was purely physical. "No complications. Friends that fuck. That's it. We're F-T-F-ing."

I stilled, hoping he'd give me the answer I needed to hear. If he didn't, I thought my insides would blow. The bunny vibrator I had at home would not be able to fill me the way I knew only he could.

"Yes," he breathed, making my whole body sing. Then I smiled at him and crashed my lips against his. I'd just given him a deal every man wanted.

BRIAN

I WOULD'VE SAID yes to anything. If she'd asked me if I was an alien from outer-fucking-space, it wouldn't have mattered. The answer would've been yes. I wanted this woman bad. My body had never screamed for release louder, especially as she rode me in the back of this cab.

I need to get home. Quick.

I threw the driver a bill. It could've been a fifty for all I knew.

Kendy's legs were wrapped around me as I carried her, holding her by the ass up two flights of stairs.

"Keys?"

"In my pocket," I said, moving my lips to her neck. Damn, she tasted so good. I'd bet my next paycheck she tasted like heaven everywhere else, too.

She giggled as she reached into my pocket. I sucked and flicked my tongue against her neck, tasting the salt on her skin as I kneaded her ass with my hands. Her scent was intoxicating, and it didn't help the major hard-on I was rocking.

When she turned the knob, I almost lost my footing, but shifted to grip her ass to get a better hold. She laughed again as our eyes connected. Damn, she was hot, even all giggly.

As we stepped through the door, she dropped the keys on the floor, and I strode toward my bedroom.

KENDY

WHEN MY FEET connected with the carpet of his room, I felt bereft, missing being connected to him, though we were only a foot apart. He slammed the door behind him, kicked off his shoes, and lifted the back of his shirt over his head, flinging it to the side.

At once, that empty space between us was filled as he pulled me in and kissed me, sending a current of shock straight to my core. We went at it again, his tongue in my mouth, his hands groping me through my clothes, and his body meshing into mine. The sensual friction caused my insides to heat to immeasurable temperatures, and my heart hammered in my ears.

I fiddled with the button of his jeans as he backed me up until I felt the foot of his bed hit the back of my knees.

He pulled at my dress, caressing me through the fabric, wanting it off. Our movements were uninhibited, erratic.

My impatience grew as I tore off his jeans and gripped his hardness. When his dick popped free from his boxers, my eyes widened, causing a hot ache between my legs. Holy shit, he was huge.

One of my boobs hung out of my dress and he caressed it, flicking his thumb against my nipple. In the next second, he circled my nipple with his tongue, sucking, tasting, and teasing it with his mouth,

My head fell back in utter ecstasy. "Oh, God," I moaned. I closed my eyes as his lips warmed my flesh.

I needed him to stop. Now. Before he made me come and I couldn't feel him inside me.

I pulled at his hair to meet his eyes. "Where are your condoms?"

"Patience is a virtue, Kendy." His mouth was saying one thing, but his body said another as he shoved my dress and underwear to the floor.

"I left patience at the club." I tugged his boxers down his legs, dropped to my knees, and took his length inside my mouth.

He gasped, his hands gripping the back of my head as his fingers threaded through my hair. I smiled, wondering where his patience was now.

"Fuuuuck." He closed his eyes and threw back his head.

My legs parted slightly as a shiver coursed through my body. I'd never heard him swear before. Not like all guys had to swear, but coming out of Brian's mouth, it made him that much hotter.

I took him in fast, feeling his tip at the back of my throat, and sucked his hardness.

Our eyes locked as I peered up at him. His look was filled with desire so strong, I needed him undone. Thank the heavens I didn't have a gag reflex.

"Damn, baby." He pulled my hair to the side as I continued to suck up and down his length, my lips beginning to numb from the motions. "You're going . . . you're going to make me bust." His voice shook like he was hanging onto his last thread of control.

Even on my knees, I knew he was at my mercy. I was pretty sure I could have made him come in my mouth, but I needed release, too.

He tugged me up, and I let him take the lead. My breathing was labored as he grabbed a handful of my ass, pulling me against him. I needed him inside me.

"I want to fuck you," I said, flicking my tongue at the rim of his ear. "Hard."

His hands locked on my chin, forcing me to look at him in the most intimate stare. "You want it hard, baby?"

My insides jolted with excitement, and my thighs tightened with anticipation. "Hard and fast." It was the only way I knew, the only way I had liked it since Cole.

I kissed him firmly in response as his fingertips dug into my thigh and his length pressed against my stomach. He pulled back to reach into the side table for a condom. Not breaking our eye contact, he tore the package open with one side of his mouth.

I plucked the condom from his hands and disposed of the package. "Let me," I said with the most seductive look I could give him.

BRIAN

I LOVED HER hands on me, her mouth on me. I wanted her like she was my next steak dinner. I hadn't had sex in a while, and I was about to combust any second. It had taken all my self-restraint to not come undone in her mouth.

This woman was hotter than most models walking the runway, and I'd dated some hot ones before. Our breathing turned erratic as she dropped her hands to roll the condom on me. The next second, I lifted her by the waist and felt her wetness rub against my stomach.

When I moved us to the edge of my bed and she fell back, I kneeled in front of her, needing to be inside her. Her eyes widened, and I stopped because she stiffened. I froze for a second, reading something in her eyes. Fear? The panic in her normally soft features alarmed me. I sensed a shift in the mood, but before I could read further, a small seductive smile crept up her face, as though she had shaken it off and I had imagined the utter dread from moments ago.

"I don't like being on the bottom. I can't come on the bottom," she said, pushing me to sit.

Without warning, she lowered herself on me before the loudest moan escaped my mouth. And I was a done man.

KENDY

"OH, GOD," I screamed.

He felt so good, so right as I bounced on him. My eyes closed and my head fell back in utter ecstasy. He cupped one of my breasts with one hand and took it into his mouth. The buildup in my core and the tingling in my spine intensified as I rode up and down his length.

It was all too much to take in as I leaned back and dug my fingertips into his thighs.

"You're so beautiful," he said huskily, his hands pressing against my ass and moving me up and down his cock.

I couldn't say a thing. I was on the brink of overflowing. A few more seconds and I felt myself tipping over, a full-on orgasm rocking my entire body. I bit down on his shoulder, breaking skin as he pumped harder and faster. The contractions shook my body in the best orgasm I'd felt in ages.

When my orgasm died down, I fell on top of him, utterly exhausted as my heart still pounded in my chest. His cock was still hard as a rock inside me as he lifted me by the waist, flipped me around, pushed me on all fours, entering me from behind.

"Oh, God," I screamed again, feeling his thickness fill me as a delicious heat spread throughout my body.

"You want it hard?" He reached down and massaged my clit as he continued to pound into me.

He pulled back and then rammed into me, making my teeth jolt and my stomach clench. He repeated the motion again and again, causing that familiar build up I had felt just moments ago to return. Panting, he moved faster, less controlled, more inconsistent, until I knew he was this close to coming.

"Come," he moaned against my ear, dropping to my back as he moved inside me. "Now." It wasn't a request as his voice came out in harsh broken puffs. "Now," he groaned again and, just like a puppy wanting her treat, I did as I was told and came undone, both of us coming together and me screaming like I'd just won the lotto, which I had—the orgasm lotto.

As we both descended from our high, he pulled me onto his chest, and a soft fit of laughter escaped me.

"What?" he asked, his breathing labored as his heart raced against my cheek.

I peered up at him. "Nothing," I laughed again.

His mouth twitched with amusement. Little did he know the real reason for my laughter. Why Beth ever passed this up, I'd never know.

An emotion I couldn't place crossed his face right before he bent down and kissed me, long and hard, leaving me breathless.

Yes, I was convinced Beth had chosen wrong. Because good boy Brian was indeed a very, very bad boy in bed.

BRIAN

HER BACK HAD to be the sexiest thing. Tan, smooth, sultry. I wanted to lick every inch of it and worship her body with my mouth.

For the past fifteen minutes, we hadn't said a word, and just waited for our breathing to relax and our pulses to return to their normal rates.

I wanted her again. The thought seemed crazy, since we were just at it moments ago. But this woman was addictive, sexy, and seductive, and I wondered, since we'd crossed that line and I'd had a taste of her, if it would ever be enough to satisfy me.

When she stilled, I wondered if she was asleep. I wrapped my hands around her waist and pulled her closer, wanting her near me. Then I ducked my head into her hair, inhaling deeply and taking in her scent, her own unique scent I could probably pick out in a lineup by now.

I moved her hair to her shoulder, exposing the smooth span of skin between her shoulder blades. I wasn't sure if she was asleep, but it was too hard to resist as I kissed her right at the nape of her neck. She stirred as I flicked my tongue at the tender spot that had driven her wild earlier.

I sensed her smile, even though I couldn't see it, and my hands trailed up her thigh to her hip and onto her breasts. I rolled her nipple between my fingertips, feeling her pebble within my hold. When she moved away from me lazily, I pulled her closer, wrapped one hand around her stomach, and tugged her flush against me, basically spooning her.

When I used my teeth to nip at her neck, I heard her groggy voice, which was sexy as ever. "Mmmm, Brian."

The way she said my name had me standing at attention, ready to take her again.

She flipped over, her stark blue eyes staring up at me in the darkness of the room. A smile played on her lips. "What do you think you're doing?"

"Kissing you," I said as I bent down and captured her lips with mine, feeling my cock twitch at the contact.

"No, you're spooning me, and under the FTF

guidelines, that's against the rules."

"Who says?" I kissed her again.

"The FTF handbook says." Her eyes danced with mischief.

When I bent down for another one, she stopped me. "And who's the author of this handbook?" I raised an eyebrow as my hands dropped to grab her ass, the most perfect apple ass. This girl had curves in all the right places.

"I am, of course." She let out a carefree laugh, and it did something to my insides.

A euphoric sensation washed over me, and I wanted to hear it again. I was addicted to her laughter.

I pinched her sides and more giggles escaped her. "I want to know the rules, just so I don't break them." I kissed her again, because I wanted to, before she could tell me that the rules indicated I couldn't.

"I don't know. I have to think about it. The first rule should be no spooning, and most definitely no sleepovers." She bit her lower lip, her face contemplating. "We can't do boyfriend and girlfriend things, so no dates." She let out a low laugh. "Except eating. We can eat together. A girl has to eat."

She scooted off the bed, but I tugged her back and pulled her on top of me, kissing her lips.

"No sweet kissing," she murmured against my mouth as she bit on my lower lip, making my cock twitch again.

Even though we were separated by a sheet, she had to know I was ready for her. I dropped my head to her collarbone and nipped at the tender skin with my teeth. She shifted and straddled me, only a white cotton sheet separating us.

"What else?" I asked.

"Hmmm, no sweet kissing . . ."

"Yes, you said that already." My tongue traveled up her neck to the side of her chin and to the outline of her lips. I flicked my tongue, entering her mouth and feeling her warm, slick tongue against mine.

I pushed my hardness against her center, and she gasped.

"How about kissing like this?" I teased and suckled her soft lips, my tongue exploring the recesses of her mouth until she had to pull back for air.

She was breathless, her lips were swollen, and there was a look of lust in her eyes which mirrored mine. I wanted to be inside her . . . again.

"What else?" I asked, grinding my length against her core.

"Last rule, no talking." She pulled my mouth back up, hers covering mine hungrily as I reached into the side drawer to grab a condom.

"That's my favorite rule."

Chapter Nine

BRIAN

THE NEXT MORNING, every part of my body ached as I thought of Kendy. As soon as she'd left last night, all I could think about was the next time we'd see each other. The deal was no commitment, no attachment, purely 'FT-Fing', as she called it. It was every guy's deal of a lifetime, only I wasn't too sure about this arrangement we had going. But I pushed aside my conventional thinking. This was exactly what I needed. Especially being so strung out over work.

I'd wanted her to stay the night so we could go for another round this morning, but she'd been adamant about not falling asleep in my bed, even though we were exhausted after our night of foreplay and hardcore sex.

I glanced at my alarm clock, noting it was close to lunchtime, so I dressed in some sweats and headed to the living room.

Trey was at the kitchen bar, wearing a smile so wide I swear I saw his molars. "Good morning, 'God'."

I shook my head at him. I guess in the heat of passion, I'd forgotten I had a roommate.

"Isn't that your name?" He was looking at me, all proud and shit. "Oh, God!" he moaned in a high-pitched voice as he undulated his hips.

Ignoring him, I reached in the fridge for the milk and searched for a cup in the overhead cupboard.

"Dude, that one was a screamer."

"My bad. I didn't mean to keep you up all night." I strolled to the kitchen island with the milk and cup. "How was your night?" I asked, moving the focus off of me.

He raised his eyebrows, still grinning. "Well, I couldn't sleep. I thought the apocalypse was happening with the moving walls, the pounding, and the screaming like someone was getting murdered."

I rolled my eyes, though I had to smile as I thought about it. He wasn't wrong. And, damn, it had been so good. "I'll try to keep it down next time."

Next time? Would there be a next time?

I didn't like the thought of last night being a one-time thing, so I shoved it to the back of my mind.

He clasped my shoulder. "I'm just happy you're getting laid, man. I was starting to wonder if you were playing for the other side." He stood and headed toward the fridge. "Who's this lucky chick?"

"You remember the nurse? Yeah, her."

He cast me an appreciative glance. "So this is more than a one-night thing? You guys met at the bar, and you saw her at the park last week."

I narrowed my eyes at his nosy ass. "You stalking me now?"

"No." He reached for the rag hanging from the fridge and threw it at my head. "You just don't get out much, so it's the only place you've been besides work, dumbass. When you seeing her again?"

I gulped back the rest of the milk and played with the glass in my hands. "I don't know," I answered honestly.

He turned around. "Dude, man." He walked toward me, carton of orange juice in hand. "You dating this girl exclusively?"

"Me?" I asked, reeling back. "No." I replied, remembering Stiff. "She has her sights set on some other dude." A loser, who was too good for her, but there was nothing I could do to change her mind.

"Whoa, man, kinky shit you got going on there." Trey chuckled, gulping down the juice from the carton. Gross.

"Bro," I huffed, "ever heard of a glass? Use it. Anyways, she doesn't like me like that. She doesn't want anything serious." I tried to shove out any unwelcome disappointment. I knew what I was signing up for here.

Trey's wheels started turning. "So she's giving you free sex for nothing in return?"

I sighed. I didn't need to go into how I was supposed to play her boy toy to get Stiff jealous. He didn't need to know about that part of our relationship. "I don't know. All I know is she's not looking for commitment. Not from me anyway." It was the truth.

He squinted and let out a low laugh before he punched me in the shoulder. "Man, that lady just made you a deal of a lifetime."

"Yeah," I answered. So why the hell was I so down about it?

KENDY

AFTER BRIAN AND my sexcapades last night, my whole body ached, but in a way that could only be cured by him. I knew without a shadow of a doubt that I'd see him soon.

I needed to get my Brian fix.

I rubbed my index finger against my bottom lip as my mind flickered to memories of last night. This slow growing addiction was a little frightening, but it was nothing I couldn't control. We were both in this relationship for the same thing—fun.

I squinted at my phone ringing beside me on my side table and turned onto my stomach to reach for it. The clock read twelve-thirty in the afternoon. And right on cue, my stomach grumbled, clueing me in to feed it.

On the third ring, I picked up the phone, my face already lighting up when I saw my mama's face on my screen. "Mama!" I yelled. "Mama, Mama, Mama." I paused and uttered again, "Mama, Mama, Mama."

I rubbed my eyes with the heel of my palm, erasing any remnants of left over makeup. Now wide-awake, I smiled as her laughter echoed over the phone. I repeated her name over and over again, like I was six years old.

"Stop it, Kendy," she said, but her laughter continued, warming me like a down jacket in below zero winter cold.

"I miss you," I finally let out as I took in the picture of us together on my nightstand. I was in my cap and gown, and had just graduated nursing school. What I'd give to wrap my arms around my mama and pinch her side pudge, because I knew she hated that.

"I miss you, too." The sadness in her tone matched mine, causing a lump to form in my throat.

I was supposed to move her out of Bowlesville. I had worked hard during college to become a nurse, and I had promised her I'd get us out of that god-awful town. Then, we could finally start our lives somewhere new, and she'd forget about my father and the heartache he'd caused.

Who knew she'd fall in love with Hank, her boss, the

guy who owned the diner she worked in?

He had moved to Bowlesville from Seattle. His wife had died two years earlier, so he'd taken his retirement money and bought Elk Diner, a local hangout my mother had been working at for years. He'd courted her for months and, after a bit, she'd finally let up and given him a chance.

I knew when I took my job in Manhattan that she wouldn't be coming. She and Hank had been slowly getting serious, and I was ecstatic for her. But I still couldn't hide the disappointment that someone else was creeping into our space. Still, I needed her happy.

"Tell me, how's work?" Mama's sweet tone oozed into the receiver. "I only have fifteen minutes to catch up before I have to get back to work."

"Mama, don't play," I teased. "You're boom-booming the boss. Don't try to pretend you work there."

"Kendy!" she exclaimed. I could picture her cheeks flushed pink, almost as red as the apron she always wore at the diner.

"Just kidding, Mama." Even though it was funny, teasing her about screwing her boss made me shift with unease on my bed.

It was weird thinking she was doing it when she hadn't done it since Dad had left. At least, not that I knew of. Hank probably had to dust off the cobwebs up in there.

I shook my head at the visual. "Work is fine. My apartment is fine. I met a doctor who's more than fine, fine, fine," I cooed as a small smile crept up my face.

The only time I mentioned a man's name to my mama was when it was serious. And to me, getting Dr. Hot Pants' attention was serious.

"Kendall Lynn Miller, you better be working, and not

working that doctor you got your sights on. You can get in trouble and lose your job over that."

I bit the inside of my cheek and twirled a blonde lock around my finger. "Mama, there are no rules that say I cannot date any doctors."

"You and your boy toys," she chided with a motherly sigh. "Do you know there are still young men calling here asking about you?"

My eyebrows shot to the ceiling. "Who?" Everyone I had dated usually called my cell phone. "Who?" I asked again. I was beginning to sound like an owl. Who, who, who . . .

"Kyle and Brad Barsell. Did you date those brothers?"

"Nope. Only Brad. Though Kyle was truly trying to get what Bradley was getting."

"Kendy!" she exclaimed again.

I chuckled. I enjoyed making my mama squirm.

"Mama, tell those boys I'm never coming back to Bowlesville. You'll crush their hearts," I smiled big, knowing my mama was rolling her eyes at the drama in my voice, "but it's better than them hoping and dreaming for something that'll never be."

"Go back to work, Kendy," she chided with a light laugh, "or whatever you're doing tonight."

"Okay, Mama." I laughed along with her, missing her so much it was almost hard to breathe. "I love you like a love song."

"I know, dear," she said warmly. "You, too."

"Kisses and hugs to Hankie Pankie." I smiled, pressing end on the phone. Man, how I missed my mama bear.

I released a heavy sigh, feeling lonely all of a sudden as I glanced at the picture on my nightstand again. I really needed a dose of my mama soon. I'd have to check my calendar at work. I needed to see her, even if it was just for the weekend.

There was nothing left for me in Bowlesville except my mama. I wished I could bring her to New York with me. I could've shipped her in a box and written on the packaging 'handle with care'.

But I knew she'd never leave.

Deciding I couldn't wallow all afternoon, I got up and reached for my phone again, this time sexting my new best friend—Brian.

> Me: Hola! Did your dick fall off from last night? Want to do a late lunch?

I didn't have to wait even a second before his answer pinged right back.

> Brian: Sure. Where at? What time?

> Me: Clyde Diner at 2?

> Brian: See you there.

> Me: Sweet.

> Brian: And Kendy? My dick is still on.

> Me: Oh boy!

I got all giddy at the thought of seeing him again, and I replaced his name in my phone with 'Booty Call'. But when I pressed save, a sinking sensation spread in the pit of my belly. I blinked at the phone as a heaviness knotted my insides. What was wrong with me?

FTF, I had to remind myself. That was all I could do. But in the back of my mind, I wondered if it was even possible.

I rubbed at my brow, thinking of every relationship

I'd been in post-Cole. Every one of them had failed and ended quickly, not lasting more than a month. And I wondered if Cole had ruined me for eternity.

No. You can't think like that.

Taking a breath, I shook off the hopelessness and thought about the psychic and her predictions about Dr. Klein.

Right. Him. Keep your sights set on him. He's the one.

But then I thought of a certain pair of blue eyes, and my stomach churned. I could only hope we could still keep our friendship intact. Either way, I needed to set expectations with Brian today.

Pushing off my couch, I went to get ready for lunch. Once we had 'the talk', everything would be okay. I was sure of it.

Chapter Ten

BRIAN

KENDY STROLLED IN, her sunglasses on top of her head and looking cute as hell in a short summery dress. When her smile widened, I let out a breath of relief. I didn't want it to be weird between us. Sometimes things could be awkward after sex.

When she tiptoed and pulled at my neck in a full-on bear hug, I knew it wouldn't be. "Hiya," she cooed, sitting down in front of me. "Did you order yet?" She placed her purse on the table by our water glasses, adjusting her sunglasses on top of her head.

"No, I was waiting for you." I took note of the way the pink spread across her face from the heat outside.

She reached for the tall glass of ice water and gulped it down in an unladylike fashion, as though she hadn't drank in weeks. "What you should've done was order for the both of us or texted me the menu." She placed the glass back on the table and started to fan herself with her hands. "Is it me, or is it hot in here?"

She bunched her hair on the top of her head, and my eyes flew to her slender neck, remembering the tender spot I'd nipped, right above her collarbone.

"Seriously, I swear I feel like I have menopause with

all these hot flashes." With her free hand, she fanned herself, attempting to cool herself down.

"You're twenty-four. You've got a long way before menopause," I chuckled, picking up my glass of water to take a drink.

"Maybe I'm pregnant then."

I coughed, choked on my water, and tried to compose myself as Kendy laughed in front of me.

"I'm kidding. So kidding." She covered her mouth to tame her laughter. "There's no way. I always use double protection."

I picked up my napkin to wipe up the water, which had trailed from my mouth down to my shirt. "I just wasn't expecting that."

"I'm for real, though. It's super hot in here." She eyed my glass of water and I nodded, letting her know she could have a drink. Then she gulped it down, faster than the first one, and slammed the glass on the table. "Okay, let's order, quick, before I have to pee." Her eyebrows pulled together as she studied the menu. She bit her pinky nail, a habit I noticed when she was thinking deeply.

When she peered up from her menu, she quirked an eyebrow. "Do you already know what you want?"

"Yeah. Chicken sandwich," I replied, entertained by her unladylike demeanor.

Her cheeks returned to their normal color as the flush from earlier left her face. "You know what? That sounds great." She stood and squeezed her hands in front of her stomach as she started to bounce on her toes. "Order two. I really have to pee. When I come back, we need to talk."

I shook my head, amused because she reminded me of a kindergartener, unable to hold her bladder. I watched her retreating back as she sprinted to the bathroom as people moved to the side.

Make way, people, I thought. *Kendy's gotta go potty.*

KENDY

I STUFFED A big bite of the chicken sandwich into my mouth, lessening the hunger pang in my stomach. I was starving. It was two-thirty in the afternoon, and this was my first meal of the day. The savory chicken had the right amount of spice, which had my belly singing its praises.

"So . . . what do you want to talk about?" He placed his sandwich on his plate and reached for his glass.

"Just about, you know . . . about us and last night." I shied away as warmth spread from the apple of my cheeks to the tips of my ears. I took in his face, knowing we knew each other on a different level now. Nothing should be embarrassing anymore. We'd seen each other buck-naked. But I still had no idea how to start this conversation, so I used humor to cover up my unease in typical Kendy-like fashion. "We need to talk about last night and the power. Did you feel the power?"

Brian spat out his drink again, throwing his head back in a huge belly laugh. "Jeez, Kendy. Give a guy a warning."

I batted my eyes at him. "You never answered my question."

He leaned in, a seductive smile creeping up his face. "Yes, you've got the power, and I want a repeat sometime."

His lusty look made my whole body tingle. I bit my lip, trying to understand this reaction. Yes, I was most definitely aroused, but there was something more that I couldn't place. I shoved down the feeling and forged forward.

When I touched his forearm, once again I felt a zap of electricity zinging between us. "You'll feel it, all right," I said, my seductive tone matching his.

My bare back hit the cold chrome seat as I rested against it. I needed some air, some space between us if this talk was going to turn serious. "First, though, we'll need to discuss some rules, expectations." I waved my hand in the air like it was no big deal. "We're just doing this for fun, right?" I wanted to know we were on the same page and he had no issues with our arrangement.

He tilted his head, thinking about it for a second, which made me nervous. Then he said, "Sure, no worries." Though, his eyes were tight. "I'm too occupied with work to think of anything else."

I must've had a distressed look on my face because he placed his hand on top of mine on the table, his thumb caressing my fist. "Don't worry. I know you're set on Stiff." I sensed a tinge of bitterness in his tone, and I suddenly felt like the biggest hoochie.

What woman had her sights set on a guy she was going to marry, all the while making arrangements to sleep around with her friend?

But as soon as I asked myself the question, the little devil shoved that little angel off my shoulder and said, *A strong woman who doesn't take shit, who knows what she wants and how to get it. If you're up front with Brian, why can't you have your cake and eat it, too? Guys do it all the time.*

The little devil was right. Why the hell not?

Still, it made me a bit uneasy. I'd feel better if he was all in and totally okay, not just saying it to make me feel better.

His eyebrows pulled together, giving me an inkling that he was having doubts.

"Does it make you feel uncomfortable?" I asked. "That I have my sights set on Dr. Klein?"

"No. Not at all." He gave me a small smile as he paused to examine me. "I just don't get it, Kendy. You're beautiful and smart, and that guy seems like a total dick. I guarantee you he's not settling down anytime soon."

So he was worried about me? The doubt I sensed earlier was caused by his concern for me, and my insides swooned at his thoughtfulness.

And he just called me beautiful. I didn't realize I was smiling so big until my cheeks started hurting.

Dimming that smile, I told him, "I'm attracted to him." It wasn't a good enough answer. "And . . ." I paused, ready for him to laugh again. "It's what that psychic predicted." The truth was, I'd been holding onto this prediction for years, my last string of hope that I could move on from what Cole had done to me, a hope for ending my tormented past.

I reached for the saltshaker and stared at the minuscule particles. My voice dropped an octave. "You have to know what I've been through to understand." I winced, the desperation I was so familiar with emerging.

Brian put his hand on mine, but I pulled it back. I didn't need consoling; I needed to move on. I had this bitter taste in my mouth, all because the psychic's last prediction had had everything to do with Cole.

"It's her last prediction. And it has to come true." I let out a heavy sigh, forcing myself to see the speck of light at the end of the tunnel.

Brian broke me from my morbid thoughts and threw

a twenty on the table. I hadn't even realized the waiter had dropped off the check. Again, thoughts of my past were keeping me from being in the present.

"You ready?" he asked, standing. "Want to take a walk through Central Park?"

He held out his hand and, after a beat, I stood and placed my hand in his as the familiar warmth from earlier spread through me.

"Sure." I smiled. "Let's go."

BRIAN

AS MUCH AS I hated that she was still going after that prick, who didn't deserve her, I needed to erase the desolate look from her face. I sensed something deeper going on with her obsession with this damn psychic, but I wouldn't press her.

Central Park bustled with people enjoying the sunny summer day. Parents were pushing strollers, and a group of girls were rollerblading around us. As we walked, Kendy's gaze wandered to the people passing us by.

"You know the great thing about this country?" she said. "We get to walk around freely, do what we want. We have free will to choose, not like some countries that live under a dictatorship."

Odd topic choice.

She stopped and moved to the side as joggers passed us. I expected her to make some comment or joke about the shirtless guys, but she just stared blankly in front of us. "When your free will is taken away, that's when all hope is gone."

I frowned at her, my muscles tensing. What was she getting at? And why did it sound like she was speaking from experience?

I wondered where this conversation was headed, but I kept quiet, because she still had that look in her eye. The spark, the light I was usually accustomed to seeing in Kendy's eyes was replaced by a desolate look of utter despair.

She turned to me and such hopelessness passed over her face. "What if that one person, the person you loved the most, who you thought would never, ever do you wrong, took away your free will . . . and suddenly you felt helpless?" Her eyes broke, and all of me wanted to cross that invisible line and ask her who the hell had hurt her so I could rip their limbs apart.

The next moment, she gripped the front of my shirt, surprising me. "Kiss me. Hard. I need to forget."

I hesitated as warning signals rang off loudly in my head. But looking into her eyes, somehow I knew this was what she needed. So I leaned down to meet her lips, even though I knew this girl was not entirely whole. I was starting to see it more clearly. Behind the façade of a confident woman was a vulnerable girl, utterly broken.

And I was determined to know why.

KENDY

OUR LIPS CRASHED together, our teeth clashing with the impact. I didn't care that we were in the middle of the busiest park in the nation. I pushed through any thoughts of Cole to feel the warmth of Brian's tongue against mine.

I needed to drown in him, feel numb again, and dull the feeling that was bubbling up in my chest. The feeling that always haunted me whenever I thought of Cole.

"Harder," I moaned into his mouth. Despair began to strangle and suffocate me, making it difficult to breathe. I struggled to drive down old memories, to forget. I needed to clear my mind, to feel emptiness and pure sensation.

I bit on his lip, because he wasn't giving it to me rough enough, and I was rewarded with a low moan. Still, all I saw and heard was Cole. His voice rang loudly in my ears. His stocky frame and face clouded my head. His anger was so real, even though it had happened years ago.

My body trembled, tears threatening to break free. "More," I begged through muffled kisses, wanting to drown the past that haunted me. I needed to push past this overwhelming all-consuming anguish.

Finally, he bent me back, and I felt his hardness through the thin material of my dress.

"We have to get out of here," I said breathlessly.

He cupped the side of my face, his thumb lightly grazing my cheek. A look of concern passed over his face, softening his features. He was about to say no; I could tell.

But before he had a chance, I pressed my body against his. "Let's go," I breathed. "Where?"

Finally, an intense look of desire replaced the concern. "Your place," he panted.

"Yeah." I tugged on his hand and led us quickly out of the park.

BRIAN

SHIT. I SWEAR I just experienced my first heart attack.

I collapsed on the bed, Kendy's beautiful body splayed on top of me.

"Oh, God," she laughed as she buried her face in my chest. "That was intense."

I was still lodged inside her, but I could barely move, let alone breathe. I couldn't formulate words. I just needed a moment to collect myself, for my pulse to return to a normal rhythm.

As my eyes raked in her face, the blue in her irises caught the sun coming in through the window. Damn, she was breathtakingly beautiful and flushed pink from our passion.

Resting her head on her hand, she said, "I broke it, didn't I? Your dick."

"Maybe." I laughed. I wondered if I would ever get tired of looking at her. She had sex hair, and it was the hottest thing.

Her chest rose and fell as she giggled, a sound that radiated throughout the room, a sound I was becoming addicted to. "It's because I rode it like an amusement ride."

"You sure did," I said, and even though her words had been funny, I softened and ran a hand through her hair. Our eyes locked and my smile faltered. I couldn't get what she'd said earlier out of my head.

What if that one person, the person you loved the most, who you thought would never, ever do you wrong, took away your free will, where you felt helpless.

My arms tightened around her, wanting to protect her in some way, even though she'd already been hurt. Her soft curves melted against my lean chest as a lump developed in my throat.

She seemed to be oblivious to my concern as her eyes twinkled with mischief, her lips still swollen from our passion. You would've never guessed she was troubled. But I noticed. I noticed everything about her.

I needed to know more. What had happened to break such beauty?

I cupped the side of her face, and she rested against my touch. My thumb grazed her cheek and, as I stared into her eyes, the blue irises, which seemed so carefree but weren't, I finally couldn't hold it in any longer. "What happened? Who hurt you?"

As if a door inside of her slammed shut, her stare turned blank. "Don't. It's nothing." Her voice was barely above a whisper.

Her eyes turned cautious, and I knew I had crossed some invisible line, but this time I didn't care, because in my gut, I knew she was lying.

"Brian . . ." She lifted herself off of me and moved to the side, wrapping the sheets around her naked body. She averted her eyes, staring out the window. "It doesn't matter. It's in the past. He's not a part of my life anymore."

As soon as those words left her mouth, my whole body tensed.

I gritted my teeth. "I want to know." My voice came out harder than I'd intended, but I didn't back down. The curiosity burned inside of me. The need to know who hurt her was so strong that I took deep and slow breaths to keep me calm. I reached for her arm. "Tell me." I ground out.

She shook her head, closed her eyes, and stood. My hand fell to her wrist and I held her, waiting for her to respond to this one question I needed to be answered.

"Brian . . ." Her eyes shone with pain when they met

mine. "Don't. If you want this to work, just don't." She wrapped the sheets around her body and darted to the bathroom.

As I sat up, my gaze dropped to the floor and I ran one hand down my face, releasing a heavy sigh. I had no idea what the bastard looked like, but I somehow formed a face in my mind. His evil eyes, his cruel mouth, a bottomless pit of a soul. I'd never wanted to punch something, someone, anything, so badly. But I needed to keep myself in check.

My lips pinched together as I reminded myself of my place in Kendy's life and our arrangement. I needed to lay off. This was her business, and I wasn't in any position to pry.

Problem was, could I?

Knowing me, it would be a hard feat to accomplish.

KENDY

I FLIPPED ONTO my stomach and then onto my back for the hundredth time, restless. Brian had left my place over five hours ago, and still I couldn't fall asleep.

I shut my eyes tightly, only seeing darkness, but my heart was pounding loudly in my chest, as though I'd run a race. Brian's concerned tone was ringing in my ears like a broken record.

What happened? Who hurt you?

After another minute, I shook my head and sat up, trying to push memories of Cole down to the hidden chambers of my brain, where I always kept him locked up.

Cole was the first guy I'd been in love with. The man I not only gave my virginity to, but the one I'd thought I was going to marry. I could still picture his sugar brown hair and eyes as light as honey. He'd swooped me up and made me his in a matter of weeks.

I'd thought he was it. Everyone thought we were it. The first time we made love, he'd rented a motel room and lit up the room with candles. I wasn't his first, but he was definitely mine. First love, first sexual partner, first everything.

The night had been perfect, unlike my friends, who lost their virginity in the back of a pick-up truck. I'd assumed I was going to be one of those girls who married her high school sweetheart, and that was fine by me.

The first six months were bliss, absolute bliss. We hadn't fought at all. We couldn't keep our hands off each other. I'd thought our love would last forever.

But slowly, I had witnessed his eyes straying. He'd become distant. And the more distant he'd become, the more jealous I became. Sweet Kendy had turned into bitchy, jealous Kendy.

I should've trusted my gut, because one night, when he said he'd be at the diner, I showed up. He was nowhere to be seen, but I had found a bunch of his football buddies chilling against the pool table. I'd searched the vicinity and walked outside, noting his truck in the parking lot. I'd found him in the back of his truck, pants down and Clary's mouth on his cock.

I had cried for ages in Beth's arms. I thought I'd never mend my broken heart, but cheating was one thing I would never, ever condone.

I didn't want to be my mother, and in our small town of Bowlesville, history did repeat itself. It was a known fact that if I had married Cole, I'd be waiting for him to come home, just as my mother had waited for my father year after year. She had turned the other cheek, even when the stench of another woman had been heavy on my father's jacket. She'd lived a life of one-way love, and that was not how I was going to live. Not one bit.

I should've known better. That wasn't love. Lust was temporary, and only true love lasts forever.

I shuddered as more memories rushed to the surface. He had stiffened, cussed her out, and shoved her off him. Then he'd chased me, begging me to believe it was all her, that she had initiated it. I'd fought him, even though he'd tried to hold me against him, continuing to use lies to calm me. But I needed my space away from him.

Unfortunately, he'd felt differently. I'd seen a different side of him—a frightening side I never knew existed.

Pulling the pillow over my head, I let out a loud scream. Then I threw the pillow to the floor, staring intently at the popcorn ceiling above me, trying to focus on anything other than my past.

I'd done so well not bringing up memories of Cole, until recently.

When would this madness end? It'd been years.

I glanced at the digital clock on my side table. It was six in the morning, and I hadn't gotten a wink of sleep. Great. Now I'd be dead on my feet for my shift at seven. I should fit in a nap in between. If I could only force my mind to stop . . . to turn off my thoughts.

I bit my pinky nail, debating whether I should call the only person who knew what had happened that night. My fingers trembled as I reached for my cell.

She picked up on the third ring. "Kendy?" Beth's groggy voice filtered through the phone. "What time is it?" She exhaled a heavy yawn.

"Six my time."

"Are you at work?"

"No . . ." I paused, feeling silly and sagged against my comforter, the tension easing just at the sound of her voice.

"Everything okay?"

I remained silent, wondering how I would tell her I was now doing the guy she used to date. I doubted she'd care, but I also doubted her ability to understand our mutual arrangement.

I let out an exaggerated sigh and continued to chew my pinky nail.

"I know something's wrong. Spill it."

I heard the rustle of sheets and a door shutting. She must've left Kent sleeping in their bed.

I let my head hit my mattress, threw my arm over my eyes, and started rambling. "Remember, I went out this past weekend to a club I knew Dr. Hot Pants would end up at?"

"Yeah," she said, prompting me to move on.

I let it out in one breath without gulping for air. "Well, he left with a redhead, which pissed me off, and let's not go into the fact that he left with a different woman last weekend. So I had this bright idea—because I always get bright ideas—that I'd use Brian to make him jealous. But when Dr. Klein left with that woman, one thing led to another with Brian and, before I knew it, we were a little tipsy. But still, holy mother of God . . . it was the most raw, animalistic sex I've had . . . ever. And it's been great . . . until I almost mentioned Cole last night, and now it's not that great."

My body relaxed as I let out a low laugh. "Oh gosh, I

feel better already." Maybe all I needed was to vomit all that pent-up emotion to my best friend.

I had stunned her into silence because she didn't say a word. I listened to her breathing and waited for her to respond.

"Beth, are you there? Where did I lose you? Before or after the animalistic sex?" I started to laugh until . . .

"How does he know about Cole?" she asked carefully.

The corners of my mouth pulled down at the sound of that bastard's name. My chest tightened as I twisted the edge of my covers between my fingertips, wondering why I'd almost slipped about the one thing I never slipped about. "I started to tell him . . . but I didn't finish. He just guessed. He knows something's wrong with me."

Of course he does. Is it so obvious that I'm damaged goods? The only thing I've ever held onto was a stable job. Everything else has gone to shit. My father. All men after Cole.

"Nothing's wrong with you. You did nothing wrong," she said sternly.

But if her words were true, then why couldn't I get over it? Why couldn't I move on?

She let out a frustrated sigh. "What're you doing, Kendy?" Her tone turned accusatory, which I didn't appreciate.

"Having fun," I snapped back, feeling my blood pressure rise.

"Don't you have your sights set on that doctor?"

My insides heated at the tone in her voice. "So?" I sassed. "Brian knows. What we're doing is mutual."

"I'm just saying. I don't want to see you hurt."

"Are you concerned about me, or about another girl hurting Brian?" It was a low blow, and I knew my words were a slap in the face, but I didn't need her to lecture me on how to live my life.

"Both," she stated plainly. "I don't want either of you hurt."

"I'm having fun, Beth." I already had a mother. I didn't need another one.

"I can't imagine this ending well. Hear me out, babe. I know him . . . the kind of guy he is, and I know you. I know you want the doctor and why you're so damn set on having him—"

"Stop!" I didn't need to hear anymore of her lecture. "I'm done with this conversation."

I was about to press end on the phone, when her voice softened. "I love you, babe. We're cousins, and we've been best friends since we were six. I know what you've been through." Her voice dropped. "But . . . you never mention his name or what happened to anyone except me. So why did you . . . to Brian?"

I didn't respond, because I didn't have an answer. I wasn't sure why I'd spilled my guts to him. Or part of my guts. He was doing something to me. Something about Brian chipped at my exterior, the one I'd been working so hard to keep up.

Maybe it was his happy-go-lucky demeanor, or his sweet concern for my wellbeing. Or maybe it was my need to connect to someone and not having a close friend in New York. Or maybe it was just him. Who knew?

Gulping down my inner thoughts, I told her, "I have to go." Then I threw the phone on my bed and dropped my head in my hands.

I hadn't signed up for this, all this chaos. I'd moved here to leave the craziness behind and move on. Why did everything seem to keep pulling me back to Bowlesville, to when I was seventeen?

Breathing in through my nose and slowly out my mouth, I let out an exaggerated sigh. After a moment, I pulled myself out of it and went to take a shower. Things with Brian would be fine. We could manage this FTF thing. Everything was going to be fine.

Right?

BRIAN

AFTER WORK, I walked into the condo, dropped my laptop bag onto the hardwood floor, and went straight to the fridge. "Hey," I said, acknowledging Trey, who was spread out on the couch. "Dude, don't you work?"

The corner of his mouth lifted. "Daddy dearest is out of town on business, so I cut out early. You look beat, man. Hey, can you grab me one of those?"

I reached for two beers, tossed one to him, and plopped my ass on the couch next to him. "I finally got the Tiggins Corporation to agree to sit through a presentation." As I lay my head back, I felt the tense muscles in my neck relaxing. Damn, this had been a long week. "Now it's a matter of making them choose us over their current bank."

He knocked my shoulder, hard. "Great job, man! That's what you've been banking on. We gotta celebrate."

I would've been more excited if I wasn't exhausted. My usual A-game had been a bit off in the boardroom today. I couldn't help it, though. My mind was preoccupied with more than work, running rampant from my night at Kendy's and our strained conversation. I still wanted to question her, and so many times I'd had to bite my tongue to prevent myself from asking about her past. But she'd use her tempting sex appeal to change course. She was a fiend, addictive. Sex with her was raw, wild, and uninhibited. I wouldn't have been dead tired if she hadn't rushed me out of her bed at two a.m.

She blamed it on the FTF handbook and her god-awful rules. I didn't understand what the deal was. If we had a mutual understanding about our relationship, why did it matter if I crashed at her place?

This morning, I had to press my snooze button twice. It took a while to wake up, even after a cold shower. My body was physically exhausted, plus the nerves from the morning meeting had worn me down. Still, I couldn't get enough of her.

Physically, she tired me out, but hanging out with her, being in her presence, rejuvenated me.

I glanced at my watch. I hadn't been home more than ten minutes, and I was already itching to see her again.

Trey took a swig of beer and rested his elbows on his knees. "Where are we going?" He had a smile on his face like he wanted to cause some trouble.

"I'm going to Kendy's." As soon as it slipped out, I regretted it.

"Oh boy. Getting some action tonight." He lifted his fist, but I stared at his outstretched hand and left him hanging.

I raised an eyebrow, tired of his teasing, and moved my eyes to the television. Maybe Kendy and I were only friends that fucked, but I didn't appreciate Trey joking about it.

"So you getting serious?" he prodded, fishing for more information.

I didn't know what to tell him. All I knew was that I

didn't want it to end.

"No. It is what it is. A fling until she decides it's over."

He ducked his head into my line of sight and asked again, "You like this girl?"

"Me?" I shook my head in response. "Not in the way you're thinking. We have a mutual agreement. That's all."

Besides, I needed to be focused. If I won this new deal, I'd make my quota for the year and could position myself for a promotion. It was the next big step on my radar.

"Hmm." Trey tipped back his beer. "Mutual understanding . . ."

I didn't appreciate his sarcasm. "Yes." I gave him a look, telling him I didn't need to be pestered any further.

Trey took another swig of his beer and stood. "Chill, man. I'm just playin'." He slapped my back before moving toward his bedroom.

I ignored him, reached for my phone, and texted Kendy.

Me: Hey, still want me to come over?

Kendy: Lover boy!!!! But of course. Be here at 8.

I blinked a couple times at her text and rolled my shoulders back. The stiffness in my neck, which had started to dissipate a few minutes ago, was back. Mutual agreement or not, part of me felt like the appetizer, not the main course, a feeling I was familiar with.

I shook my head. This mutual relationship was my choice. I already knew what I was in for. In my prior relationship with Beth, she'd chosen the other man. I hadn't previously been prepared for that. There was a difference.

I rubbed at my brow to ward off an oncoming headache. Before I contemplated what our relationship was any further, I placed my phone on the table and got ready for our next date.

Chapter Eleven

KENDY

THE SCENT OF coffee from my mug filtered through the air of my one bedroom apartment. There was nothing more refreshing than a fresh brewed cup of coffee.

"So, you wanted to talk?" I prompted, bringing the mug to my lips.

Sarah sat on the stool at my kitchen island, holding my Mickey Mouse mug as she blew at the steam rising from the cup. She had some important news to tell me about Dr. Klein, so of course I'd told her to come right over.

"I'm sorry. Super Cupid failed you. I just wanted to tell you this in person, since we've been on different shifts lately." Her eyes dropped to my granite countertop, one of the many beautiful features which had drawn me to the place. "I'm working my magic on the other side, promise you. I've been dropping your name whenever he's around."

I rolled my eyes, thinking back to Saturday night when I had been dressed to impress, but had bedded the man I hadn't been expecting to leave with. I didn't know what more I could do. "Well, that night you got a stomach virus and left me without a wingman, the night you abandoned me . . ." I gave her a joking narrowed eye. "He left with another woman. If I wasn't Kendall Lynn Miller, I'd be losing hope here, and be on the verge of giving up." I didn't need to mention that he'd left with another woman the next week too. Saying it out loud would only increase the blow.

"Forget that girl." Sarah waved her hand in dismissal. "That was a one-night thing. You're going to be a forever thing, so you can't give up." Her eyes turned sympathetic as she shook her head before she placed her hand on my forearm. "On a good note, he asked about you," she sang, her eyeballs practically popping out of their sockets. "He wanted to know if you were dating anyone."

I perked up, her words sinking into me. Had I finally caught his attention?

She blew her dark hair from her face. "I have never, ever failed in a hook-up situation. I set my sister up with our neighbor, my friend with a boy who works at Wal-Mart, and my old roommate with the personal trainer at my gym. All have ended in successful relationships and marriages," she said proudly. "God has graced me with a talent; a talent for leading everyone in the right direction to their true loves. I guess the only person I can't set up is myself." She shrugged like it was no big deal, but I heard the sadness in her tone as she slumped against her seat and focused on my Mickey mug. Maybe Sarah had been hurt before.

I leaned over. "Don't worry," I said, giving her arm a consoling pat. "Someone's going to scoop you up, take the arrow from their back pocket, and shoot you themselves, right in your fine ass."

She smiled, but it didn't meet her eyes. It made me wonder if she'd been burned before. She shook it off and perked up. "Don't you worry about me. I'll just keep at what I know best."

Sensing the sour mood in the atmosphere, I changed the subject. "So what do I do now, Miss Cupid?" I wondered how long this waiting game was going to drag on. When would the prediction become true? I was getting impatient.

"You just wait right there." She pointed a finger at me. "I'll be back to work on him tomorrow. It's just a matter of time." She got this glint of excitement in her eyes as though her mind was turning, solidifying her plans in her head. She raised one hand in the air, like she was going to take flight. "Super Cupid to the rescue."

At that, we both laughed.

A KNOCK AT my door jolted me from the couch and had my heart skipping a beat, maybe two. Sarah had left an hour ago, and I was glad, because if she had met Brian, she'd ask questions I wouldn't be able to answer.

Opening the door, I was greeted with a panty-dropping smile as he stepped in, holding a bottle of wine.

"Hiya!" I waved him in, greeting him in my usual Kendy bouncy ways. "You come bearing gifts," I said, taking the bottle from his hands.

"Why, yes I do." He smirked, his hands in his pockets as he rocked back on his heels. He was wearing a Cubs T-shirt, a baseball cap drawn low, and his signature dark jeans, which made his rock hard thighs look amazing.

My eyes moved to the large clock dial in my kitchen. It was eight on the dot. He never failed. As always, Brian was punctual. It was one of the many qualities I admired, especially since I was always the one running five minutes late. I called it Kendy-Standard-Time.

I placed the wine in the fridge and spun back to his charming smile. A whole bunch of awkwardness filled the air as I shifted from one foot to the other. I locked eyes with him, baby blue to crystal blue, and the next second, I angled my head downward.

I knew why he was here. He knew why he was here. It was too early to get it on, yet here he was. I sighed heavily and chewed on my bottom lip as heat moved to the tips of my ears. It seemed we had forgotten how to hang out.

Finally, he stepped forward. "Come here."

I wrung my hands together. Nervousness bubbled to the surface, though I didn't know why.

When I didn't move, he inched closer and cupped the back of my head. Then he bent down and kissed me, and I melted against his soft lips as smoldering heat rushed through my entire body. I pushed my body against him, my nipples pebbling with arousal. The effect this man had on me was undeniable, instant.

Damn. What this man could do with his lips. Hands down, the best kisser I'd ever encountered. He should teach a class he was so damn good.

When I tilted my head to feel the tip of his tongue, his lips slowed down.

He lightly brushed his mouth against mine then pulled away, leaving me with a burning desire, an aching need, for another kiss.

With one thumb, he grazed my cheek tenderly. "Did you have dinner?"

I blinked a couple times, in a daze and still high from his kiss. I took a slow, level breath to calm my stammering pulse and shook my head. "No, not yet. You?"

"No," he replied, flashing me his sweet smile. "Let's get dinner, pretty girl."

Our eyes locked and I drowned in his. Warm. Sweet. The deep blue reminded me of a clear ocean, one you'd like to dive into, swim in, and never come out of.

My breath caught at the loving look in his gaze. "Okay," I said softly.

His hand traveled from my cheek to my arm, interlocking our fingers and leaving a trail of goose bumps where he touched.

I peered up at him through my lashes, shying away as the warmth spread to my cheeks. "You know you don't have to buy me dinner to get laid. You already bought me wine."

He chuckled and then winked, wiggling our interlocked fingers. "Don't worry. I'm feeding you so you can work it off tonight."

I squeezed his hand back, offering him my seductive smile as my insides tingled with anticipation. Though, I had to admit I was looking forward to our dinner date, too.

Hanging out with Brian was easy, like breathing, effortless. It didn't feel like work being in his presence; our conversations flowed easily. I craved his attention, and he always had a way of making me feel wanted, as though he also craved my attention.

Admittedly, a part of me would be sad when this arrangement came to an end.

BRIAN

AFTER DINNER, I paid and led her out of the restaurant, pulling her in close as we maneuvered through the crowd.

Luckily, we were still close by and could walk back to her place. It would have taken forever to hail a cab.

A few blocks from her apartment, she jerked us to a stop in front of a post office. "Can we stop in here?"

"Sure." I followed her inside and into a booth, where she reached for a pen in her purse, took out her checkbook, and started filling out an envelope.

"What're you doing?" I asked, leaning against the counter. I was strangely impressed by her neat handwriting.

She smiled her golden smile. "Sending my mama money." Her eyes lit up as she said it, like it made her happy to send her mother money. "She works hard at the diner, but I've been sending her more money so she can cut back on her hours."

I cocked my head, lifting an eyebrow. "I thought she was dating the boss."

She slapped my shoulder before taking the paper and heading into line. "It's Mama, and my mama is not going to take one thing from that man, even though Hank is sweet as pie. She's not taking anything from him until he puts a ring on her finger."

She stepped into the line and the guy in front of us eyed her up and down. Of course he did. Kendy was gorgeous. There wasn't an ounce of makeup on her, yet she was captivating. Her summer skirt lay mid-thigh, accenting her shapely legs, and her fitted white tank top was short enough that when she moved in certain angles, you could see a small span of her stomach.

When she smiled her sweet smile up at him, he

returned her gesture and then he eyed me up, most likely wondering if I was the boyfriend. My lips pressed together in a tight line, my eyes telling him to face forward and carry on, which he did.

This boiling feeling inside of me was foreign. It surprised me. I'd been protective of my sisters, and maybe of my girlfriends in the past, but never jealous. Something about Kendy brought out this new side of me.

I rubbed the base of my neck as tension rose to my shoulders. It was an emotion that made no sense, especially since we weren't officially together.

She folded the check in half and then in quarters, like she was trying to hide it in her fingers.

"You're going to stick it in the envelope like that?"

She shrugged. "Yep. Maybe she'll think I sent her an empty envelope for once and then *bam*, it drops out like a nice surprise. I'm sure she wouldn't put stuff past me. I've wrapped earrings in a small box before, and placed it in multiple larger boxes. Then I gift wrapped that baby in duct tape."

I chuckled, displaying a wide smile. She and her mother seemed to have the best relationship. I wondered if she got her happy-go-lucky personality from her, too. "Do you send her money often?" I felt like a shitty son all of a sudden. I'd thought I was good, because I'd always remembered to send birthday and anniversary cards.

"Yep. Every other week, when I get my paycheck. I started doing it when I graduated and began working. The first time, she sent the check back and wouldn't accept it. I just about flipped on her." Her infectious laughter rippled through the room. "She's so used to taking care of me. It's just a great change to take care of her." She peered up at me with pride in her eyes. "I love my mama. She's been through a lot." Her voice trailed off as her smile dimmed. "Being a single mom is hard . . . and I'm just happy I can finally give back."

Behind the counter, the older attendant with a full head of grey motioned for Kendy to step forward. I stood behind her as my jaw tightened, a slew of emotions filling me. There were so many facets of Kendy's life I didn't know about. Her cheery exterior was a façade, holding in a young woman who'd been through her own struggles in life.

When she was finished, she strolled out the door and, once again, I followed.

She went on as we walked down the crowded street. "My father left us when I was eleven. From eleven to seventeen, I waited for him to come back. It wasn't until that psychic told me to stop waiting that I knew he was never coming home."

A sad smile passed over her beautiful face. "It's hard waiting and wishing and thinking that every day I might wake up and he'd be right there beside me." She shook her head as her chin trembled. "I hoped and prayed he'd come back, just to mend my mama, who would not stop crying. I never told her I saw the psychic, though. I didn't have the heart. I didn't know which was the lesser evil, breaking her heart or letting her hope with no future."

She dropped her lashes to hide the hurt. "The next week, just like Evangeline had predicted, I saw him with his new girlfriend at a county fair, one town over. Fucking bastard. He saw me and just turned away." She nodded once and, as she lifted her head, I sensed a glimmer of hope pass through her eyes. "That psychic was the best thing that ever happened to me. I stopped waiting for something that was never going to happen."

As I stared at her profile, I noticed she looked lighter. Like a little bit of her shell had broken off. I reached for her hand, locking our fingers. If anything, our connection made *me* feel better.

A tiny smile touched her lips. "Now I'm just waiting for this last prediction to come true."

I nodded once, slowly coming to the realization and understanding why she needed everything she'd been told to come true. "It will." I patted her hand to reassure her. What I said was meant to comfort her, yet it had an opposite effect on me as my stomach churned at my own words.

KENDY

I HAD RUSHED Brian out of my apartment in the early morning, hoping I could get a little shut-eye before my twelve-hour shift.

Today, the hospital was unusually chaotic. We had already treated two gunshot wounds, both cases I'd been assigned to. When my butt finally hit the seat at the nurses' station, my whole body collapsed against the chair. I felt like I'd been on my feet forever. All I wanted to do was soak them in some warm water and get a pedicure.

My hand moved the mouse, bringing the computer to life. Once in the system, I typed my write-up for my last case. When I spotted Dr. Klein from the corner of my eye, I perked up, looking studious.

But remembering him walking out of the bar with that chick had irked me.

I pulled all my hair to the side, flattening my unruly

mane, probably crazy from the long day. My eyes flickered discretely in Dr. Klein's direction. He looked hot as hell, which eased up the annoyance a little.

Karen, the charge nurse, wheeled out Mrs. Calley from room two-oh-one. She had been admitted for dehydration and was on observation. The woman, no younger than seventy-five, brightened when Dr. Klein raised his head.

The scene broke my mood, the corners of my mouth pulling up as it unfolded in front of me. I could tell she had a little crush on a certain doctor as she smiled big and spoke fast. Her loud voice could also be blamed on her hearing aid, but it was more likely Dr. Klein.

Get in line, Mrs. Calley, I thought humorously.

"Adeline, I see you're doing much better," he said, easing next to her. "Looking good now. In a few days, you'll be back to a hundred percent. You'll have to keep drinking liquids and stay out of the heat."

Her wrinkly hand patted his as she peered at him. "I'm just glad it wasn't anything more serious. I could've fallen again and bruised my hip. That would require a longer stay."

He chuckled lightly. "How is that hip of yours doing?"

"Better." She nodded. "Still a little sore after that surgery, but better."

Observing her cheerful demeanor, I wondered if she'd ask Dr. Klein to massage it. I would. Even at the tender age of seventy-five, I was sure my personality would never change.

He patted her hand this time. "Don't worry. Nothing a couple of Tylenols and rest won't cure."

Her laugh was carefree, making my smile widen at her display of affection toward my doctor. Normally, jealousy would surface, but not when the woman with a full head of grey hair looked giddy staring up at his face. The woman reminded me of my own nana, my grandmother I had loved so much.

"Thank you, doctor," she cooed, her eyes lighting up.

"You take care and do call us if you have any concerns." He placed her hands back on her lap and smiled sweetly before touching her shoulder and sauntering my way.

I ducked my head back to the computer, pretending to type, which ended up with random letters and a word I didn't understand on my screen.

I sensed his presence looming above me. When I looked up, there he was in all his handsome glory. My pulse quickened in my throat, and the insides of my palms formed tiny sweat beads.

Boy, was he dreamy; even more so up close.

Inwardly, I sighed. But I composed myself and peered up. "Hi."

He leaned into me, like he wanted to be closer, and my whole body went into overdrive. "Did you do something with your hair?" There was this sly grin on his face. He was definitely flirting, and now it was my turn to play coy as I glanced down at the keyboard.

"Well, Dr. Klein, I didn't get it cut or anything, if that's what you're asking." I flipped my hair over my other shoulder, making eye contact. "But I did curl it today."

The side of his mouth twisted into a half smile as he took a strand of hair between his fingertips, making me die of utter happiness. "It looks great, Kendy. You should curl it more often. Oh, and from now on, you can call me James."

He winked then walked away, and I watched his

perfectly sculpted ass move down the hall. My stomach stirred, full of butterflies. *Holy hottie.*

If he loved curls, I'd seriously consider getting a perm.

I scanned the area, searching for anyone who had witnessed the love fest that had just happened. Then I touched my cheeks, just like the kid in *Home Alone*, trying to get my pulse to return to a normal rate.

It worked.

I couldn't believe it frickin' worked!

The scheme to make him all jealous at the bar with Brian had gotten me noticed.

No one could break my high.

With no one to share my giddiness with, I texted Brian.

> *Me: We did it. Our plan is working. Dr. Hot Pants loves me.*

It took a few long seconds before he texted back.

> *Brian: How could he not?*

> *Me: Truth*

I replied and tucked my phone back in my pocket with a smile. "Now this weekend, I'll help you with the women," I muttered out loud.

Brian had held up his end of the deal, and it was time for me to fulfill mine.

BRIAN

I SHOULDN'T HAVE been annoyed that Stiff had flirted with Kendy, but I was. He hadn't made a move since her

167

text, though, and I doubted the dick would make one at all.

Maybe I was in denial. I couldn't tell.

She had worked three twelve-hour shifts in a row and wanted to recuperate, but we'd been texting daily. Her funny jokes and my one-liners were comic relief during the boring yet stressful workweek. Still, I missed hanging out with her in person and seeing that beautiful face of hers. I didn't want to miss her, but shit, I did.

Tonight was going to be hysterical. She was determined to set me up. I would've rather stayed in with her, but I knew her whole game plan this evening would be entertaining.

I sat on the bar stool against the kitchen island. The black granite countertops were a stark contrast to the white Sports Illustrated magazine with the model, Kate Upton, on the cover.

I heard the jingle of keys and looked up to see Trey strolling in.

With one hand, he undid his tie, and sauntered into the kitchen. "Man oh man. Daddy dearest made me work my ass off today."

I laughed out loud, thinking how ironic it was that his father made him work harder than any of his execs or other partners.

"I feel you." I sighed as my shoulders released the tension from the long day of customer calls.

Trey swung his suit jacket off and threw it on top of the bar stool next to me then went to sort through the pile of mail on the counter.

"One day, you're going to be King of Manhattan like your daddy. I'm jealous, man," I said.

He shook his head, an air of sadness in his face. "He's

got all the money in the world, but he's lonely. Don't be jealous." The air in the atmosphere shifted to cold, as though I'd hit a nerve with my comment.

"You can buy company," I joked, trying to lighten his mood.

"And I'm sure he has." Trey reached into a drawer for the letter opener. "Anyways, what're we doing tonight?" he asked as he tore through his first piece of mail.

"I'm meeting Kendy."

He raised an eyebrow, but didn't ask the question I knew he wanted to. "You headed to the bar? Mind if I tag along?" He threw me my pile of mail.

"You can hang out, but not at the after party at her place." I smirked. "Sorry, I don't swing that way."

"Dumbass." He rolled his eyes. "I can get my own."

"We're leaving at ten," I told him.

A part of me wanted Kendy to myself since I hadn't seen her all week, but I knew that was plain stupid. We weren't together, and yet I missed her. It was becoming harder and harder to lie to myself.

Was it possible to miss someone who wasn't even yours?

I looked at the clock on the wall. We still had time to grab something to eat before I was going to meet her. "Hey, want to grab dinner?"

"Sure," he called back before strolling to his room.

"I'm going to snooze off for a bit. Wake me up when you're done with your hair."

KENDY

"NO, THAT GIRL was a skank, a wannabe good girl. Gold digger through and through." I slapped Trey's shoulder as we chilled, reclining on the lounge chair of Clayton's Wine Bar and checking out the slew of women in front of us.

After who knew how many rounds of drinks, we'd tried to look for Brian's type. Trey and I had been arguing playfully for hours, not even letting Brian get a word in.

One thing we agreed on was that Brian needed to pick himself a keeper. We both knew he was ready to settle down.

"Kendall, you just don't know your women like I do," Trey joked, a heavy, drunken smile on his face.

I gave him my own drunken smile. "Trust me, I'm the queen of manipulation, and that girl was a skank to the tenth degree." I flipped my golden locks over one shoulder. "And you say you know women, pfft. I know how women work because I'm from the species."

"How about that girl?" I pointed to a beautiful tanned woman sitting by her friends on the opposite end of the room. She had legs that went on forever. Her face had a sweetness about it, and she was attractive, not super skinny, but where she had curves in all the right places.

Trey tipped his beer in the blonde's direction. "That girl?"

"Yes, that girl." I nodded. "Seriously, I'd date her. Look at her."

"You'd date her because she looks like you." He threw back his head as he laughed, which made me flush pink.

"Hey, hey, hey," Brian said, getting in between us. "Don't I get a say in who I'm going to end up with?"

"No!" Trey and I said in unison, making us all crack

up.

Trey ran one hand through his dark hair and looked at me pointedly. "You were picking out all the uptight, granny-looking ones. I mean, you can't do that for my man over here." He threw one arm over Brian's shoulders and pulled him in for a brotherly side hug.

"Well, you're choosing the half-naked ones, with their titties hanging out. Seriously, that's not settling down material." I threw Trey a face.

Brian had been quiet most of the night. He had this lazy, drunk look all over his face, and he was take-me-to-bed adorable.

I patted his chest, letting my hand linger there as warmth spread up my arm. "Brian, tell your best friend that I'm right. You liked Chloe from Midtown, the beautiful blonde with the cutest outfit."

Trey's eyebrows shot to the dark night sky. "Um, that woman had jacked up teeth. Dude, messed up teeth is a deal breaker." Trey pointed to the bar in front of us, where Chloe stood with her group of friends. "You want to get with Kendall's girl with the jacked up teeth?"

I peered up at Brian, looking at him expectantly. "Oh, so you wanna marry flapper? She's used and abused. Her shit's so loose her lips down there are starting to flap." I jutted my chin out, waiting for his reply. "Brian?"

He just shook his head at the both of us as the beginning of a smile tipped the corners of his mouth. "No comment."

I huffed and crossed my arms over my chest. "Whatever. You know I'm right. How about the bartender, the girl with the bouncy curls and a sweet smile?"

A slow secret smile crept up Trey's face as he glanced back at the bartender tending to her patrons. "Kendy, have you noticed you're only approving of the women for my boy over here," he slapped Brian's chest, "who look just like you."

An awkward silence filled the air as Brian turned to me, and the tips of my ears heated as I glanced from the tall tanned woman, to Chloe, to the bartender with the blonde bouncy curls.

Shit! Trey was right, and I hadn't even realized it.

I rolled my eyes. "The only thing we have in common is that we're all hot. Don't you think your boy deserves an attractive girl?" I played it off as a nervous chuckle left my lips.

Here I was trying to keep my distance and the friendship lines intact by setting Brian up with a woman who was worthy of him. But as I took in his beautiful face, a face that I'd been seeing on a weekly basis, I wondered where my place would be when this girl became a part of his life. I'd grown fond of hanging out with him, and the selfish part of me didn't want to let that go.

Chapter Twelve

BRIAN

AS WE WAITED for the cab, Trey and Kendy argued back and forth about my future wife. She would lean into him and slap his shoulder, and huff and puff at him. I didn't know why, but that familiar jealousy boiled up inside me again. I fisted my hands as I fought a strong desire to yank her away from Trey, take her home, and claim her.

Trey laughed at whatever Kendy had just said, and it made my face steam. I'd never been mad at my best friend over a girl. Probably because he'd been dating my sister for a huge chunk of our time in high school.

I knew he didn't want Kendy, but I couldn't help it. This jealousy was an animal all its own.

When he reached out and grabbed her forearm, I stiffened. The next moment, I laughed awkwardly and possessively pulled her closer to me. It was a smooth move, and one I didn't think she noticed as her giggles continued. But Trey did. I saw his smile falter as he stared at me questioningly.

Trey had never been a cock blocker. That was one of the things I'd never have to worry about him. One quality that oozed out of Trey was loyalty, but still . . . there was something about tonight, or maybe it was just Kendy who brought out this jealous bastard in me.

A moment later, he stepped away from her. Just when a cab pulled in front of us, Trey scratched the top of his head. "Hey, I'm gonna go meet some friends at the Bud Lounge."

Well, shit. I hadn't meant to make him feel bad. But I didn't say anything to stop him either.

Kendy released me and tugged on his shirt. "No, come on. You said drinks at your apartment. It'll be fun. Let's go."

I clenched my jaw and shot him a look, silently telling him to beat it. I'd have to apologize for my caveman behavior later.

"You're such a party pooper," she sassed, grabbing my hand and pulling us toward the cab. "Brian and I are about to get crazy wasted. We're going to play drinking games, right?" She winked back at me before ducking her head to get in the cab.

I glanced back at Trey, who mouthed, "Have fun." He wiggled his eyebrows as he motioned between Kendy and me. He put his two fingers together in a kissy motion, and then in a more vulgar move, circling his thumb with his index finger.

I gave him the finger before I shut the door behind me, sliding thigh to thigh beside Kendy. In the next second, I recited my address to the cab driver and pulled Kendy into my lap. Both of my hands moved to the bareness of her lower back, shoving her against me, and I kissed her. Hard.

I heard her sharp intake of breath right before her mouth opened to let me in. I needed to tame the beast inside of me, the jealous one that needed to calm the hell down, and I knew the only cure was her.

KENDY

FOUR BEERS LATER, I felt pretty damn good. I was sitting cross-legged on the couch, dressed in only Brian's t-shirt. As soon as we'd stepped into his apartment, Brian had carried me into his room. There was a fierce possessiveness in the way we had sex tonight, but never once had I felt threatened.

It had always been hot and heavy with Brian, but tonight was a notch higher. I didn't want to read too much into our sexcapade, but it was as though he was claiming me with his body.

Brian was on the living room floor, shirtless and only in his boxers. His chestnut coffee table sat between us. As I rested against the couch in his oversized t-shirt, my body warmed all over from the liquor coursing through me. I swallowed back another swig of Miller Lite as my eyes flickered to his well-defined six-pack. I had to appreciate a guy who took care of his body, and Brian did that well.

We were playing the card game High/Low, and I kept on losing.

"You suck major," I said, laughing as I said it, a warm flush creeping up my cheeks.

There was no way he was as toasted as me. Still, he had a heavy smile on his face to match mine.

"Go." I pushed the cards toward him. There was no way. I couldn't lose four in a row.

He flipped the card, revealing the four of hearts.

I shook my head, my smile widening. "And here is where my losing streak ends." I grabbed the card on the top of the pile. "The odds are forever in my favor." I bowed and flipped the card over. "Booyah!"

And then I frowned at my two of clubs. Damn.

"I hate this game," I pouted, childishly messing up the cards into one pile as I emptied the last of my fourth bottle. "I want to play another game." I frowned like the sore loser I truly was. No denying it. But who wants to lose all freaking night?

"Can't play a drinking game without a drink." He grinned at me and lifted off the floor, strutting over to the fridge to get me another bottle.

"If you're trying to get me drunk so you can take advantage, know that you already did that thirty minutes ago," I joked. "Don't you love our mutual agreement?"

He spun around, holding our beers. His eyes turned unreadable, somehow shifting the mood in the air. He sat next to me on the couch this time, not smiling, just meeting my gaze. I could sense some sort of emotion behind his look, and it had my heart racing.

Shifting in my seat, I averted my eyes and focused on the cards on the table. I didn't want to read something that wasn't truly there, or maybe I was refusing to see it.

He handed me my beer, still silent, and I bumped my shoulder into his. "If we were in a relationship, I'd be griping that you were drinking too much. Bitching like a girlfriend does when her man has a little too much fun. We wouldn't be this carefree, and we wouldn't be playing these type of games on a Friday night."

"Yeah." He nodded slowly, his voice off yet gentle. "Want to play another game? I want to play 'I never'."

BRIAN

I'VE BEEN THERE before with the controlling girlfriend who didn't like it when I had too much fun. That had been in college, when I'd had more than enough fun for the both of us.

As I watched Kendy's blue eyes gloss over, a smile still heavy on her face, it was hard to picture her as the type to go all crazy on her boyfriend.

I decided I wanted to know as much as I could about her, so I picked the game that would give me the inside scoop into that beautiful head of hers. The 'I Never' game was a popular drinking game, where one player would give a statement, and if the other players agreed with that statement, they took a drink.

"I'll go first," I told her. "I've never FTF-ed before you. Not with anyone that I wasn't seriously dating."

She wrinkled her nose. "You make me seem like a hooker." She pretended to push her bottle away, like she wasn't taking a drink, but then she slammed it back, which didn't surprise me. "And for your information, I've only FTF-ed one other time before you, so there." She tucked her feet under her ass. "Why so serious? Let's lighten this up, shall we?" She extended her beer bottle, and I tapped mine against hers. "I've never had sweet and sour pork."

I let out a carefree laugh and guzzled down my beer. "Really?" I asked, genuinely surprised. Out of all the 'I nevers' she'd picked that one. While this was a way for me to take a playful game to get to know the real her, she brought this game back to the light side.

She shrugged. "I love Chinese food, but there's something about sweet and sour. It's a food contradiction. You can't be sweet and sour. It's just not right." She tried to suppress a giggle. "One more," she said, raising her index

177

finger. "I've never been to the Statue of Liberty. I'm afraid of heights."

I brought the bottle to my lips again. "Heights?" I didn't know why, but I found this surprising as well. Maybe because Kendy seemed so brave, and there was nothing she was afraid of.

She gave off this tough girl persona, which was sexy as hell, but when I got glimpses of her little insecurities or fears, it only drew me to her even more. As though her insecurities gave me an inside look into Kendy, only fueling my desire to want to know more about her.

She scrunched her nose again. "Yes. If I stood on this couch right now, I'd be terrified of falling." She leaned into my face and pointed to her chin. "See this?"

I had to squint to see a tiny scar that was barely noticeable.

"In the fifth grade, I stood on top of the monkey bars, trying to show off to the boys." She chuckled in spite of herself. "Epic fail, because I needed four stitches after that little stunt."

"Come here," I said, inching closer. I closed the gap between us and kissed her chin lightly. "There, boo-boo gone."

A tiny blush touched her cheeks as though she wasn't expecting that, and then she pointed in my direction for me to go.

"I've never . . ." But nothing came to mind.

There were a few random coasters scattered on the table, my beer sitting on top of one made of glass. But what caught my eye were the white letters against the black cork coaster, a Shakespearean quote.

"The course of true love never did run smooth," it read.

The first thing that came to my mind flew out of

my mouth. "I've never had someone write me a poem." Dumb. I should've skipped my turn.

Her eyes danced with amusement. "Poems," she cooed. "The boys loved writing me poems." She pointed her beer bottle in my direction again. "You get one more, because I took two turns."

I tried to think of something good, something light, but nothing came to mind. I had started this game to get to know more about her, and I was beginning to realize how truly boring I was.

"I've never been in love," I finally said.

It was such a weird guy thing to say, but it was true. I'd only experienced puppy love, not the true, all-consuming love. I knew once I felt that all-consuming part, I'd make it a point to marry that girl.

Her eyebrows scrunched together. "Jeez, Brian. What's up with the serious 'I nevers'? And wait. So you, Brian Benson, have never been in love."

"Nope. Never." I shook my head. "Not where I couldn't live without a girl, couldn't function." I'd thought I was in love many times, but now knew it hadn't been the real thing.

I waited to see what she would do—would she drink, or would she not? She didn't move or speak, so I prompted, "You've been in love?"

Immediately, her smile left her face, and I knew her relationship with this Cole guy hadn't ended well. I gripped the bottle tighter, wanting to know about this bastard, particularly his address.

Her tone was disconnected, quieter. "Yep. A long time ago." She seemed closed off all of a sudden, and I felt a chill in the air at the change in mood.

My instincts told me to drop it, but I couldn't. Not

now. Not today. Not this time. "So what happened? He let a girl like you go?" I used flattery to try to change her mood, but she didn't give an ounce of a reaction. I knew this guy had hurt her, but I had to tread carefully because, knowing Kendy, she'd close up like a clam, like she'd done every time before.

"It was a long time ago." Her stare turned vacant as her breathing slowed. "Cole was my first and last boyfriend in high school." Her tone was acidic, hatred ringing in her eyes. "Fucker cheated on me and stole more from me than you can imagine. He walks the streets of Bowlesville like he owns the fucking joint, when he's a piece of dog shit." Her voice got louder as she spoke. "I hate him." The way she said it, the way her eyes filled with pain, even though her voice reeked of hatred, had my insides on fire with a rage I'd never felt before.

I clenched my jaw from revealing any emotion.

I wondered what guy in his right mind could cheat on Kendy, or even cheat in general. Was this the guy she'd been talking about at the park? Had he been abusive toward her?

Her words rang out in my head. *Took away your free will, where you felt helpless.*

I wanted to ask her more, though I knew she wouldn't answer. Still, I needed to take away the cold, disconnected look in her eyes.

The next second, I was inching closer, ducking my head so I was in her line of sight. "I've never kissed a nurse before you."

KENDY

ONE MINUTE MY body was shaking, and the next Brian's handsome face was in my line of sight. I didn't take a sip, because I had never kissed a nurse, either. I had only ever kissed a doctor, but not the doctor who I had my sights on.

Cole's asshole face was imprinted in my head. His cocky ways, his arrogant self. *"Bitch! You think you're better than me? You think you can just leave me?"* Trembling, I shook my head to get the visual of him looming over me out of my mind.

Being in love was blind. He was hella hot and the most popular guy at Bowlesville High. Maybe that was why I'd had my eyes on him. I'd felt flattered when he'd asked *me* out. He was the only guy I'd ever dated all through high school. I'd thought he was the one, maybe because he was the only one I'd ever known. There was a difference.

When you were young and in love, you thought love lasted forever; you thought love could only ever be pure. You expected it to be perfect and drama free. I had expected it to be like those princess books, when the prince scooped up the princess and whisked her away in the pumpkin that turned into a carriage.

You never expected a relationship to leave you gutted and heartbroken.

The more I thought about Cole, the more my hands shook with anger. The next moment, I rammed my lips against Brian's, wanting to have some essence of control. I needed to be in control.

I shoved him down on the couch, his head hitting the cushions, and ran my hand down his chest. I reveled in the firm span of his six-pack, which instantly made me wet. My tongue moved from his chin to the outer shell of his ear while my hands gripped his hair.

"I've never done it on a brown leather couch," I breathed, flicking my tongue against his.

He shifted beneath me, and I could feel how ready he was. My insides clenched with anticipation as I pulled at his shorts. I guess the 'I never' game was over, which was fine by me.

BRIAN

I RUBBED MY eyes and stood. My head was spinning from the abrupt movement, and from one too many beverages last night. The last thing I remember was putting Kendy in a cab and giving the driver one too many bills. I walked slowly into the living room, shielding my eyes from the bright light.

Trey was already dressed and sitting on the couch. Leftover pizza from whenever was on the coffee table in front of him.

I didn't say a word as I strolled to the windows, pulling the curtains together to lessen the light in the room.

"Holy shit," I said, rubbing my eyes with the back of my palms. The roof of my mouth felt like sand paper. I was probably dehydrated, but I needed to sit before I toppled over.

I plopped next to Trey, who had this amused smile on his face, which didn't help my mood.

"Why you smiling like an idiot?" I practically growled at him.

"Don't know," he joked, still looking at me like I was the funniest thing on the planet. I'd seen him butt-ass wasted before, and I'd been more sympathetic.

"Got something to tell me, bro?" He leaned forward, resting his elbows on his knees.

My eyebrows pulled together. "What?" My headache coupled with my queasy stomach was giving me major issues with my mood.

"Come on, man. Don't hold back. What're friends for? Lay it all out on the table."

"You're speaking a foreign language, dude. And a little too loud." I let my head hang between my hands and massaged my temples with my fingertips.

"When did you start falling for her?"

My head shot up, causing the whole room to spin. "What're you talking about?"

"You and the blondie. The one you're doing. When did you—"

"I heard you. But I told you, we're not like that," I snapped, glaring at him.

He scratched his jaw, casting me a 'yeah, right' look. "Is that why you wanted to kick my ass for looking at her too closely?"

I didn't bother answering him. His statement did not warrant a response.

"Well, if you guys aren't serious, and maybe she's into me, maybe I'll take a shot at—"

Before I could even stop myself, I shoved his chest so hard he shifted on impact. "Don't fucking say it. I'll knock you out cold. She's not some sex toy."

His eyes widened and he raised both hands. "Easy, easy. I don't see what the big deal is. If you're not *together,* and she's up for a one-night . . ." His voice trailed off, probably from the scary-ass look on my face.

I stood. "Stop," I commanded. "She's off limits. End

of story, shithead."

"Whoa, whoa, whoa." His mouth trembled with a need to smile. "I'm just playing. I want nothing to do with your Kendy. I'm just trying to prove a point."

"What point?" I ground out.

"That you're falling for this girl." He softened then, and I wanted to punch him for that, too. I didn't need his pity. "Hey, look, I've been there."

"I'm not there. There's no 'there'," I growled. "Quit being such a dickhead and leave it."

Trey sighed, stood, and placed one hand on my shoulder. "I've been there before, bro. With your sister. I tried my hardest to win her back, and part of me wishes . . . part of me wishes I'd tried even harder."

Win her back? He'd had my sister. They'd been together. What was he talking about?

Pain flashed in his eyes as he let his hand fall to the side. His look turned serious, like he was finally going to go into what had happened between them, but then he shook his head instead. "You can win this girl. Don't regret it and walk away without trying." He turned toward his bedroom, glancing back one last time. "Don't use work as an excuse, man. You let her walk away and be with that doctor without telling her how you feel, you'll regret it. Trust me." When he shut the door behind him, I contemplated heavily on his words.

My mouth slackened as I let myself drop to the couch. The sane part of my mind was screaming at me that I had the deal of a lifetime. Every guy's dream. No strings attached.

But the crazy part of my mind wondered 'what if'?

I let my head fall between my hands again as it pounded more painfully than before. I ran my hands through my hair, gripping the tips in my fingers as I re-membered how jealous I'd been last night. I slowed my breathing, inhaling deeply through my nose and exhaling slowly through my mouth.

Why? Why had I been jealous?

Trey was being a bastard, but maybe he wasn't all wrong.

I pressed my palms hard against my eyes, seeing only darkness, when the truth started coming to me. No, Trey wasn't all wrong. Because he was right.

I was falling for her. Hard and so fucking fast.

Shit.

I'm screwed.

Now the question was—what was I going to do about it?

Chapter Thirteen

BRIAN

IN TYPICAL BRIAN-MODE on a Sunday night, my computer was on my lap and I was tapping away, trying to write a proposal and figure out questions that I could ask the company when I met with them for our first meeting.

My manager had just added a new prospect in my portfolio that he wanted me to call on after my Tiggins Corporation meeting. Here I'd thought that if I landed Tiggins Corp., I'd be sitting pretty for a while.

Not at the nation's biggest bank. There were probably a hundred young professionals willing to take my position tomorrow. I had to wear my game face.

Kendy had called and wanted to hang out, because she was bored at home, so I invited her over. After what Trey had said, I shouldn't have. And even though she'd be a distraction, I knew there was no way I could say no to her.

Kendy flipped through the channels from where she sat beside me on the couch. "What time are you going to be done?" She had asked the same question five minutes ago, reminding me of a child in a car asking, 'Are we there yet?'

I lifted my head and noticed her signature pout. I

wondered if she was doing it on purpose, or if it was just a natural reaction for her. A big part of me wanted to bite her bottom lip, which was jutting out, then maybe we'd just have dinner in bed.

I shifted to adjust myself. "Give me thirty minutes." I promised her dinner after I finished, and I wasn't about to go back on my word. This boy needed to eat, too.

She only bit her bottom lip then stared at the TV as though she was upset by the reality dance show she was watching.

As I focused on the financials in front of me and studied the manufacturing company's business, my stomach churned. I had an important customer call with the client tomorrow. If I impressed the CFO, I could secure a meeting with the decision maker, the CEO of the company. I had to convince the Tiggins Corporation why they should leave their current bank and bring their business over to Financial State.

I rubbed my brow, squinting at the write-up on my screen. I had memorized my pitch, yet somehow I knew I could tighten it up, make it even better. Letting out a heavy sigh, I tilted my head from side to side to ease the tension in my shoulders.

When I peered up at Kendy, I couldn't help but smile as her knees bounced to the hip-hop music the dancers were performing to.

Something about this girl calmed me. There was an overall lightness to her aura that was contagious. A minute ago, I was about to pound my head against the computer. Now, just watching her, I felt my whole body loosening up. She was like my own personal beer on legs. All I needed was a dose of her at the end of a long ass day to relax me.

But as I let that sink in, I remembered Trey's assumptions, and my smile slowly faded. Jackass was haunting my thoughts.

I debated telling her that maybe we could order in, but I didn't want to see her famous pout again. I didn't want to disappoint her when she'd come down specifically because I'd promised her dinner. This woman was my distraction to my every day. I didn't know what to do with this newfound realization.

My fingers worked faster on the keyboard, trying to finish my work up so I could satisfy this hunger in my belly and feed my girl.

My girl?

Closing my eyes, I took in a slow, jagged breath. Funny how the subconscious knew before the mind made a decision.

Now what was I going to do about it?

I guess I needed to finish the task at hand and eventually feed *my* girl.

KENDY

BORED OUT OF my mind, I had the sudden urge to mess with him, but that would prolong me getting fed. But then an awesome idea entered my head so I poked his side.

His stare was intently glued on his screen that I startled him, and he jumped at my touch.

"Hey, do you want to watch a movie after dinner?" I poked his side again as his eyes remained glued on the screen in front of him. "Come on," I cooed coercively.

The side of his mouth curled up in a slight smile. "I

just have to get this proposal done, and we can do whatever you want." He was so focused that he hadn't glanced my way. I was throwing him my Kendy sex look, but it didn't help my case if he couldn't see it.

I started to unbutton my shirt, and then laughed when his eyes flickered toward me. Now I had his full attention. My fingers stopped on the third button, revealing my pink polka dot bra, which was a large contrast to my black button down.

He quirked an eyebrow, amused.

Seizing the moment, I shut his laptop, placed it on the low center table and climbed into his lap, straddling him. "That'll be here when you get back. Come on, they're showing that Zombie movie. Oooh, scary," I taunted him, wrapping my arms around his neck. I pulled him even closer and gave him my pretend sad face, knowing he couldn't resist.

He smiled back at me, but his eyes flickered down at his watch. I saw the indecision in his eyes. I was about to convince him with kisses when he ran one hand down his face and let out a low sigh. "What time is the next showing?"

"Eight!" I yelped, jumping up and down on his lap, knowing I'd won.

"Easy, beautiful." He chuckled darkly. "You keep doing that, and we won't be making the movies."

I kissed his lips long and hard as his hands wrapped around my waist.

Pulling back, I said, "I want popcorn, a Slurpee, and Snowcaps." I kissed his cheek again then instantly debated if this was crossing the FTF line. But I wanted to watch this movie, so I pushed down the little voice of reason in the back of my head.

He stood, forcing me off his lap. "Let's go before it gets too late. I have to finish this proposal. I need to secure this deal tomorrow."

I barely refrained from groaning. I was a selfish little witch. I knew he had work to do, but still . . . I wanted to watch my movie. And for whatever reason, I wanted to watch it with him.

"We'll have to grab a quick dinner." He piled his work papers in the center of the coffee table.

"Better yet, let's grab a hotdog at the movie theatre." I wasn't normally into greasy food, but my stomach was suddenly grumbling for a hotdog.

He snaked one arm around my waist and pulled me in. "Great idea." He pecked my lips sweetly, which awakened the butterflies in my stomach.

I bit my lip and peered up at him through my lashes, studying his strong yet handsome features. I drowned in the sea of blue looking down at me, and a lightness spread throughout my limbs.

Releasing a silent sigh, I went up on my tiptoes and kissed him again. "Thank you," I whispered against his lips.

BRIAN

HER MAKEUP WAS scattered all over my bathroom counter. She told me she needed five minutes to freshen up, but as I rested against the frame of the bathroom door, I wondered how long her five minutes would actually be. Probably as long as Trey's five minutes.

I rubbed the back of my neck, forced stress off my face

and tried not to let my impatience show. My watch indicated it was almost time to go, and I counted the number of hours I had left before tomorrow's morning call. I was torn. My responsible side needed to get my shit together and get the proposal done, but my fun side wanted to let loose and enjoy the evening with Kendy.

She cast me a look and flung her makeup brush in my direction, barely missing my chest, which made me laugh. "You will not be thinking of work when you're with me."

"Yes, ma'am." I lifted my hand to salute her.

With her, all sensible logic flew out the door. This woman, I swear, had a way to get me to do whatever she wanted, where there was no way I could say no to her.

Funny enough, my father was the same way with my mother.

My jaw locked automatically as soon as the thought filtered through.

"Loosen up. Going out tonight will do you good. Work smurf. That stuff will be there tomorrow."

"All right then, Ms. Fashionista. You don't want to be late for your movie, so hurry your ass up." I picked up the brush and tossed it with a swish back in her bag.

I was constantly having this internal struggle within myself, listing reasons why I shouldn't be with her, reminding myself that she was ready to hook up and marry this other guy.

I'd played our conversations over and over again in my head. Her constantly talking about him. When I thought of Stiff, I pictured myself knocking him on his ass, staking a claim on her as they had in the caveman days.

True, I didn't know him, but I didn't like that he was still somehow the center of her world. I told myself that I'd promised her we were only 'FTF-ing', though I'd grown to hate that word. It seemed like weeks ago I'd promised myself all I needed was a little excitement, some fun, and a break from my day-to-day stress.

I had thoroughly screwed myself. I knew this, because I watched her every move, and as she looked in the mirror and held up two different pairs of earrings, I thought it was the cutest thing. Everything she did was damn adorable.

I wanted to tell her we should forego the movie and make a movie of our own. Or just rent one instead and make a point not to watch it.

She finally decided on a pair and looked at me for approval. "Beautiful," I said, but I wasn't talking about the earrings. *Damn me and my inability to keep our relationship purely platonic.*

I was screwed. I should cut myself off because the more we prolonged this relationship, the harder it was going to be on me. But I knew I wouldn't. I just couldn't. I knew myself. So I needed to formulate a plan.

I would have to convince her to pick me over Stiff. As irritating as it was that I even needed to prove myself over the prick, I knew that's what I would have to do.

Smiling to myself, a thought pushed to the surface. Going forward, I'd break every FTF rule there was in that damn handbook of hers. Every single one.

I PULLED HER to the elevator and pressed the down button. As we stepped onto the main floor, I held her hand and opened every door that led us to the outside without breaking contact.

We hailed a cab, and I kissed our locked fingers,

making sure I was breaking some unspoken rule. She had this look in her eyes, like she was quietly questioning my affection, yet she didn't stop me.

I opened the door as we stepped into the cab, and she babbled on about how she hadn't seen a scary movie in forever, since she'd left Bowlesville. I wondered if she knew she had repeated herself three times.

"Are you scared of zombies?" she asked, lowering her tone in a scary way, which had the opposite effect on me.

"There's nothing I'm scared of, Kendy," I told her with confidence.

She laughed and flipped her blonde locks over her shoulder. "Silly me. Thinking this blue-eyed bad boy was scared of anything." She pushed at my chest with her index finger.

I laughed and pulled her in closer, taking in her intoxicating scent. I hadn't felt like this in a long time—fully content, like nothing was missing—and I couldn't help but feel as though it had everything to do with her.

I didn't tell her that I was lying. Instead, I released a shallow breath and remained quiet. Because the truth was, there was only one thing that scared me . . . losing her to Stiff.

Losing her to anyone who wasn't me.

KENDY

WE WERE STILL holding hands as we strolled down the street. I'd never mentioned holding hands was against the rules, but really, I should've added that to my made up list. If we were going to keep our relationship strictly platonic, there didn't need to be any handholding business.

I didn't want to lead him on, but he knew what our relationship was. I glanced at his profile, wondering what he was thinking. A little stubble had grown on his chin, and I wanted to run my fingers down his face—better yet, my tongue. But then we'd never make the movie.

As we stepped in front of the attendant, I pulled out my wallet. I had to pay for my own ticket. I needed to make sure this wasn't a full on date and keep the friendship lines clear.

"What're you doing?" he asked incredulously.

"Paying for my movie."

He moved my hand away from the window. "No, you're not."

I leaned in so no one could hear me. "We're already boom-booming, and you're taking me to the movies? Nope. I'm paying for my own. FTF handbook." I winked at him to soften the blow.

A muscle moved in his jaw, but his face remained unaffected. "You and your damn make-the-rules-as-I-go handbook."

Giving him a satisfied smile, I shoved my money toward the attendant through the small window. "One for Zombies Take Over." I flashed a flirty smile, causing the teenage boy to blush, but then Brian blocked my path and moved my money to the side.

"Here, I have this. Two for the eight o'clock showing." He reached for my hand and held it tight.

I squeezed his harder, surprising him, and threw the ten through the window. But Brian reached for it and shoved the cash in between my cleavage. My jaw dropped as I stared at him.

Unbelievable.

The teenage boy, no more than sixteen, laughed at our interaction.

I went in to reach for it, but Brian took my free hand captive. "Don't." His eyes were stern, and I gave it right back to him, jutting out my chin.

"You don't tell me what to do."

"You're not paying," he said with finality, his voice hard, causing a havoc on my pulse. "I was raised better than that. It's what we do. Just let it happen."

I rubbed my thighs together, getting heated at the look in his eyes. There was something about his stance that demanded authority, and it was a total turn on. I'd only seen him act like that in the bedroom.

A second later, his eyes softened as he bent down to peck my lips then

his finger dipped into the span of perky cleavage peeking out of my black shirt, leaving goose bumps prickling my skin. He took the money out and placed it in my hands. "Thank you, Princess." He winked and nodded to the attendant.

I decided to let things be. I'd make it a point to get the next movie we saw together. "Chivalry is not dead after all. I'm telling your mama she raised a good boy."

I was awarded with his sexy-ass smile.

BRIAN

ONCE WE STEPPED into the theatre, Kendy tugged us up the stairs toward the back row. I noticed the bounce in her step. I loved her aura, the energy that surrounded her. She always seemed to have it, even after her long shifts at work.

"When was the last time you watched a scary movie?" I asked, trying to keep her pace.

She glanced over her shoulder. "Right before I left Bowlesville."

"Are you leading us to the very top, so we can make out?" My eyes focused on her perfect apple ass, admiring the sexy sway as we made our way up.

"But of course," she said, twirling her thumb up and down the inside of my palm, making my cock twitch. She turned toward me and raised her shoulder to her chin flirtatiously.

She chose the center of the top row. "Best seats in the house are at the very tippy top. Plus," she angled herself in my direction, "if the movie gets boring, maybe I'll let you take advantage of me." Her devilish smile lit up the room like a meteor shower in a dark sky. Hell, I couldn't breathe. There was no way I could not be affected by this woman, even if I tried. She was seeping into every part of my life, and I had to admit I was enjoying it.

When her stomach growled, she laughed and curled in. "Me needs food."

Since we were cutting it close to show time, we had decided I'd get snacks after we'd claimed our seats. "Okay, I'm going to grab us some grub."

Her nose wrinkled in the cutest way when she was confused. "I'll go get it. I can't live without popcorn, and of course butter, lots of it. And I have to have my cherry Slurpee." She raised a finger for an exaggerated effect. "Let's not forget the hotdog."

She stood to leave, but I placed my hand on her arm. "It's okay. I told you I'd grab it. I promised you a meal."

She leaned down quickly, pecking me on the lips. "I'll

do it, babe." Then she winked and skittered down the aisle, skipping down the steps.

I blinked at her retreating back.

She'd just called me babe.

And I swear I just died a little, because she just broke her own rule, and was so damn sexy doing it, too.

THE MOVIE WAS way more cheesy than scary. Bad actors, horrible makeup and costumes, and fake as hell. A few people even got up to leave and never came back.

Though I yawned twice already, bored out of my mind, what I did enjoy was watching Kendy's engrossed reaction. A half hour ago, she'd gripped my shirt, fisting my sleeve with one hand like her life depended on it. Her other hand was holding the armrest on the opposite side like she was going into labor. Her tight grip on my shirt cinched my sleeve and was beginning to cut off my circulation.

"No! Don't go there!" she yelled, causing the people in front of us to shush her. With one finger, she pointed to the screen. "Movie is in front of you," she sassed before smiling her adorable smile.

I angled closer to whisper in her ear, "Do you want to get us kicked out?"

Without warning, she turned and jammed a handful of popcorn into my mouth to silence me. "Quiet, I'm watching."

I laughed as a few kernels fell to the floor. After her gaze went back to the screen, she jumped onto my lap in one leap, pulling her knees to her chest as she threw her hands over her eyes and peeked at the movie between her fingers.

I chuckled and wrapped my arms around her, simply holding her tight.

When the zombie caught the human, Kendy buried her head into my neck, her breath tickling my skin when she exhaled. "Stupid girl. Stupid. Stupid. Stupid," she murmured into my collar. She peered up to take a peek at the screen and then cowered into me again.

I pulled her closer against me, secretly wishing the movie would never end. I liked being her protector, especially since she gave off this rough and tough persona. Part of me hoped she'd have nightmares and ask me to sleep over just to watch over her. I inwardly laughed as I imagined declaring a solemn oath to protect her from the zombies, to be her zombie-slaying hero.

When I returned my attention to the movie, I stifled a groan. The zombie was eating a woman's limbs. It was gruesome and stupid at the same time. Kendy peeked up at the screen again as the zombie went to town, chowing on the human like it was Thanksgiving.

My hand threaded through the ends of her hair as she whispered how stupid the now dead woman had been. I exhaled heavily, a weightlessness spreading through my limbs.

I could get used to this.

I kissed the top of Kendy's head and relaxed as she pressed into me.

When the scene ended, she began to maneuver to her own seat, but I tugged her back against me. She complied and relaxed in my arms, making my insides soar.

I linked my fingers together against the cotton of her shirt, and as I tightened my hold, my stomach rolled. I didn't know where this was heading or what the future held. All I knew was that I never wanted this to end.

There was an internal struggle inside me. I was afraid of getting hurt again, afraid of rejection, so the possibility of being in love with this girl absolutely scared the shit out of me.

WHEN THE MOVIE ended, we waited outside for a cab. The air was charged with good energy, and I loved that I felt this intimacy growing between us. I gazed down at her as her blonde curls blew in the wind. Her laugh was euphoric. It was like working out. It gave me a high, and I needed her to do it again.

I whispered something unintelligible in her ear, and she laughed again, causing that same feeling to bubble in my chest and my cheeks to hurt from matching her smile.

She wrapped her hands around my waist and peered up at me, resting her chin against my chest. My breath caught as I took in how unbelievably beautiful she was, in a non-trying kind of way, unlike most women I'd met.

The gleam of the moon cast a light upon her.

"I had fun. Thank you for taking me to get my zombie fix on."

"Anytime." I cupped the side of her face, my hand cradling her chin, my thumb lightly grazing her soft skin.

She rested her cheek on my hand, relaxing in my hold. It was crazy how she fit perfectly against me, almost short enough that I could tuck her under my chin. And holding her like this felt crazy right.

She closed her eyes briefly and, when she opened them, she suddenly looked tired, worn down. Very un-Kendy-like. I knew she'd been busy at the hospital, but my gut told me it was something more.

"What're you thinking?" I grazed her chin gently with my thumb.

"I miss home."

I could see the sadness in her eyes. For all the sass that Kendy had and however worldly she pretended to be, there was still a sweet innocence about her. All that rough around the edges young woman was gone, and all that remained was a small town girl.

"Where did that come from?" I asked, dropping my hand and wondering how her mood could change so easily.

"It's been months since I watched a movie. I used to do it every weekend with my mama." She let out a heavy sigh. "I didn't think I'd miss her so much when I came here, but I do. I miss everything. Having hot cocoa with her before bed. Watching our late night talk shows together. I even miss fighting with her. Maybe . . ." She hesitated as she fidgeted with her fingers.

"Say it."

She peered up at me, looking vulnerable for the first time tonight, which tightened my chest. "Maybe I rushed into things. I wanted to move to a city where no one knew me, but now I just want to go home. Every part of me wants to go home."

I tried not to let those words slam into me like the reality they were. Maybe she wouldn't stay here; maybe New York City wouldn't become her permanent home. And I would lose her if she didn't stay.

Then an idea came to me. I breathed quietly, trying to keep my racing heart in check. "Want me to take you home to Bowlesville?"

I waited for her instant rejection, for her to bring up

those fucking FTF rules again, argue that friends that fuck don't take their temporary lovers home to meet the parents or friends.

But she didn't do that.

She smiled.

It was small at first, and then grew until it lit up her whole face, and it made me want to bust out my credit card and charge two tickets to Chicago right this second.

"You'd do that?" she asked, her voice filled with awe.

"There's nothing I wouldn't do for you," I replied honestly, feeling like I was laying my guts out on the table.

She bit her bottom lip, which was the cutest thing, and everything in me wanted to do the same thing, so I did. I leaned down, caressing the side of her face, and captured her lips with mine.

I kissed her softly, sweetly, and poured my feelings into that one action. I wanted to savor her, take it slow. She molded into me and, once again, she fit perfectly against my chest between the span of my shoulders. So crazy perfect.

And I knew I was in deep shit.

When I pulled backed and glanced down into those stark blue eyes, in that instant, I knew I was screwed.

I'd fallen in love with this girl.

The girl who only wanted to play the game.

Chapter Fourteen

KENDY

HIS KISS LEFT me breathless, making my heart pitter-patter against my chest, and there was something behind it that I couldn't put my finger on. It was the type of kiss that was frightening yet addicting all at the same time. Either way, it made me want more, something I wasn't used to.

We stood under the moonlight, lips locked like we were on our own movie set. I sensed people around us, passing us by, but I didn't care as I melted into his arms. After a moment, he slowed to a few pecks, pulled back, and the look he gave me made goose bumps break out along my skin. There was such reverence in his eyes; his look alone made me feel . . . cherished, a feeling that seemed so foreign to me.

Letting go of my face, he reached for my hand and intertwined our fingers. As he stepped away, the energy from that kiss left my body.

My shoulders slumped, my body exhausted from the long week. I was overworked, tired of constantly chasing James, and tired of missing home. My feet hurt, my back hurt, and I needed sleep.

"I'm tired." It slipped out before I even had a chance

to stop it. I sounded like such a party pooper, when I had practically begged him to go out.

"I'm taking you home," he said sweetly.

I laughed, because I didn't think he'd heard me correctly. "I said I'm tired. I think taking me home is going to equate to being more tired after you work me out. Plus, you have that proposal and big client meeting tomorrow."

He let out a low chuckle. "I just wanted to make you some homemade hot cocoa. You know, bring some Bowesville here."

Homemade hot cocoa? Made from scratch?

I swooned, my knees growing weak. The selfish yet homesick side of me wanted him to come over, but my reasonable side didn't want him to be tired at work.

"Plus," he said, "I need to run to the grocery store, since I'm out of condoms."

I pulled back so I could see if he was kidding. "We've used a box of condoms? How big was the box?"

"Pretty big." His smile turned devilish. "And yes . . . we're out."

I shook my head, smiling. "You know what? Hot cocoa sounds so good right about now."

BRIAN

AS THE CAB pulled up to the local mart, I took her hand again, stepped out, and led us through the doors.

Funny how easy my lie had been. Now she thought I knew how to make hot cocoa from scratch. Hell no, I had no clue, but I wasn't about to tell her that.

Before we'd hopped into the cab, she had excused

herself to take her evening call from her mama. That's when I'd Googled how to make authentic hot cocoa. I would fake it for this girl. It was that or go home, and I wasn't ready to leave her yet.

I was conflicted because I had that important call and proposal, but being with Kendy, spending more time with her, outweighed work at the moment. I'd probably regret it tomorrow morning when exhaustion hit me, but right now, it didn't matter.

"Alrighty, where are we off to?" Kendy asked, stuffing her phone into her oversized purse. It was amazing how much shit a girl could fit in those things. The oversized accessory reminded me of my sisters.

"Baking aisle." I took a screen shot of the recipe. The first recipe I saw was Nutella Hot chocolate. It looked so damn delicious I couldn't resist.

If Google said it was the best, I doubted they'd lie. Hope rose within me, thinking this was one of the many ways I was going to win her over. By making her the best hot cocoa, better even than her mama's. That was the goal, at least.

"You're going to make me homemade, fresh from scratch hot cocoa?" She popped her hip out and raised an eyebrow in disbelief. "And I'm not talking about that dirt in a can that you mix with milk."

"Yes, ma'am," I said with a nod. "It's going to be the best. I can guarantee it. You allergic to nuts?"

"Not your nuts." She tugged on my belt suggestively, making me laugh.

"Not the kind of nuts I'm talking about."

"Nope. I'm not allergic." She laughed. "And I love all kinds of nuts."

KENDY

BRIAN WAS ON a mission. I couldn't help but be impressed that this young man knew his way around a grocery store. I mean, it wasn't hard to make hot cocoa, but still. How many twenty-five year old guys made anything but frozen meals at home?

He searched the aisle twice before stopping in front of the baking section then grabbed the Hershey cocoa powder and cinnamon and placed it in the shopping cart.

I tugged at his shirt, forcing him to look down at me. "Cinnamon?"

"Trust me," he replied, bending down to kiss me on the lips.

"Okay." I waved my hand for him to lead the way as I pushed the cart beside him.

We walked a few steps down before he dropped another ingredient into the cart.

"Marshmallows." He threw me his boyish smile before walking ahead of me.

I continued to follow him up and down and through the aisles as he dropped every ingredient in while also announcing to the world what it was.

"Nutella."

"Vanilla Extract."

"Sugar."

My eyes zoned in on his tight ass. He was getting me hot and bothered. Anyone could tell he worked out, and he had the ass of Hercules. I loved the feel of it clenching between my hands when he'd come.

"All right. I think we're done here."

I curled my finger in a 'come hither' gesture. "We're missing one last thing." I pointed to the economy box of condoms that I'd grabbed earlier.

His smile turned devilish, and I hooked one finger around the loop of his jeans. "You're going to make me hot cocoa, which reminds me of home." I kissed him gently, outlining his lips with the tip of my tongue. "And then I'm going to ride you like I'm at the rodeo, make you come, and bring you home." I closed my eyes and kissed him with reckless abandon. I wasn't quite sure what he was doing to me . . . but I liked it.

BRIAN FOLLOWED ME into my place with his bags of goodies. The clock on the microwave flashed eleven-thirty p.m., and I released a silent sigh, thanking the heavens that I didn't have work tomorrow. But then I bit the inside of my cheek, remorse eating my insides, knowing Brian had that big client call tomorrow morning.

The selfish part of me wanted to spend all night with him, sweating up a storm, but I knew he had to get going.

"What's the matter?" he asked, setting the bag down on my kitchen island. He pulled out the ingredients, placing them on the counter one by one. "What's the sad face for, Princess?"

I smiled at his endearment. "You need to get your proposal done, and I'm feeling a little guilty about forcing you to watch that zombie movie."

His eyebrows pulled together as though he was thinking of his deadline, but in the next moment, he shook it off. "Don't worry."

"No, really, Brian, we have all the ingredients. Maybe we should just continue another night."

"I'm a big boy. I can handle my business."

He reached into my overhead cupboard for a pan. I didn't know if I should feel happy that he knew where everything was, or if that indicated just how blurred our relationship was starting to get.

"Brian . . ." I started to protest.

He gave me a pointed look. "Push in that lip of yours, or I'm going to bite it."

As commanded, I stopped pouting.

"Kendy, I'm the type of man to always get things done. Even if it takes me the whole night," he said with another mischievous look.

I flushed because I knew how much stamina Brian truly had. I was sure he was talking about doing an all-nighter for work, but my mind had strayed into the land of dirty. "Oh, I know."

He winked before turning to the stove and pouring some milk into the pan. Then he pulled out his phone, checked something, maybe a text. I noticed he'd been glancing at his cell frequently, and I couldn't help but wonder who'd be texting him this late.

Without warning, the green-eyed monster rose to the surface. I was about to ask him, but really I had no right. I had made that loud and clear these last few weeks.

So, in sneaky Kendy fashion, I advanced toward the stove to see if I could get a glimpse of his phone. I didn't like someone else having his attention when he was here with me. I, at least, had that argument.

As he stirred the milk and scooped out the cocoa powder from the jar, I stepped behind him and wrapped my arms around his middle, my hands moving under his shirt and palming the span of his six-pack.

Instantly, the horny little devil came out to play. My hands moved south as he continued to stir. I rubbed the front of his pants, and he hardened at my touch, his length standing at attention.

He moved from my grasp, grabbed my hand, and pressed a kiss to my palm. "You're never going to taste this hot cocoa if you don't slow down." He bent down to meet my lips and spun back to the stove.

When he picked up his phone again, I felt irritated, because I couldn't get a good glimpse at the screen.

After he opened the cinnamon and shot two dashes into the pot, I finally asked, "Who's texting you this late?" I tried using a sweet and curious tone, hoping he didn't hear the jealously in my voice.

"Trey." I didn't miss his hesitation before he answered and then poured the sugar in the pan.

He was the worst liar.

For the first time, I was realizing I always talked about my doctor, but Brian never talked about another woman. I had never asked him if he was seeing someone else, and for some reason I couldn't imagine Brian with another girl. Not like he couldn't get any, I just assumed he was too busy with his job. Though he wasn't solely mine, the thought made my chest hurt.

I stepped back while he hummed to himself. As he stirred his concoction, the scent of chocolate filtered through the air, and my whole body stiffened.

There were always the three days when I was working where he could maintain a relationship. If there was a girl, I wondered who this chick was. Was she beautiful? Blonde or brunette? Was she taller than me? Maybe someone who worked for the bank, like Beth?

I was making up all these different scenarios in my head, and it was starting to drive me bonkers. When he focused on his phone again, an almost growl escaped my throat. I unbuttoned my shirt and threw it on the counter, disposing of my bra in the process, then slipped off my jeans and underwear and stood naked behind him.

He squinted, so focused on his phone that he didn't even notice me without an article of clothing on.

Then he reached to the overhead cupboard and grabbed two cups. "All done," he said, twisting toward me and reaching for the pot to pour the warm, light brown liquid into the mugs.

Abruptly, he spilled some of the drink on the counter as his eyes greedily roamed my body. "Ow, shit," he said, before dropping the pot onto the stove. "Jeez, Kendy, I'm gonna have third degree burns because of you."

He held his finger with his hand, and I reached for it. "Does it hurt?" I asked seductively. "Because as you know, I am a nurse . . . with healing capabilities. I can make your boo-boo go away."

He didn't respond, but his eyes darkened when I stepped forward. Without losing eye contact, he turned off the stove behind him, and a ripple of excitement coursed through me.

I guess my hot cocoa will have to wait.

Taking his finger between my lips, I sucked hard and was rewarded by his deep intake of breath. As I sucked his finger in and out of my mouth, a delicious shudder went through me.

When I released him, we crashed together, his tongue down my throat as both of our hands worked on his belt. I pulled back, coming up for air as he dropped his jeans and stepped out of them. I reached for the hem of his shirt, peeling it off his body, and he complied by lifting his arms and tossing it behind him.

The bright florescent light from the kitchen heated up the room even more as it highlighted every defined muscle on his toned body. It was odd, but we'd never had sex under this much light.

I didn't have time to be self-conscious as Brian picked me up by my waist, my legs wrapping around him as our lips crashed together again. He gently eased me onto the kitchen island as his lustful eyes raked over me. With one powerful hand, he trailed his fingers from my neck to my stomach to the swell of my hips, finally touching my core. He slipped a finger in me without warning as he trailed kisses along my stomach. I moaned, my back instinctively arching at the sensations running through my body.

I bit my lip and peered down at him as he watched my reaction. My moans increased with each passing second as his stroking fingers sent jolts of pleasure throughout me. And the louder I got, the more intense his movements became. His warm tongue dipped into my navel, then moved to my hip, and then to my thigh and lower, until I felt him kissing my inner thigh. When his tongue reached my center, I gripped the tips of his hair, not knowing what else to do.

I raised my bottom, coercing him to go deeper. "Brian," I exhaled. I wasn't going to last long. Not when his mouth was working its magic.

BRIAN

HER BODY WAS exquisite, beautiful. The light

illuminated her curvy figure perfectly, and the flawless span of her skin had me wanting to lick every part of her. The way she writhed under my hold had my cock ready to burst.

My tongue teased her sensitive nub, and I tightened my grip on her thighs, knowing she was close. As many times as we'd been together, I'd memorized her movements, knew when she was about to come. Losing patience, I slipped my finger in as my tongue moved with sensual purpose. I need to be in her. Soon.

Then, with one more flick against her sensitive clit, she came undone, screaming my name so loud her body shivered in ecstasy. Then I withdrew myself and reached for the box of condoms on the counter, thankful I'd remembered we'd ran out.

I slipped it over my length as she came down from her high, her breathing still erratic. I didn't even wait for her to come back to reality before I swept her up.

She hooked her arms and legs around me as I carried her, our lips crashing together.

"I want you again," she said breathlessly.

"Good, because I'm far from done with you."

This girl was insatiable and, if anything, I was ready to give her what she needed, and be here to satisfy her every desire.

She pressed herself against me. I didn't even make it to the bedroom as I crushed her within my embrace, pushed her against the wall, and entered her.

I bit her lip as I slowly moved in and out of her. The slapping of skin echoed through her apartment as our tongues danced against each other.

"Move to the couch," she begged, gripping my hair tighter, pulling at the ends like she wanted to rip it out by its roots.

I wheeled around, obeying her command and, when I dropped to the couch, we lost connection. She moved from beneath me, pushed me back to a sitting position, and then she straddled me, riding my length hard like she'd promised earlier in the grocery store.

My mouth circled around one of her breasts, sucking and teasing her nipples as she bounced up and down my length.

When her movements became erratic, my lips lost contact with her body, letting my head fall back. "Shit." That familiar sensation rose up, intensifying, starting from the base of my shaft.

Gripping her by the waist, I controlled her movements. I lifted my head and saw the stark blue eyes of the hottest woman alive. As hard as it was, I refused to come before she did.

I felt the contractions beginning in her core, which relieved me, because I didn't know how much longer I could hold off. She let out a loud moan as she moved faster, wrapping her arms around me, and burying her head into my neck as she shivered, her orgasm taking control and taking me with her.

The pleasure was pure and explosive. We held onto each other as our panting subsided then I swept her hair to the side and kissed a searing path down her neck and shoulders.

I trailed my fingers down her delicate back and cuddled with her, feeling whole having her in my arms. Somewhere deep inside me, I knew we were breaking the rules. And before I realized what I was doing, I almost broke the biggest rule of them all. It was on the tip of my tongue, those three little words which would reveal how

I felt about her.

When I was in this woman's vicinity, all logic flew out the door. I knew what I needed to get done for tomorrow's meeting, yet when I was with her, nothing else mattered except being with her. She completed me in a way I hadn't realized I needed, until she'd flown into my life. Now I didn't know what I'd do without her in it.

I whispered softly into her neck. "Kendy, I . . ." But I couldn't say it. It would freak her out.

I thought I'd been here before—in love. But I knew I hadn't, because an undeniable connection drew me to this woman like nothing I'd ever experienced, and this time, I couldn't fathom walking away. Either way, I knew this was where I was with this girl. She was what I wanted.

KENDY

STILL IN MY post-orgasmic state, I lay back on the couch as my body relaxed and turned into Jell-O. Everything was absolutely perfect. Brian was absolutely perfect. And not only did we have hot, skin-slapping sex, I still had his hot cocoa to look forward to.

I was in absolute heaven, resting against him, when he almost dropped the bomb of all bombs. I knew what he was about to say. The emotion was written all over his face, and it was something I was not ready for. Something that we had decided could not happen.

"I . . . I," he whispered, causing me to still in his arms.

I stopped breathing. Stopped moving. Just stopped.

As crazy as it seemed, even though we'd talked on and on about what we were to each other—of what we *weren't*, rather—and although I continually gushed about James, a part of me would want to say it back if he did.

Over these last few weeks, I'd realized I'd never felt such emotion toward another guy since . . . since Cole.

Cole . . . Cole . . . Cole.

The moment his name resurfaced, I froze.

I knew more than anyone that love could lie, make you think you felt something when you didn't. I clenched my jaw as nausea settled in my stomach.

Standing up, I avoided Brian's gaze. This was exactly why I couldn't fall for him. Love was scary; love could be wrong. Love was blind. One minute, it elevated you to an unbelievable high, and the next, it could crush you to the ground, leaving you broken. Most of all, love was uncontrollable, and that was one thing I promised I wouldn't relinquish—control.

I kissed his cheek and headed to the bathroom. "That was amazing, lover boy," I teased, thanking the heavens that those words hadn't slipped out.

BRIAN

I STARED AT her retreating, naked form then went to the garbage and disposed of the condom.

Ah, fuck.

I can't believe I almost did that. But I couldn't help how I felt, and a huge part of me wanted to throw open that bathroom door and tell her, make her believe me. Because then she'd know. She'd know that I was utterly in love with her.

But I knew my calmer side needed to chill out and

give her some time.

I decided I would continue to break every damn rule in her book from this day forward until she was my girl. I had almost broken the most important rule. It was only a matter of time before she heard it.

One thing was certain—I was not going down without a fight.

Chapter Fifteen

KENDY

I STARED AT the red numbers on my digital clock and gripped the pillow tighter to my chest. Brian had texted and called, but I hadn't returned either. He most likely wanted to tell me goodnight or that he'd gotten home okay. Nothing too personal, but I couldn't get past the 'almost' that'd happened tonight. I didn't know what I was going to do with him or with our relationship.

As juvenile as it sounded, I needed my mama, but if I called her, she'd be on the first flight from O'Hare International Airport.

Instead, I picked up my phone, my fingers hovering over a different name on the screen. I knew she'd be sleeping, but I needed to talk to someone right now.

"Kendy?" Beth asked, her voice groggy. "Is everything okay?"

"Yeah," I whispered, even though I knew she knew everything was not okay. I wouldn't be calling her in the wee hours of the morning if everything was okay.

"Kendy!" she said louder, making me jump. "What's the matter?"

Kent's voice boomed in the background, trying to calm her down.

The last time I had called her in a panic was to tell her that our Nana had died, so I made sure to have a relaxed voice this time.

"Relax, Beth. No one's dead. I'm pregnant," I said, trying to break my own mood.

She didn't say anything, but I pictured her jaw on the floor. "Is it Brian's?" she asked, her voice barely a whisper.

My attempt to turn a dreary conversation into comical one had turned plain awkward. "I'm kidding," I said softly, grimacing at the reality of that possibility. I was not ready for kids. Let alone having them with . . . well, with someone I was not going to spend the rest of my life with.

Her soft voice was muffled against the phone. A door shut in the background, and then there was silence. "Does he know?" she asked, her voice more level.

I shook my head, realizing maybe if I was, it would make it easier. There would be one clear-cut choice. My mama wouldn't have me knocked up and single. That was not what we did where we were brought up. I'd be shunned to the ends of the earth.

"I'm not pregnant. But it's worse," I finally fessed up. I collapsed on my bed, my soft down pillows surrounding me.

"Kendy," I heard the sympathy in her tone from just one word, just how she said my name.

I wished I hadn't called. "I'm sorry. Seriously, what was I thinking calling you this early in the morning? Especially since you have to work in a few hours."

"It's me, Kendy. Your best friend. Spill it. Your story can't be any crazier than mine."

I nodded as I recalled Beth's path in life. She had been through her own set of trials and had a funny way of fixing them. I was just glad it had all worked out for her.

"I'm staying on this phone until you tell me what's going on." Determination was set in her tone.

She would, too. We'd been best buddies since childhood and nothing had changed. There was no one else I trusted more.

"I think . . ." I shook my head at the reality of it all. As soon as I let those words slip out of my mouth, I knew I couldn't take them back. They'd be true. Vocalization of thoughts only solidified the truth.

"I think I'm in love with Brian." I rushed out the words in one quick breath and closed my eyes as my heartbeat throbbed in my ears.

It was silent at first, and then I heard it.

Laughter.

Beth was laughing at my freaking misfortune. Before I chewed her out for being a lousy friend, she laughed again.

"Thanks for nothing," I grouched, ready to end our phone call. I had called to gain some sort of sympathy from my cousin and closest confidant, but instead, I was getting ridiculed.

"Stop! I'm not laughing at you. I'm smiling, because you've finally found your someone. I knew you'd fall for him. And," she laughed again, "Kent and I had a sort of bet going. I, obviously, predicted the outcome."

My face was aghast. "How did you know?"

"Kendy." Her voice turned serious. "Brian is the real deal. He's once in a lifetime material. I know this, because, at one time, I thought he was *my* 'once in a lifetime.' I'm a true example of how you can't choose who you fall for."

I thought about that, while I wrestled with all these strange feelings inside me. "But what about the psychic and all she predicted? They've almost all come true. This doctor is it for me. He has to be."

He had to be it for me to heal and move on from my past. I didn't repeat the last part, but Beth knew. It didn't have to be spoken out loud.

She sighed heavily. "Kendy, people's futures change all the time. Yes, everything that psychic had said has come true. True to an eerie science, but that doesn't mean your course in life hasn't changed."

"She was specific, Beth. You were there. You heard what she said." I shook my head. "I can't, Beth. He reminds me . . ." I closed my eyes, instantly seeing Brian's face, his charming smile. "He reminds me of Cole. The way I felt for him." And look where that had gotten me. I had trusted Cole with my heart, never realizing what a monster he truly was inside.

"Oh, honey. This is good." She sounded elated, and I almost wanted to slap her as nausea hit me harder, just thinking about the bastard.

"No, it's not. It's not. " I punched my fist against the pillow. "Did you not hear what I said? I'll forever be broken if I choose him. He's too close to Cole."

"Kendy, Cole happened seven years ago," she tried to reason. "You were dumb, naïve, and blinded by first love's symptoms. Brian is nothing like Cole. You would've weeded him out by now if he was."

"I don't know. I'm . . . I'm scared," I whispered, my voice leaving my mouth in broken puffs.

And maybe that was the real truth here—I was so damn scared I couldn't see straight, not even to read my own feelings. Cole had left such a deep gash inside of me, I wondered if I'd ever truly be able to read love when it came along.

That's why it had to be James. He was the safe choice

for me. The one the psychic had predicted. He was more mature, older, and more importantly, the one she had chosen.

"Don't let fear stop you from being happy. Unless you're a hundred percent sure this doctor guy is it."

But I wasn't sure. I was realizing that I really didn't even know him, yet I wanted to give him a chance. I needed to give him a chance to prove the psychic right, but that was beyond my control. He wasn't even giving me a second glance lately. How could I make a guy love me? I couldn't force a thing like that.

"Kendy, I love you. You know I do."

I gripped the phone closer to my ear, needing to hear those words, letting them wash over me and calm me. "I know," I exhaled, wishing I could blink her across the country and into my apartment.

"Sometimes, we only see what we want to see and miss the very thing that's right in front of us. Don't miss the opportunity with this awesome guy, just because you want someone else to be it for you. From experience, I know that sometimes you don't realize the perfect guy could be right in front of you all along."

I rubbed at my brow, still unsure.

"You don't need to decide today. Go to sleep, honey. Let that mind of yours rest."

"Maybe you're right." All of the day's energy was leaking out of me, exhaustion hitting me straight in the face as I yawned into the phone.

"I love you, Kendy."

"You too. Bye." I let the phone drop onto the bed, and then turned over, taking in the scent of my pillow.

As I closed my eyes, all I could see was Brian's handsome face as he stood over the stove, making me my hot cocoa. I hadn't even tasted it. It was the drink that usually calmed me, but not tonight. Not when an internal battle was brewing inside me.

My heart wanted this man with such certainty; the one who made me laugh, the one who I cared for, and the one who I knew I could count on.

But my mind was fighting my heart's every instinct, using fear as its sidekick to push down all those inner desires and screamed at me to stay in control.

And as I fell asleep, I decided I had to think with my head. Thinking with my heart would only get me hurt.

BRIAN HAD CALLED all week. We had exchanged a couple of texts, but luckily I had been working back-to-back twelve-hour shifts, so I didn't have to lie to him about not having the time to see him. As the light from the morning sun filtered through my window, my phone vibrated with a text.

> *Brian: Morning, Beautiful. There's Fourth of July fireworks tonight at the East River. Wanna go? We can meet at eight, right before dusk.*

After a couple of minutes, when I didn't respond, he texted again.

> *Brian: I impressed the Tiggins Corp and landed a meeting with the CEO and their board members tomorrow, so I'm aiming to just go out and have fun. Put this work alcoholic out of his misery.*

I sighed. How long could I avoid him? He'd know something was seriously wrong, if he didn't think that already. And I wanted to see him, but fear was the heavy-duty steel door keeping me at a distance.

He looked nothing like Cole. Cole was tall, dark, and handsome. Brian was the all-American male with the bluest eyes—eyes that sucked you in.

Their outward appearance was nothing alike, but the way I had felt for Cole, the deep attraction and passion, was the same, or even stronger for Brian, which frightened me to no end.

But I couldn't deny I missed him.

Without thinking, my fingers moved across the screen, texting him back. Maybe I could set him straight, reiterate what our platonic relationship entailed. Or maybe . . . I was lying to myself, and my mind was already losing the battle against my heart. Either way, I wanted to see him. If lying to convince myself that I was in control of this situation would justify meeting him, then so be it.

Me: Okay. Meet at my place.

BRIAN

AS I KNOCKED on her door, my palms began to sweat. I had no idea why I was so damn jittery. I wasn't usually the nervous type, and this wasn't a first date.

Still, I hadn't seen Kendy in almost a week, and a part of me was a little worried, because she had been so brief over our texts. An unsettling feeling came over me. Had Stiff finally made his move? Was she done with me?

The thought of either scenario made me sick to my stomach, but I'd made the decision that I was all in with her. Just like a game of poker, even though I didn't know if I had the winning hand, I was going to fight for her, and I'd fight dirty if I had to.

Today was the day. I was going to claim her, make her mine—tell her how I feel.

My knuckles were about to hit her door again when she opened it. At first, she seemed hesitant, and then she bit her bottom lip, a telling sign that she was nervous.

Half of her hair was pulled back into a ponytail, the rest cascading down her back. Her short shorts revealed the span of her toned legs, and her fitted Cubs T-shirt was straining against her chest, the red 'C' stretching to the max. She didn't have on an ounce of makeup on, but damn was she gorgeous.

A second later, that hesitation washed away and she smiled, stepping aside to let me in. I swear if I hadn't seen her smile before, today it would've knocked me on my ass.

KENDY

BRIAN STEPPED INTO my apartment and wrapped one arm around my lower back, leaning in to me to give me a kiss on my cheek. I swear he inhaled me as his arm tightened around my waist, and his head dropped to the crook of my neck. My whole being felt content just being in his arms, but I was having a hard time shaking this nervousness.

I bit the inside of my cheek and told myself this was not a repeat of history. I repeated Beth's words in my head: *paths can change; futures can change.*

His hug lingered a tad bit longer than what could be considered just friendly. Not that I minded.

My body molded to his, fitting against the span of his chest like this was my natural place, caged in his arms. Just like a book in its natural spot on a bookshelf, snug between two other books.

I inhaled his masculine scent and let out a soft exhale. I hadn't realized until now how much I'd missed him this past week.

He released me and tucked an escaping strand of hair behind my ear. "I missed you." The way he said it, the seriousness in his tone, made my heart race faster than before, faster than I should've allowed it to.

I shied away. "I know why you missed me, you horny little man." I was playing off how much his words affected me. I stepped away from him and tried to calm my raging pulse. "Let me grab my purse." My voice sounded shaky when I hadn't meant it to be.

But he reached for me, squeezing me from behind. "I missed *you*. Your smile. Your laugh. I've had a very uneventful, boring week without you."

I closed my eyes, my eyebrows pulling together. He didn't even realize he was going from zero to one hundred, not giving me a chance to breathe. I headed down the hallway, not meeting his eyes. "I need to potty first." Torment was happening inside of me, a battle brewing between my heart and my head, and I was confused as hell. *What do I do?*

I rushed to the bathroom. Resting my back against the door, I dropped my head into my hands. His words had made me swoon, but as much as I tried to deny it, I couldn't resist his charms.

And there it was, the real truth—I was slowly but

undeniably falling for this man.

BRIAN

I WAS MAKING it a point to break every rule in her book, ones mentioned in passing and even the rules left unsaid. I wasn't even hiding it anymore.

I held her hand as we got off the train and kissed her palm when we were stopped at a crosswalk. I didn't break contact as the crowd weaved past us, rushing to the same place. I led us toward the entry ramp to the Manhattan Bridge, where we could catch a good spot. She didn't say a word, just let me lead.

When I took side-glances of her, I noticed her sagging shoulders and there were faint bags under her eyes. She had told me she'd worked twelve hour shifts three days in a row.

Damn.

I should've suggested we stay in, but knowing me and how much I'd missed her, not much resting would take place.

Just being in her vicinity had me itching to touch her. If we'd been alone, I'd bury myself deep inside her, make love to her until we were too tired to do anything else but lie there. Just the thought had me wanting to forget the fireworks and take her back to my place.

When we reached the bridge, the area was bustling with families and couples, all ready for the firework celebration. A set of triplets were wearing matching red, white, and blue shirts. They glided in front of us, holding their parents' hands. A woman held an American flag proudly above her head.

I sensed Kendy's excitement as she bounced on her tiptoes while we walked. Her tiredness from a moment ago was disappearing.

"Can we get closer to the front?" she asked giddily as she took the lead and forced us through the crowd. "I want a better view."

She tried to break contact when the crowd didn't budge, but I didn't let up on my hold. Instead, I pulled her back, stepped in front of her, and used my upper body to weave us to the front.

I stopped behind the little kids sitting on top of their parents' shoulders. It wouldn't have been fair to block their view.

Satisfied with our spot, I moved Kendy in front of me, caged her with my arms and rested my chin on top of her head. We watched two little boys light up sparklers in front of us.

Kendy's eyes lit up as she watched their interaction, their laughter matching hers. When the dazzling flame burned slowly to the end and they lit up another, I had an undeniable urge to kiss her. The way the light caught the aqua blue in her eyes left me breathless. I turned her slightly, cupped the side of her face, and ran my thumb up and down her cheek.

KENDY

BRIAN WAS ABOUT to kiss me. And I knew it was going to change things. We'd kissed so many times, but this, here . . . it felt different. *We* felt different.

Most importantly, I was slowly coming to realize what I wanted, and I knew I wanted more. I wanted him. The movies the other night and now this had given me glimpses of how our relationship would be, how effortless it would be to be with him.

As I peered up at him, the bridge's lights highlighting all his boyish features, I found myself wondering about a future with him. Would it be possible? What would it be like to be solely his? There was something so incredibly gentle in his eyes. A look of adoration and awe. For me.

Excitement fluttered in my belly. Everything as I knew it was shifting. I could feel it. In his hold, when we had sex and in everything we did together. I should've stopped the building of this budding relationship, but I wanted to accept it, even though the stars and that psychic's prediction had lead me to James.

Brian bent down farther, and just before he kissed me, I caught that look again, as if he thought I was the most beautiful girl in the world.

I had an undeniable urge to meet his lips, and when he brushed his mouth against mine, my knees weakened and I felt like a puddle of mush within his hold. His lips were soft, sweet, and caressing, as if he was telling me something with that one kiss alone.

I inhaled deeply, taking in his masculine cologne, the kind I'd remember if someone else was wearing it and passed me by, but that scent would always remind me of Brian.

He pulled back, cupping the side of my face, and my heart stammered in my chest. I rested my cheek against his palm. His hold, his aura, something about him, calmed me. Even with the chaos of the crowd around us, just being near him relaxed me.

As the crowd of people continued to push against us, I sighed, feeling content and oddly whole.

If there had been a sea of beautiful models in our vicinity, Brian wouldn't have even noticed. His eyes were solely focused on me, making my cheeks warm and the butterflies to work up a frenzy in my stomach.

Slowly, he turned me to watch the first booms as he lightly rested his chin on my head. I took in the colorful array of blazing lights shattering against the dark night sky before breaking up into tiny sparks, that trickled down like teardrops. Silence filled the air for a few second before a sonic boom shook the ground, followed by a stream of red, white, and blue whirls into a spiral against the backdrop of the Brooklyn Bridge.

I turned to Brian, yelling above the noise, "Isn't it beautiful?"

He nodded, smiling down at me.

"Almost like I can reach up and touch the fireworks. Be that much closer to the stars."

A sudden hint of amusement crossed his features before he reached for my waist and started to lift me.

"Wait," I said in a panic, feeling my feet leave the ground. But before I could protest more, he sat me on his shoulders like I weighed no more than a feather. "No, no, no, I'm afraid of heights," I started to argue, hating being so high up.

Ignoring me, he pushed me up higher. "Don't worry, baby," he said with pure confidence. "I've got you."

I've got you. Such innocence in those three words. Nothing like what he almost said the other night, or what I thought he was about to say. And yet, those three words had tears budding in my eyes.

He's got me.

"Okay," I replied quietly, unable to find my full voice.

He gripped my thighs so I wouldn't slip, and I slowly but surely decided to trust him. I reached up toward the sky as another array of fireworks colored the darkness. Then I sat taller, throwing my head back and stretched my fingers as if I could catch a star and, if I did, I'd make a wish. Just one. For happiness.

I let out a loud scream, followed by laughter, feeling free. Lighter.

It was the Fourth of July fireworks, not a baseball game, where I'd be cheering, but still, I felt like the queen of the universe as I sat above the crowd of people below me.

He chuckled like I was the funniest thing on Earth, and I smiled down at him, my cheeks hurting. Laugh lines would probably forever be etched on my face.

I knew when it was almost over when bursts of fireworks exploded consecutively one after the other, ending with a glittery shower trickling down until the sparks disappeared against the black back drop.

I wiggled to let him know I wanted down.

"You sure? We can keep you up there all night long."

"Yep, ready." Trust or no trust, I didn't need to be up here longer than necessary.

"Okay, on the count of three," he started. "One, two . . ." Then, without a three count, Brian turned me so I slipped down the length of his body until we were chest-to-chest. Tingles traveled from where we were connected to my core, arousing me. It was crazy how his body affected me.

When my eyes met his, I read desire in them. I had no doubt what was playing in his mind, because it was playing in high definition in my mind, too.

My feet touched the ground, and we stared at each other for a moment, then he bent his head and crashed his mouth into mine. This was the kiss I had felt at the bar, my whole body hyperaware of his lips on me.

His fingertips gripped my waist, leaving indentations against my skin. His tongue danced with mine. We were in the middle of a crowd, but it didn't matter. It was just the two of us and this all-consuming kiss.

After a moment, I pulled him into me, fisted the back of his shirt, and felt his arousal against my stomach. My breathing intensified, and I knew if he didn't take me home this instant, I'd have to resist the urge to drop my panties in front of this massive crowd.

I pulled back slightly, just enough to catch the look of desire on his face. I went on my tiptoes and whispered, "Let's get out of here."

He blinked once, but didn't hesitate. Grabbing my hand, he led me out of the crowd.

An inner warmth radiated throughout my body at our connection, and my hands trembled within his, because I would've let this man lead me anywhere.

I HEAVED IN exhaustion as I lay on Brian's chest. We'd just had marathon sex, and my stomach suddenly grumbled against him, hungry from the workout.

The only light filtering through his window was the moonlight cascading a blue shadow over his grey blanket, which encased both of our bodies.

Sleep was calling my name as my heart rate descended, finally returning to its normal pace. Brian ran his hands through my hair, over and over, contributing to my drowsiness.

Don't fall asleep. Stay awake.

I couldn't fall asleep here, not at his place. Not before I had consciously made my decision about us.

He kissed my hair. A week ago, I would've told him that was against the rules, but we were definitely past rules now. Those rules had been broken, destroyed.

He kissed my temple and his hands moved to trace circles along my back. And just as I was thinking about the rules, or lack thereof, I heard his gentle voice. "Stay. Stay the night."

I shut my eyes tight, letting the words wash over me. I was tempted, so very tempted, but I couldn't. Not when I hadn't totally thought things through.

This one slight move would be the final change. It would solidify things. It would be an unspoken act of affection on my part, a proclamation that I wasn't sure I was ready to make.

I shifted off of him and smiled to soften the blow. "I can't," I said regretfully. My stomach churned as I watched disappointment filter through his eyes.

Without saying a word, he swung his legs over the side of the bed and stood. He didn't even look at me as he headed into the bathroom and shut the door behind him.

Wait. What just happened?

I sat there for a moment, debating going after him as his cotton sheets rustled against my naked body. Should I go? Should I let him stew alone?

No. I wanted to know. I had to know what he was thinking.

I jolted up and clutched the sheets against my chest, but remained stoic on the bed.

Chickenshit, I scolded myself. I was a chickenshit. I

was usually much braver than this.

I knew why I wasn't going to barge through the bath-room door and question him. It was because I didn't want to hear the truth. In my heart, I knew what he was going to say. It would've been the switch in our already blurry relationship, and nothing would be the same.

It was fear keeping me here. Fear from the past. Fear of the unknown future. Fear of falling in love again and letting myself be open to the kind of vulnerability that came with being in love.

At times, I thought I was dauntless. But with Brian, I was just a coward.

Chapter Sixteen

BRIAN

I'D MESSED UP. Asking her to stay the night had been a total fuck up.

I could sense everything changing between us, yet I couldn't stop it, nor did I want to.

I had my client call tomorrow morning, and I needed to bring my A-game, but the only thing that occupied my thoughts was her. This was my last meeting with Tiggins Corp, and it included their CEO. This was it, so I should've let her walk out the door and called her tomorrow.

But somehow I knew I'd sleep better in my bed with her in it.

This woman had walked into my life with a simple solution to help her get the other man. Yet, she was the ultimate solution to mine, and I didn't even know it. My parents had been married for almost thirty years, and when I was ten, my father had told me that when he'd met my mother, he'd known she was the one. I hadn't understood him before, but now I did.

When they said opposites attract, wasn't it the truth? I'd never felt an undeniable connection with anyone else, an attraction so strong there was no way I was walking away from her.

I splashed water on my face and stared at my reflection. How the hell did I get myself into these situations? For once, why couldn't this work in my favor?

But as I asked myself these questions, I knew the answer. The problems weren't mine. They were hers. Her old pains, her old insecurities, kept this hidden barrier and chains against her heart.

I could see the torment in her eyes. I sensed the internal struggle she was going through in her actions. What she said versus how she acted was a constant battle. One minute, she was sighing into my shoulder, relaxing against my hold, and the next, she was denying me, not wanting to sleep over.

It didn't matter though, because I knew myself. I'd fight to banish her insecurities, be her safe haven and squash her fears.

Before I could think any further, I rushed out of the bathroom, afraid my girl had left.

My girl.

I was already claiming her, and she didn't even know it, but I couldn't help it. My heart belonged to her now. We were forever linked.

When I stepped out, I exhaled a low sigh of relief that Kendy hadn't left. She was out of bed, though, and dressed in her jean shorts and red, white, and blue tank. She was crazy beautiful, just as she'd been this evening.

My eyes traveled the length of her legs, and I had the strongest urge to drag her back to bed. Her eyes flickered to mine for a second then moved to her purse on the ground, but not before I sensed the hesitation, the tear in them.

Almost as if she had to keep busy, she picked it up and began rummaging through her belongings. "Thanks for taking me to the fireworks." Her voice sounded shaky. Not a good sign.

"Kendy," I said gently, approaching her slowly so I wouldn't spook her.

I reached for her waist, and then brushed her hair away from her face. I peered down at her, our eyes locking. My insides softened as I saw some of that hesitation melt away, and then I bent down to kiss her. Again she didn't stop me. I told her with my lips how much I wanted her to stay the night. My true feelings and emotions rushed to the surface, and I savored her with such passion that she turned liquid beneath me.

She was the first to pull back. She blinked a couple of times as confusion crossed her face, and something else. It was an emotion I was familiar with, an intense look of longing, and it gave me a tinge of hope that she felt as deeply as I did.

I didn't give her another chance to deny me. I cupped the side of her face. "Stay," I whispered urgently. When she didn't protest, hope bloomed in my chest, and I brought her closer by the nape of her neck. "Stay," I whispered again.

When I caressed her lips with my tongue, she didn't open at first, but then I flicked my tongue against her. "I need you," I told her. I didn't give her a chance to respond.

Tonight, I would do anything to keep her here. I didn't want her to walk out that door, not again. We'd played this game long enough. I was done with the game, done with FTFing, or whatever the hell she thought we were still doing. I was over it, and if making love would keep her here, I'd happily oblige . . . all night long.

There was no way I was letting her leave, not without a fight. Tonight, I wasn't taking no for an answer, not when I knew I had fallen hopelessly in love with this woman.

She moaned into my mouth as her hands moved, urgent and aggressive, over the front of my boxers. We broke contact just enough for her to reach for the waist-band of my boxers, but I lifted her hands and brought them to my lips. Kissing her delicate fingers, I stared down at her. I wanted to savor and cherish every inch of her body. Tonight, I'd take things slow, make love to her the way she deserved.

I cupped the back of her shorts and picked her up as she wrapped her legs around my waist. When I pushed her against my hardness, she dropped her head back, and my tongue found the tender spot below her ear that drove her mad. This was her spot, the one that got her panties wet just from one flick of my tongue.

As many times as I'd been inside her, I'd memorized every inch of her. I knew the tender spot on the inner part of her thigh, how to make her moan and, even better, how to make her scream louder.

If her body was a road map, I could trace every birth-mark, every freckle, and every part of her body that drove her over the edge.

Her feet touched the ground, her tender eyes locked with mine. Bending down, I lifted her behind her knees, carrying her like we were crossing some sort of threshold, and maybe we were. Maybe this was some monumental shift in our relationship. Either way, I knew there was no way she was leaving tonight because I wasn't letting her go.

I JOLTED UP from my peaceful state of sleep when I heard a scream. It was Kendy. She was lying beside me, thrashing around, blonde hair matted to her face. And then she stopped.

I leaned in, listening to her tiny mumbles to see if I could decipher something . . . anything. There was only one word I could make out.

"No."

She spoke so softly. It was barely above a whisper, but she repeated that one word over and over. Her face was distorted and her eyebrows pulled together as though she was in pain.

When she started to whimper, I moved up to my knees. It was like taking a punch in the gut over and over again, watching her struggle. But then I noticed that her cheeks were wet from tears, and any indecision on whether or not to wake her up flew out the window.

Her tears were my undoing.

I shook her gently. "Kendy . . . Kendy . . ." I pulled her to my chest, wiping away the wetness on her cheeks.

Finally, her eyes flew open and she reeled back, throwing herself up against the headboard. The action was so abrupt, my eyes widened. Her limbs shook as her face flashed with fear then confusion.

I raised my hands like I was approaching a scared animal. "It's me. Brian." Of course she knew it was me, but I'd just woken her from her nightmare, and she seemed disoriented.

The next minute, she rushed toward me and started wailing into my chest.

Listening to her cries was like tiny knives shooting straight through my heart.

"It's okay," I whispered, smoothing a hand down her

back. "It's okay, baby; it's okay. I've got you." I tucked her under my chin and she curled in, unresisting.

I didn't know what had frightened her. All I knew was that I wanted to fucking jump back into her nightmare and beat the boogie man to a pulp.

I rocked her as she cried in my lap. I'd never felt so helpless, wanting to do something, but not knowing what she had dreamt about.

She wouldn't talk, so I didn't know what I could do or say. I just comforted her the best I could and rocked her within the confines of my arms as my insides contracted at her uncontrollable sobs.

When her cries died down, she pushed at my chest, and I loosened my hold. She wiped the tears from her face with the bottom of my oversized T-shirt, that she was wearing.

Pulling her knees under my shirt, she backed up against the headboard again. I knew in my gut what her nightmare had been about. There was no confirmation, but my gut was never wrong. Whatever this was, I was certain it had something to do with her ex-boyfriend.

She wouldn't even look at me, and I couldn't take it. I inched closer, wanting to be near her. I sensed that she didn't want me to even touch her, and I yearned to hold her again, but I kept a small distance.

"I'm sorry," she said sadly.

My stomach dropped at the sorrow in her beautiful blue eyes. Why the hell she was apologizing, I had no idea. I could see exactly how broken she really was, and I knew she was embarrassed. She had let her guard down, something she'd never done with me, but I had to show her that it was okay.

"There's nothing to be sorry about." I reached out to

hold her, but she cowered, backing up farther.

She nodded, barely, then hugged her knees closer to her chest and rested her chin on top. She looked so tiny in my oversized t-shirt.

"What were you dreaming about?" I asked carefully, gritting my teeth. My muscles tensed as I waited for her response. Time seemed to tick by slowly, painfully. The seconds seemed like an eternity.

Her eyes met mine for a brief second before she turned away again. "Cole."

I gritted my teeth again as my body tensed. I wanted to ask her more, but I waited for her to tell me. If I pushed her, she'd clam up. I had figured that out by now.

Her lip quivered as she spoke. "He held me . . . he held me down the whole time. Even when I begged him to stop." She spoke softly, though she sounded tormented.

I gripped the sheets in my fists, my eyes losing focus. Everything made sense. No wonder she didn't want to be on the bottom when I made love to her.

I want to fucking kill him.

Tremors overtook my body, but I breathed heavily and concentrated only on Kendy's face to keep me steady. "What else?"

She gulped, seeing how angry I was. She'd probably kept this secret all this time. "I found him in his truck with his pants down, with Clary," she said quietly. "I told him I didn't want to see him anymore . . . and . . ." She stifled a cry in her sleeve. " . . . and he wanted to make sure I knew what I'd be missing."

My hands trembled at her revelations and, automatically, I advanced toward her, because, shit, I had to hold her. I needed to feel her beside me, but she held up her hands to stop me.

"I was embarrassed. I didn't think people would believe me, since we'd already been together sexually. And by the time I could absorb what had happened . . . I just wanted to forget," she said before tucking her feet under her butt, her tone heart-wrenchingly soft. "I'm fine. I got my revenge. I busted his nose."

She was trying to make light of the situation, when there was nothing funny about it. If all that asshole got was a broken nose, he got off fucking easy.

She shook her head, offering a sad smile. "Don't feel sorry for me."

"I don't." It was the truth. Kendy was strong, no question. I didn't feel sorry for her, but she needed to know she didn't have to go through this alone. She had me now.

She peered out the window, wrapping her arms around herself in a cocoon of anguish. "I haven't had that nightmare in a while." Her eyebrows pulled together like she was studying me, gauging my reaction maybe.

Then I paused and somehow found myself asking, "Do I look like him?"

She shook her head, biting her lower lip. "No, not at all." Letting out a soft sigh, she added, "But sometimes you remind me of him."

Ice spread through my stomach. I didn't want to be compared to that asshole in any way, shape, or form.

My jaw locked right before I spoke. "I'd never hurt you, Kendy."

My voice came out strong with conviction. There was no way I'd fail her when every man in her life had. Her father had left her at such a young age, and the only man she had ever loved had hurt her beyond repair. I'd restore her faith in men again. I would. She'd gain trust and faith in me.

"No, the good parts of him. The way I felt about him."
She lowered her head, her bottom lip quivering. "You remind me why I fell in love."

I choked down all the emotion from her words and extended my hand. "Come here." I just needed to touch her. If not for her then for me because I was anything but fine. "It's me," I reassured her.

Her eyes held a haunted, distant look in them. She glanced at my extended hand, her face filled with caution.

"I've got you," I said, coaxing her toward me. Everything had to be on her terms, not mine.

Finally, she extended her hand and locked our fingers. I watched the light from the bathroom shine on her beautiful face.

"Stop worrying about me," she said. "I told you I'm fine." She said the words, but I didn't believe them. Her forced smile didn't reach her eyes. It wasn't the genuine smile I was so used to seeing.

"Well, I need to hold you, because I'm far from fine. I'm about to hunt this bastard down and leave him with more than a broken nose."

She bit her lower lip, emotions rushing to the surface. Then she crawled into my lap, and I wrapped my arms around her.

I heard her heavy exhale as she leaned into me, her whole body relaxing. Maybe she too felt steadier around me, wrapped in my embrace.

This was good. Really good.

I took this as a sign she was slowly trusting me, getting used to me. At least this time she wasn't pushing me away. My chest tightened as a fierce protectiveness overtook me. As though this newfound purpose reigned throughout my veins, and it was to protect and love this woman for eternity and ensure that no one would ever hurt her.

"I'm okay." Her hands moved under my shirt, her fingertips trailing along my waist, the bareness of my back. "I'll be okay." Her words came out stronger with more force, but they weren't directed at me. She was speaking to herself.

Her hands turned more urgent, not as gentle, as her fingers dug into my skin, and the mood shifted. I tensed, confused at the quick change, yet wanting her all the same.

She rested back on her heels, seduction written all over her face as she gripped the back of her shirt and lifted it over her head. Her perfect nipples pebbled against the soft bathroom light, which was shining into my room.

She positioned herself over my boxers. She still had her panties on, but as soon as she sat on me, I was hard as a fucking rock. Then she gripped the tips of my hair, pulled my head back, and slammed her lips against mine, ravenously kissing me.

Warning signs rang loudly in my ears. A moment ago, she'd been so vulnerable, and now her possessive movements seemed so erratic.

I wanted her, too. Shit, did I ever. I always did. But it felt wrong, when moments ago she'd been crying.

She pulled back and rubbed her tits against my chest. There was a devilish smile on her face, but I stopped, my jaw tightening. What I noticed in her eyes was what broke me. She was disconnected from this moment, the passion I was used to seeing gone and replaced by an eerie coldness.

"I'm going to fuck you. Hard."

The way she said it tugged at my heart. I was

beginning to realize maybe this was how she forgot. This was why she always had to be in control. It was all she knew.

Looking up at her stark blue eyes, I wanted to tell her that I didn't need anything else, just her. With me, in my life.

But I didn't say anything, because I had a feeling she wouldn't believe me.

She shoved my chest until I was lying on my back and moved her hands to the edge of my boxers. I pulled on her hands, bringing them each to my lips. Then I lifted her toward me. Our eyes met in the darkness, mine softening, trying to get her to be present with me in this moment.

When she paused, I sensed the wall weakening, the uncertainty in her eyes lessening, and I framed her face, pulling her flush against me. "Kiss me," I said gently, sensing I was chipping away at her hard exterior; her defenses were deteriorating.

When her eyes lost focus at my words, I pulled her face down to mine, and our lips met. When her body tensed in my arms, she retreated and I stopped. Then suddenly, her mood changed like a switch had been flipped. Her kisses turned urgent and rough as her lips crashed against mine. It was desperate, cold even. She was forcing that wall up again, sealing me out, and I couldn't let her do that.

I wouldn't let her do that.

I framed her face to slow down and savor her mouth, outlined her lips with my tongue, and touched her lips gently with mine. I looked up at the woman who had claimed my heart, peering deeply into her eyes so she knew, so she understood. "Do you know how crazy beautiful you are? Why are you so perfect?"

She seemed lost, pain shinning in her eyes. Her voice was barely a whisper. "It's because you want something from me." When it slipped out from her mouth, my heart sunk. Was sex all she thought she was worth?

Suddenly, she looked so vulnerable that I pulled her flush against me once again. This was a side of her I'd never seen before, and I made it my mission to prove her wrong.

"The only thing I want to do is kiss you." I framed her face and kissed her lips. "Here." I kissed her button nose. "And here." I placed a small kiss on each of her eyelids as my lips feathered across her tender skin.

She shivered as her breath caught in her throat, but she didn't resist, her body molding to mine as I pushed us both up to a sitting position.

"And here." I flicked my tongue over and over against the tender skin on the side of her neck.

Her breaths increased as I sucked at the soft spot below her ear.

That's my girl. Let go. Let me love you like you deserve to be loved.

I feathered kisses along her jaw and made my way to the other side of her neck, teasing her with my tongue until my lips found their way back to hers. All I could hear were the sounds of me worshiping my girl.

She moaned into my mouth as I slowly guided her down the length of the bed and onto her back, so gently, like she was a porcelain doll. I hovered above her as her head hit the pillow, and that was when I saw it—the fear in her eyes, a panic so alarming that it was like jabbing a knife in my gut.

"Trust me." I didn't break eye contact as I peppered

kisses along her jawline. "Beautiful. Sexy." I worshiped her with my words and with my lips. "Perfect."

When she stiffened, I backed up an inch. I wanted her to feel adored, but I wanted her to trust me first. I had to do this right, on her terms. All in good time; she'd believe me eventually.

My lips trailed to her neck and then brushed against her nipples. I ran my tongue around her breast, resting on her nipple and feeling it pebble in my mouth. Her breathing became labored as her hands threaded through my hair. I sensed she was still holding back, but that cage confining her heart was opening slightly.

She was absolutely perfect in the way she tasted, the saltiness of her skin. I was rock hard, but I ignored the throbbing as I concentrated on her.

Then a look of longing replaced the fear in her eyes, and I took my tongue lower and lower until I was kissing her outer thigh.

Her chest heaved with anticipation, and I wanted to drag this on, lick every inch of her flesh and cherish this moment.

"Please," she begged as I dragged my tongue along her inner thigh.

She wiggled beneath me and, because I couldn't prolong it any longer, because I needed to feel her against my tongue and taste her sweetness on my lips, I moved to her core, flicking my tongue against her folds. She tasted like heaven. I continued to savor and suckle her sensitive nub then gripped her thighs so I could move deeper but slowed down, to prolong the buildup.

A moan of ecstasy slipped through her lips, and I knew she was close. Soon enough, she gripped the ends of my hair, pulling hard. "Brian. Please," she begged, wanting release.

With one more flick of my tongue, her body convulsed, contractions overtaking her. She was too gone in ecstasy as I crawled up and kissed her mouth, moans of pleasure rippling through her.

This was a small success, but I was determined.

I'd cherish this girl, make love to her over and over again until she understood the magnitude of my feelings for her. I'd eradicate any memories of any man who'd ever hurt her, replacing them in her mind with new memories of us and convincing her to trust me.

KENDY

WHEN MY ORGASM slowly died down, he trailed kisses up my body, meeting my lips. I trusted him. I did. And as he slowly made his way on top of me, my knees fell to the sides and I cradled him between my legs.

His kisses felt heavenly. I'd never been to Heaven, but I was pretty sure this was how it would feel—heart overflowing with sensation, love, and pure joy.

I could feel his hard length against my stomach as he entwined our hands together. With my free hand, I threaded my fingers through his hair, loving the thump of his heartbeat against mine, as though we were one, and I stifled a cry as the enormity of the emotions flooded my insides.

He stared deeply into my eyes, and I knew I was his. Words didn't have to be spoken to know he loved me, and though I'd been trying to deny it, trying to fool myself into thinking our relationship was purely physical, the deepest part of me knew it wasn't. Our connection went beyond the realm of physical.

He traced a finger from my brow to my temple, then to my chin. The look of adoration in his eyes clearly showed he was enamored with me.

I was hypnotized by him, my skin tingling where he touched, draining all my doubts and fears away. I had never felt so cherished, and a euphoric feeling washed over me, like there was nothing in the world that existed except the two of us.

Then out of nowhere, he said, "I love you." It was effortless, like he'd known it all along.

I gulped, my heart beating faster in my chest. Normally, I'd be afraid, but . . . I wasn't. I couldn't be, because I found that I trusted him. Brian's purity was putting me back together somehow, making me whole.

I released a soft sigh, noting the panic-ridden Kendy was no longer present, and I lowered my hand and ran it up and down his length, feeling his cock twitch between us. I positioned him at my entrance, wanting nothing between us. I was on the pill, and I knew we were good about getting tested on an annual basis.

As his eyes filled with such unyielding love, he thrust inside me without restraint, and I gasped. I bit my lip as he cradled my cheek with his palm. The act was so gentle, so tender, tears threatened to spill over. I'd never been handled this carefully, and I knew in the deepest part of my being that Brian could never hurt me the way Cole had. He wasn't perfect, but maybe . . . maybe he was perfectly made for me.

His lips moved to mine as he continued to move above me, filling me with an amazing sense of completeness. My eyes fell shut at his fullness, which caused my body to prickle with sensation. Every move increased the hypersensitivity of my body.

"Open your eyes," he said huskily.

I looked up at him and felt overwhelmed by what I saw, by his presence inside me, surrounding me. As he peered down, he continued to tell me how much he loved me, how I was so perfect, so beautiful. Not only did he tell me with words, but he showed me with each thrust of his body as his eyes smoldered with desire.

I let his words wash over me, fill me, and put the broken pieces of this girl back together.

Our passion flowed through me. We had this undeniable, intense connection, where all I could feel, sense, and breathe was Brian. I was so overcome with emotion that a tear formed in the corner of my eye, and then it all hit me—I loved him. I was in love with him. There was no way on earth I couldn't be.

He touched his forehead against mine, his movements becoming erratic as he pumped faster. "I want to come inside you." His breath left him in broken huffs, and I could feel his restraint slipping.

Because he felt so damn good, and because I loved him, I answered, "Yes."

"God, baby, you feel so amazing," he grunted in the heat of passion. He rested his forehead against mine, and my eyes fell shut as I felt the contractions taking over. "I love you so damn much." Such passion and emotion leaked from his voice.

And then—explosion.

I saw damn stars behind my eyes as he transported me to another planet. We came down together and, as he stilled and collapsed on top of me, I held him against my body, wrapping my legs around his waist in a tight vise, never wanting to be disconnected from him, ever.

Keeping us whole.
Keeping us one.
Keeping us together.

Chapter Seventeen

KENDY

HIS ARMS WERE draped across my waist, and I watched the moonlight from the window cascade shadows on his face. I kept silent, watching him sleep soundly beside me as his eyelashes fluttered over his cheek when he exhaled.

Everything had changed tonight. I felt it when we touched, when he moved inside me. I'd been here once with Cole, but that had been before he'd taken my free will and forever changed my thoughts about love.

After that painful time in my life, I had sworn to never let a man control me, my body, or how I felt about anything. I was my own and would be no one else's until I gave myself away in marriage. To James. Or so I'd thought.

Until tonight . . .

Doubts still plagued me. About my future. About Evangeline's predictions.

Chaos ruled my mind and my heart, because tonight, something had happened between Brian and me. I'd relinquished control. I hadn't held back. I'd let him have me, touching my heart in a place I'd locked up for a long time. And I didn't know why.

Maybe it was him—his gentle spirit and his kindness,

that was breaking free the exterior I'd spent a lifetime building up.

And though I wanted to deny it, I couldn't anymore without lying to myself. I was in love with him. It felt foreign to admit that to myself, but it was true.

I touched my temple while closing my eyes, trying to reign in my thoughts and steady myself. With him, all my sanity flew out the door.

I had to remind myself that what I'd had in the past wasn't normal, wasn't real. This was real. History had tainted my view on life. I'd always treaded on the cautious side of being happy. Once I let myself feel happiness, I was always suddenly afraid things were too good to be true and all would come crashing down.

Not this time.

This was how love was supposed to be—uncontrollable, undeniable. I was in love with this man, and he loved me.

Let yourself be happy, Kendy. You deserve it.

Brian is no Cole.

My phone vibrated in my purse on the floor. I sat up as my eyes raked in the smexy man next to me—*my man.* I tilted toward him, mere inches from his face, and inhaled deeply before placing a light kiss on his lips.

As I reached for my phone, my pulse quickened when I saw fifteen missed calls and five missed texts from my mama. My adrenaline spiked and the worst possible thoughts crossed my mind. I hoped she was okay.

I swiped my finger against the screen, revealing a text.

Mom: Hanky Panky proposed and I accepted. Wanted my favorite girl to be the first to know. Call me back, Sweetie.

The words should've had me elated, but I wasn't. I

mean, I was. For her . . .

I went back and read the text.

Again.

And again, but more slowly.

My heartbeat thudded in my ears, and I squeezed the phone in my hand as hot tears prickled my eyes. Maybe if I stared at the text long enough, the message would read something different. But it didn't.

Evangeline had predicted that my mama would re-marry. It was the second to last prediction. The last was my prediction, the one which had led me to James, the man who'd given me the moon, the man I was supposed to live my happily-ever-after with.

My insides suddenly crumbled as the reality of it all slapped me in the face. Hot tears coursed down my cheeks, and I gulped down small breaths to minimize my cries. This was it, the finality of it all.

There was what I wanted in life, and then there was fate. It was as though fate was laughing in my face, telling me that my life was already predestined to follow a certain path. This final prediction foretold the guy to give me the moon, and that he would set me free. Brian was never it. He was never supposed to be.

My hands trembled at my side, hating this, hating Evangeline. I had once thought her predictions were a blessing which used to give me hope and peace, knowing the outcome of my life. Now, those predictions were my own living curse.

I stared at the handsome man sleeping soundly beside me, and closed my eyes to stop the tears from falling.

And then I saw him.

Cole.

Behind the darkness.

I would never be free of him.

My hands began to sweat as a nervous, gut-wrenching sensation came over me, and I suddenly felt the walls were closing in, a feeling of claustrophobia hitting me.

I needed fresh air.

I needed to leave.

Now.

I pushed myself off the bed, careful not to wake him. Then I reached for my clothes and slipped them on. Turning, I risked one more glance at his beautiful face, taking in the features I'd memorized over the weeks we'd spent together.

God, was he gorgeous, but even more beautiful on the inside than he was on the outside. Who'd have thought I would fall for Brian? It was a mystery, even to me.

But then, it's not such a huge surprise. Nice guys are the best ones. The ones you fall for, the ones you marry.

At that thought, the tears started anew. I had to get out of here. I didn't know if it was because I was in close proximity to Brian or if I was losing control of this life, that had already been planned out for me by Evangeline's predictions. Either way, I couldn't deal with the enormity of the one prediction that I no longer wanted to come true. The prediction that controlled my life and only heightened my fear of relationships, crippling me from making any decisions on my own. Any semblance of control on my life seemed like it was slipping, and I knew I would fall apart if I didn't gain it back.

As I tiptoed out of his room, a heavy sadness washed over me.

Bending down, I planted a kiss on his cheek as my vision blurred from my tears. I rubbed the heel of my palm against my chest and used all my strength to keep myself upright as sobs wracked my body.

"Goodbye, Brian." My voice quivered as I spoke, while my world bottomed out and despair swallowed me whole.

I awarded myself one last look then turned to leave.

This was it.

The end.

I RUSHED INTO my apartment and jumped into bed, desperate for the comfort and normalcy of my own place—the scent of citrus candles in my apartment, the softness of my down pillows, and the comfort of my own mattress.

But even in my own home, my thoughts were occupied by the man I had left soundly sleeping in his bed.

The thoughts of Brian were overwhelming me. Though he wasn't here, his presence still lingered.

My eyes focused on my couch that we'd made love, the kitchen where he'd attempted to make me an upgraded version of my mama's hot cocoa, just because it reminded me of home, and the empty bottle of wine he'd brought before our date.

I wrapped my arms around my knees, rocking back and forth, and stared at the phone by my foot, knowing I had to call my mother. But I couldn't. Not now.

Picking up the phone, I chucked it off the bed and it fell onto my hardwood floor. I clenched my eyes tightly, wishing I would see anything other than Cole.

When I had caught him cheating on me, I knew it was over, that I needed to break up with his ass, and move the hell on. So I'd showed up to his place. I'd wanted to show I was mature and properly break up with him, as I would've liked someone to break up with me.

Cole wouldn't have it. He'd torn his room apart in the process of trying to explain to me that nothing had happened. When I'd tried to leave, he'd pulled me to him and kissed me hard.

"Tell me you don't feel that," he had said.

I had shoved him off with both hands.

At one time, I'd felt every touch, every kiss from Cole, but not anymore.

"No," I had replied, only disgusted by his behavior.

Cole was immortal. I had put him on a pedestal, enamored at the fact that he'd picked me. But that night, all I could see was Clary and him together every time I closed my eyes, and I knew I would never get over that.

"Bye, Cole." I had turned to leave, finally done with him and ready to move past my heartache.

He'd reached for me, tugged me toward him, and kissed me hard again. Then he reached to cup the front of my pants with his hand. Pulling back, I saw anger and darkness in his eyes. Chills shook my body and dread filled my veins.

"This is fucking mine," he'd growled. "No one else's."

My throat closed up as my mind regressed back to the day he'd raped me. The restraint, the suffocation, and the overall feeling of being powerless to someone I had once loved and trusted. I'd seen his violent side when he'd been in fights before, but never once had he unleashed it on me. . . . until that night.

That night, I had fought like my life depended on it as he forced himself inside me, taking away my power to choose. He'd broken me that night. Seven years later, I was still broken. Just a shell of my former self, unable to hold a real relationship, unable to feel anything other than the sensation of sex when I was physically with any man.

Then came Brian. He was everywhere, bringing back memories of Cole, because I felt everything with Brian. Somehow he had torn through the barriers I'd spent years building up. When I was with him, I felt every single touch, every kiss . . . everything. As if, when Brian touched me, he was reaching into my soul, breaking away all my insecurities, making me feel somewhat whole.

These past few weeks, I'd caught a glimpse of how it could be with Brian. My future, free from my past. But tonight, the dream vanished after hearing of my mother's engagement. It was as if I was predestined to follow a path, and if I veered from this path, the consequence would be my happiness.

My comfort had always been in this future, which had been foretold to me. That had been my semblance of control since I was sixteen, since Evangeline had given me the reality to stop wishing for my father to come home and what she had predicted about me . . . about my future and about my happiness.

And then came Brian, and I felt okay just by being with him, but being with him meant I had to let go of my past and let go of the predictions. Just let go.

Tremors shook my body, and I couldn't. I just couldn't because I was afraid, so very afraid of the unknown, of letting go. Being in love meant you let someone else take the driver's seat, and the only time I'd been in love, the driver drove us off the cliff, crashed us, and obliterated the carefree girl that I once knew.

I swiped at my face, threw the comforter to the side, and cried a goddamn river into the sleeve of my shirt. "Stop!" I screamed at myself, pushing my palms against my eyelids. But the more I willed myself not to cry, the more tears fell down my cheeks.

I shook my head and stood, biting my cheek and loving the pain. Maybe the physical pain would make the tears go away, or at least change their purpose. "Stop!" I said, pinching the inside of my wrist. "Stop crying over that fucker!"

He'd taken so much from me that night. My free will, how I saw men, and my 'glass half full' mentality. Now, at any moment, I was fearful that someone might tip the glass over, causing it to empty.

I turned the TV on, volume on loud to drive these thoughts deep down into places inside of me that I didn't touch anymore. The ones of my dad and his new family. The ones where Cole was on top of me, hurting me, restraining me against my will, and using force to have his way.

When it didn't work, I turned the volume up higher. When that didn't work, I cupped both ears with my hands, but it was no use. The memory was taking me under.

Finally, I threw the remote and heard it thud against the television, then I dropped to my knees on the floor. That thud was a comforting sound compared to hearing myself plead with him over and over. My cries, my begging, and my screaming had not stopped him from violating me in the worst possible way. He had only wrapped his hand around my throat, suffocating me and restraining my cries.

And once it was over, he'd left me to clean myself up and leave.

I let my head fall into my hands, my shoulders shaking with sobs. I couldn't. Not with Brian. Not when our relationship was unpredictable and all-consuming. If I let go with him, I wouldn't be in control of my life anymore. This had not been our arrangement, our plan. I needed to take charge of my life from this day forward or I'd never be fixed. I'd forever be broken.

BRIAN

I REACHED OVER to the side of my bed, feeling around for the warmth of her body. When my hand patted against the empty sheet, I jolted up and searched my room for Kendy.

My stomach churned with dread as I leapt out of bed, put my boxers on, and rushed to the living room. "Kendy!" I yelled, searching every corner of mine and Trey's tiny place. But she wasn't in the living room, and she wasn't in the bathroom.

"Kendy . . ." I stopped in the kitchen as realization hit me.

She left.

My hands gripped the kitchen counter, and I let my head hang as my eyes fell shut. Tonight, I'd seen the same emotion I felt mirrored in her eyes. I knew she loved me; these feelings didn't only go one way. But maybe I'd rushed her. Maybe I should've given her more time.

"Fuck!" I growled, slamming my palms against the marble. At the sound of heavy footsteps, I peered up.

Trey slipped a shirt over his head as he strolled into the kitchen. "What happened?" His voice was low with concern as he advanced toward me.

"She left." I rushed back to my room in search of my phone then pulled it from the back pocket of my jeans, which were on the floor, and dialed her number. It went straight to voicemail.

With a frustrated growl, I glanced at the digital clock on my nightstand. It was six-thirty. In a few hours, I'd be in the boardroom, trying to land the biggest client of my career, with every important board member from the company in attendance. This would make or break my hopes of getting a promotion . . . yet all I could think about was Kendy. Had she made it home safely? Were we okay?

I tilted my head from side to side, trying to ease the tension building in my muscles. I focused on the clock again, doubting my ability to get to work on time if I went after her. At this point, though, I didn't fucking care. I wanted to talk to her, make sure we were okay. Make sure *she* was okay.

With my mind set, I pulled my jeans up and reached for my oversized shirt folded neatly at the edge of the bed, the one she'd worn to sleep. Slipping it on, I inhaled deeply, taking in her scent, which lingered on the cotton, and relived last night.

Yes, this was the right decision.

I marched to my closet, placing a pair of grey dress pants, a white crisp shirt, a tie, and a suit jacket into a garment bag. Then I picked up the keys I had dropped on the floor and rushed to the living room.

"Where're you going?" Trey blocked my path to the door. "Don't you have that big meeting this morning?"

I narrowed my eyes at him, not wanting the reminder. "I need to talk to Kendy first."

I maneuvered past him, but he grabbed my arm. "Whoa! Listen, calm down. What happened last night, bro? What's going on between you guys?"

I swallowed hard. "I love her," I said, my voice

breaking. "I want to make sure we're okay."

He nodded slowly then placed one hand on my shoulder and stepped out of my path. "Go then. Go get your girl."

My girl . . .

Was she? I didn't know.

I gave him a sad smile and rushed out. I only had a little over an hour to get to her and make my meeting. Time was ticking away.

I SLAMMED THE door behind me, stepped into the apartment, and undid my tie with one hand. "Fuck!"

This had to be the worst day I'd had in a long ass time. The biggest deal of my career had gone down the drain, because my head had not been in the game. I had gone to her apartment and . . . nothing. She hadn't answered her phone, or the door when I incessantly pounded against it for over thirty minutes.

When I arrived at work, everyone was already in the boardroom, including our prospect. Disoriented, I'd started off on the wrong foot and dropped the ball. I'd been unable to answer questions like I normally did. My pitch and my normal confidence had not been there. All because my mind was focused on her.

"We'll get back to you." Their words.

Clearly, my manager had expected a different outcome.

I'd staggered out of the office, embarrassed to face the team. Then I'd gritted my teeth, sensing any semblance of control on my life slipping through my fingers.

Any chance I had of getting promoted this year had

gone down the drain with my horrible presentation.

I dropped against the couch, resting my elbows against my knees. Running one hand down my face, I exhaled an exaggerated breath.

What the hell? What am I doing with my life?

I let my head fall back against the cushion and stared at the ceiling. All my hard work in the toilet, because of a girl? A girl, who'd left me in the middle of the night. A girl, who wouldn't pick up my calls. A girl, who most likely didn't believe I deserved an explanation.

With both hands, I tugged at the ends of my hair. Life was spiraling out of control, and I was going fucking crazy.

A moment of silence went by, and then my phone rang in my back pocket. I picked up and answered with an angry, "Hello."

"Brian!" My mother's excited voice echoed through the receiver. As much as I loved her, I didn't want to talk to her right now, not when I was in a foul mood. She didn't deserve my wrath.

"Mom." My voice came out harsher than I'd expected it to. I closed my eyes, trying to calm the anger brewing inside me as a long, jagged breath left my mouth. "Sorry," I said, forcing my voice to soften.

"Oh, honey . . . what's wrong?" Her motherly concern echoed through the receiver. It was the same voice she used to soothe me when I was upset.

"Work."

"Oh, Brian, you can't fool me." She sighed. "I carried you for nine months and raised you until you went off to college. Spill it."

And there she was—my mother, the woman who knew all. The one who always knew I was getting sick before I even felt any symptoms. The one who had bandaged all my wounds. Call it a sixth sense or mother's instinct, but there was no way of fooling her.

"Work?" She sighed. "What's my saying?"

I shook my head. She always had one-liners for every situation. Maybe that was where I got it from.

"Honey, are you there?"

"Don't stress; do your best," I droned with a small smile. The tightness in my shoulders lightened as I heard her soft laughter.

"Yes. Do your best, because that's all you can do, and laugh. When in doubt, laugh it out."

And that was how my mother dealt with my rigid father. That was why she looked younger than her years. If only it was that easy.

Her laughter died down, and a second later, her voice turned serious. "Does this go beyond work? I haven't heard you this down in a while. Usually you love hearing from your mother." She tried to use humor to break me, but nothing would alter my mood.

"Mom, let me call you later." I didn't want to take my sour mood out on my sweet mother. I needed time alone, by myself, to work out the mess I'd made of my life.

"Nope. Not until I know what's wrong."

Life had been so much easier in high school. Mom and I had the best of relationships. It was so effortless. She knew all my girl drama and gave me insight on the woman's mind.

I finally let out a long sigh. "It's everything, Mom. I just don't have control of my life anymore. I needed to land this big deal I've been working on for a while, and I blew it. All because my head wasn't in that boardroom. It was on a girl."

"Oh," she let out, her voice full of understanding. "You know why this is, don't you?" Her tone increased in volume, sounding confident. "It's because you, of all your siblings, live with your heart on your sleeve. Everything you do, whether it's football, school, or whatever, you live your life through your heart. In college, you played football hard because you loved the game. Your heart leads your life. Honey, it's one of your greatest qualities. I know you. You weren't in that boardroom because your heart was somewhere else. There's nothing wrong with that."

I sighed, both wanting and not wanting to believe her. Maybe I did live through my heart, by my heart. I let my heart rule me. Was that a safe way to live, though? Probably not, but I wasn't going for safe, was I?

It took less than one second to get the answer—hell, no, I didn't want to play it safe. I wanted Kendy.

I closed my eyes and pictured Kendy's beautiful face against the darkness. Her stark blue eyes piercing me, touching my soul.

"Ma . . ." My voice was barely a whisper. "What am I gonna do?"

"Work will always be there," she said tenderly. "But you're going to do what you've always done. You're going to follow your heart."

She made it sound so simple.

Was it?

Chapter Eighteen

KENDY

BRIAN HAD TEXTED and called, his voicemails turning from sweet to solemn. I didn't respond to anything. I wasn't one to avoid confrontation . . . but with him, I wanted to avoid conflict like it was my deathbed.

I had called my mother back, congratulating her on her engagement, but I was mad that my past was even preventing me from being genuinely happy for my own mother. I cursed my history for leaking into the present and taking this moment from me.

My only saving grace, other than sitting in my apartment and hating myself for being a total bitch, was that I had to work. For the next three days, I'd be working my twelve-hour shifts.

I debated texting him that I had to work, but it would mean he'd have hope for after work.

Strolling the ER floor in a daze, I checked into the nurses' station, got my list of patients, and started to make my rounds. About three hours in, I strolled to the coffee machine, needing the extra jolt of caffeine tonight, especially since I hadn't slept well after leaving Brian's place.

Leaning against the counter, I rubbed my temple with two fingers, attempting to ward off an oncoming headache. I could already feel the beginning throbs at my temples.

I didn't get headaches often, only in high stress situations, and this would definitely be classified as high freaking stress.

When I peered up, Sarah was strolling in, smirking like she'd won the lotto. She stopped in front of me, but her cheery self didn't affect my mood. Happiness was contagious, but not with all the confusion reigning over my life.

"Guess what?" she said, her voice peppy and bright.

I squinted up at her, because opening my eyes at full mast only intensified my oncoming migraine.

"What?" I asked, rubbing my temple like I could imprint my fingerprints onto my brain and force the throbbing to cease.

"I heard rumblings that a certain someone is going to ask you out." She practically bounced on her toes, while nausea crept up my throat at the thought.

I'd heard that one before. I gave her a dubious expression, as if saying, 'So?'

I should've been excited, over the freaking moon about it. Finally, after weeks of pining after James, I'd caught his attention, but my thoughts were constantly on Brian. He was the one who occupied my head and my heart, and I doubted I would get over what had happened so easily.

"I thought you'd be happier to hear my news report. What's wrong with you?" She quirked an eyebrow, taking in my hunched posture.

"Well, there's kind of a party going on in my brain. These little drummer boys are in competition with who can be the loudest."

"Cheer up." She bumped her shoulder against mine. "Your Dr. Hot Pants is on the market," she swooned. "And I'm pretty positive you're next on his list."

"That's great," I said with no inflection in my voice.

She angled toward me as if there was some big secret that no one should know about, which was odd, because there was no one in our vicinity. "He's interested in you," she said with a sly grin. "I'm so sure."

"What do you mean?"

"He asked if you were seeing someone and I specifically told him no. You were free as a bird, ready to fly and soar and get married. I told him you were sweet as pie and talked you up," she squealed, her eyes brightening. "He's been asking about you nonstop."

I pressed my thumbs harder to my temple. Her pitch was only intensifying the pounding, so I shut her out. She kept talking and talking, but I didn't hear anything. I only saw Brian in my head. Brian's smile. His blue eyes staring down at me.

Sarah snapped her fingers in front of my face. "Hello. Earth to Kendall. Are you listening to me? He's going to ask you out."

I dropped my head, focusing on the floor. The little drummer boy pounding in my brain was turning into a Marine firing a machine gun.

What was wrong with me? This was what I had wanted. This was what I had planned out, what the psychic had predicted. The answer was laid out in front of me, clear as day. So why was I so conflicted?

There was an emptiness in the pit of my belly, and I knew it had everything to do with Brian. I raised my head and squinted up at her. "I don't know what I want anymore." My voice was soft as the truth finally leaked out.

Her mouth flew open, wide enough for a fly to pass through. "What do you mean?"

I shrugged, shocking myself with what I was about to say. "I'm just not sure if he's it anymore."

Sarah stalked to the other side of me and filled up a cup with water. She pushed the Styrofoam toward my face and held out a Tylenol she'd dug from her pocket. "Take it. I think your headache is interfering with your ability to think clearly."

I did as I was told because I needed the headache gone, but that wasn't what was hindering my thinking. Not all of it, anyway.

"James Klein, the hottest man in the universe, who also happens to be a doctor, is going to ask you out." She tilted in, her face stern. "Don't make my efforts go to waste."

I reeled back, wondering how sweet Sarah had been replaced with this pushy chick from Jersey.

But her face softened a moment later. "I'm just saying." She placed her hand on top of my arm. "You asked me to help you land him, right? Well, here I am, helping you. He's doing rounds around ten. Just do what you regularly do. I'm sure he'll be excited to see you. It's perfect."

I didn't answer her. All I wanted to do was go home and sleep, forget about all the chaos ringing through my head and in my heart.

"He gave you the moon, remember?" she whispered conspiratorially. "Your soul mate, as that psychic once put it."

All I could do was nod. Before, all I had wanted, all I had wished for, was a chance with him, and it looked like I was going to get it.

But did I want it?

IT WAS A slow night. Not a lot of patients with broken arms or gunshot wounds. Not that I was hoping for either, but I needed something to keep my mind off of things, and blood always seemed to help occupy me.

I watched James pace back and forth around the nurses' station. It was as if he was purposely trying to get my attention. In normal circumstances, I'd be up and out of my seat, giddy at the thought of him noticing me. At one time, I would've craved any bit of attention he would throw my way. Now I felt blasé about it. I didn't care anymore.

I sat in the chair, rested my elbows at the edge of the desk, and stared blankly at my computer screen. I was bored out of my mind as I waited for my next patient. When James finally approached the desk, I smiled up at him, feeling polite but nothing else.

It was funny. Odd. Almost freaky. Just a couple weeks ago, I'd been like a teenage girl with butterflies whenever he was around. I groaned internally at the irony of my life.

I wished I could just get this over with, fast forward five years to see where I'd be. I wanted to confirm I'd be as happy with him as Evangeline had predicted because with all that Beth had said about futures changing and all my feelings for Brian bubbling to the surface, I had major doubts.

I looked away from his hopeful grin. If he was going to ask me out, let him do it. If not, I vowed to remain celibate with my vibrator for life. No complications. No expectations. Me and my energizer bunny, that never told me he was tired, unless the batteries ran out.

When James walked away, I huffed out a sigh and went back to my computer screen, charting my last patient. After ten minutes, I headed to the coffee machine. I felt his presence behind me before I even turned around. When I moved to face him, he threw me his winning smile, the one that used to make my heart pitter-patter and my knees go wobbly.

But as I stared up at him, I started to notice everything Brian had pointed out, things I had never spotted before because I was too infatuated with a guy I hardly knew, a guy I had put up on a pedestal.

He awkwardly rested his hip against the counter where the coffee machine was stationed, not at all suave. He looked uncomfortable—stiff. Just thinking of that word made me laugh internally.

"Slow night," he remarked with a forced coolness that made me believe he'd never once been cool.

Disappointment seeped into me. It was hard to believe that, not so long ago, I'd thought he was the epitome of the perfect man. But he was only a character I'd made up in my head.

His eyes roamed my face then drifted to the curvature of my breasts. If this had happened even last week, his look alone would've probably given me goose bumps. But it didn't today. Slowly, I crossed my arms over my chest so he'd stop undressing me with his eyes. My boobs weren't his to look at.

"Dr. Chan is already down here. I'm wondering if I should go home," he said, his eyes still on my chest.

Rude much?

I didn't answer. Instead, I just closed my eyes and let his voice wash over me. I pictured us buck naked, doing it like rabbits as I had imagined so many times before.

"Hey," he said, "I was thinking maybe we could go out to dinner. Me and you. On a date. I checked your schedule and we're both free Friday night."

A date?

Brian's face popped into my mind, and my mouth went dry. I felt sick.

When I opened my eyes, I forced a smile for his benefit and mentally cursed Brian for ruining something that was supposed to be perfect.

This was Karma biting me in my sweet ass because every time I closed my eyes, I knew he was the only man I'd see.

Being with Brian had ruined me for eternity.

FOR FOUR DAYS, I avoided Brian's calls and texts like a dark alley in the ghetto. It felt like an eternity since we'd seen each other, and I was willing to keep that going. It would be easier to pretend we never happened.

All was going as planned until Thursday night, when I walked up to my apartment and saw him in front of my door.

He was hunched over, sitting on the floor. His legs were stretched out in front of him, his Cubs hat drawn low, so I couldn't see his eyes. I stopped moving as a flood of emotions engulfed me, a dizzying current racing through my veins. Damn, I'd missed him.

There was no denying it as my heart raced in my chest. There was this pull, this energy forcing me toward him. It took all my self-control, all my power, to remain a few steps away.

When he saw me, he pushed himself off the floor. "Hey," he said as he lifted his cap.

"Hey," I replied softly.

He pointed to a traveler's mug on the floor. "Hot cocoa," he murmured. "Since you missed the opportunity to taste it the other night . . . I tried to perfect it at home."

I swallowed hard and bit the inside of my cheek.

How much more perfect can this guy get?

When our eyes locked, there was such sadness in the span of blue looking down at me, and I knew I was the bitch who'd put it there. It hadn't been intentional. The last thing I ever wanted to do was hurt him.

When he stepped forward, I took a step back. The hurt in his eyes intensified, and my gaze dropped to the floor as a nauseating feeling of despair began to take over. I couldn't bear to see all the pain I'd caused him without breaking down myself.

When he reached for me, I pulled away, putting even more distance between us. If he touched me, I'd cave. I'd lose all resolve, and I wasn't sure I could give myself to him, lose myself completely.

"We need to talk," he said firmly.

I nodded once and inserted my key in the door before stepping inside. He followed right behind me. I dropped my purse on the floor, fidgeted with the edge of my scrubs, and backed up against the wall. All my defenses were up because I was scared shitless.

Right now, I needed an absolute guarantee that our story would end happily, and Brian couldn't give me that. I couldn't stand another heartbreak. My breakup with Cole had severed my heart and tore me down. I wouldn't be able to live through another failed relationship again. Would I even be able to trust Brian completely after all I'd been through? That wasn't fair to Brian, either. Brian was no Cole, but how could I overcome this?

All I knew was I had to protect my heart, the beating organ, which pumped life into every vital part of my body. If I couldn't protect my own self, who would?

I crossed my arms over my chest, placing another barrier between us. My lip quivered as I forced up the shield I was so used to.

He approached me, but I couldn't retreat any farther. I was already backed against the wall. His presence blanketed me and bombarded my senses, which only reminded me how much I longed for him.

He was a foot away now, and my fingers twitched at my sides, yearning to touch him. With one more step, he closed the gap between us and cupped the side of my face. Heat spread through my body, and I didn't pull away this time because I wanted to feel his hands on me. Though I knew it would only be temporary and painful when it was over, I'd deal with that later, because I needed the now so much more.

I was a puddle of mush against his touch, the shield crashing down. My self-control slipped. I was losing the inner battle between my heart and my mind. With his other hand, he reached for my arm, forcing me to uncross them as he stepped into me.

Emotions rushed to the surface as my breathing became labored. He frightened me beyond belief. I'd never felt so vulnerable, like I could crumble between his fingertips. Problem was, I yearned for him so badly, and there was nothing I could do to stop my heart from wanting what it wanted.

I rested my cheek in his hand as exhaustion hit. For once, I wished I could relinquish control of a life I used to be so sure of. And I wanted Brian to take the lead.

But then my jaw tensed as my messed up thoughts brought me back to Cole, the way I'd let him in, let myself become vulnerable, and, ultimately, he'd broken me. My father and Cole had crushed any semblance of hope I'd had in any other man.

Brian made me feel the way Cole did, but worse. I felt naked in front of him, even when I was fully clothed. He could see the damaged me, not just the spunky, fun Kendy, but he'd also seen all my broken pieces. He knew my past about my father, and about my tormented, violent history with Cole, and yet . . . he was here, with me.

He ran his thumb lightly down my cheek, and I tilted into his palm. Being this close to him was a living contradiction. There was a direct pull between my brain and my heart. My heart melted at the look in his eyes, yet I was torn, knowing I needed to stay away.

He pulled me into him, and I let him, again.

Because I was weak, and he was my kryptonite.

He lifted my chin, his eyes telling me all I needed to know. I swallowed, heat forming behind my eyes. I wanted to tell him he frightened me, that what was happening between us scared the shit out of me, but I didn't, because I was on the verge of tears.

He bent down and kissed my lips, so softly, so sweetly, as though he was breathing all his emotions into me, then he pulled back. "I love you," he said with so much intensity all his sincerity poured into those three words.

And then it was over.

I broke down in front of him. Big, fat tears spilled down my cheeks. I hadn't cried in front of anyone other than Beth before, but I couldn't seem to stop.

I trembled in his arms, but his hold only tightened as

he rested his forehead against mine. He knew I was shattering. "I know you're scared, but I'm never going to hurt you. I promise."

I wanted to believe him. For once, I wanted to believe and put my trust in a man and know he wouldn't fail me.

"I'm not him," he said, his voice filled with emotion. "I want to be with you. I love you, baby. Don't push me away. Please let me in."

I wanted to. I wanted to so badly. Why was it so damn hard?

"Look at me, Kendy."

When I opened my eyes, I could see his heart in the blue of his eyes.

"The best thing about this—about us—is falling," he whispered. "Fall back, baby, and know I'm never going to let you hit the ground." He wiped my tears with his thumbs. "I want you to pick me. I want to take care of you, be your *'it'* guy. If you want the moon, I'll give you the moon. I'll give you twenty fucking moons, if that's what you want," he said lightly, even though the moment was serious. "Your psychic predicted he'd give you the moon, but I'd give you the moon, the stars, the universe, and everything in it. Everything you want. I want to be the man to give it to you."

It was all too much. Me crying, his words, his presence. I swiped at my cheeks, trying to dry my tears. I tried moving away from him, but he reached for my hand, stilling me in my spot.

His jaw was set, his mind made up. "This is where everything changes. Where I make it change. In this story, the good guy doesn't finish last. This is where he gets the girl he wants, the one he's in love with. I'm not walking away this time. Not when you're it for me."

I sniffled and took a deep breath, searching his face. My feet were on solid ground, yet I felt unsteady. Brian had done this to me, just by being himself. He'd broken down my defenses, made me feel helpless, uncovered, and susceptible to anything.

All I wanted was to be whole, to know I'd be happy and in love, with four children and grandbabies for my mama.

Sarah's words rang loudly in my head. Once again, my stomach sunk to the floor when thoughts of the commitment I'd made to James tomorrow resurfaced. How did I know this other guy wasn't it? All I wanted was a chance with James, and now that I had it, I no longer wanted it.

It slipped out before I could bite it back. "I have a date with James tomorrow."

The hope on his face disintegrated as he clenched his jaw. "Tell me you feel nothing. Right now. Tell me you don't feel what I feel between us."

It was a challenge. He knew. He could see it in my eyes, feel it in the way I couldn't turn away from him.

My mouth went dry, and I looked away. "I don't have feelings for you." My voice came out strong. Not just because I wanted him to believe me, but because *I* wanted to believe me. It would be easier on both of us.

"Bullshit!" he snapped.

I raised my chin and squared my shoulders as the fight rose within me. It was a mechanism I knew so well. It was how I was built and what I did when I didn't want to face the truth.

"I don't have feelings for you." This time, my voice was even firmer. I faked confidence as though I'd been born a liar, my eyes locked on his, not backing down.

A pained expression crossed his face as he stumbled back, like I'd sucker punched him. I watched as hurt seeped out of every wilting part of him, and through the reflection in his eyes, I could see the bitch I truly was, jutting out my chin and stubbornly moving away.

"Don't do this, Kendy." The way his voice broke, half commanding me, tore at my insides.

I knew I was hurting him, but this was better for both of us. I clenched my jaw to prevent any emotions from coming to the surface, though a sensation of intense desolation swept over me.

If I didn't rein this in now, I'd lose. I couldn't afford to be weak, not in front of him, though inside I was dying.

I swallowed and spoke firmly. "You're the one who changed the game. This was not how it was supposed to be."

He reeled back. "Why does everything have to be a game for you?" His voice turned harsh.

"Because it is!" I shouted. My body trembled as I tried to maintain composure. "We agreed. You never told me you wanted anything different."

"Kendy, things happened. Things changed. For me, at least." He lowered his voice to barely a whisper. "I thought you felt something."

"Yeah. Orgasms." A suffocating sensation tightened around my throat as those words left my mouth. It was mean, but it was all I had left.

He shook his head, shuffling back another step. "No. Something more, something real." A shudder left his body as he drew in a sharp breath.

I crossed my arms in front of me and stared at him like he was the stupid one, the only one who had felt our connection. Maybe I was a better liar than I thought.

I held my breath, counting seconds for what seemed like an eternity as he stared at me, hoping I'd take back what I just said, but I was stronger than that. I've had eight years of practice to toughen up my skin.

The mask was in place as I fixed my eyes on him. But slowly, my insides crumbled as I witnessed his eyes drop to the ground, all hope in them crushed.

"You're right. You made the rules, and I decided to play the game. I get it." His voice turned cold, disconnected. "I should've known that when you break the rules, you get burned."

"Bry," I whispered.

I wanted to say I was sorry. I wanted to tell him this was the last thing I'd meant to happen. I wanted to tell him *this* was as much for him as it was for me, that he didn't deserve a messed up, broken woman afraid of her own future. My traitorous feet wanted to move toward him, but I knew I shouldn't. That would've brought me back to square one.

His tone was rough as he said, "If you go out with Stiff, I don't want to see you. Ever. I walk out that door, and it's going to be forever. You hear me?"

His voice was cold, lashing, as his eyes met mine, not breaking contact. An inkling of hope passed through his eyes, as if he thought I might change my mind in the next two seconds, but as I straightened my stance, not letting any weakness show, that glimmer diminished, his eyes turning hard.

"Good bye, Kendall." He nodded once and stepped out the door.

I stared at the empty space and my open door as my tears betrayed me, falling to my cheeks. The tough girl act had left with Brian . . . when he walked out my door and out of my life. The sinking anguish caused me to stumble and slide to the floor. My head fell into my hands as I let the vulnerable girl cry it all out, alone.

Trapped in my own lie, I was defeated.

Chapter Nineteen

BRIAN

I STEPPED INTO the condo and dropped my laptop bag to the floor. I was functioning like a walking zombie lately, not speaking, not socializing, just going through the motions, typing at my computer, and answering only when spoken to at work.

In the end, Tiggins Corporation had decided to drop their current bank and move over to Financial State. My manager was ecstatic. When he'd heard of the news, he'd slapped me on the back and sang my praises. I was now a shoo-in for that promotion, and everyone was raving about this great win for the bank. Funny how that worked. Weeks ago, this had been all I'd wanted, to land the account and be the big shot. Now there was not an ounce of me that was excited because work wasn't as important to me anymore.

I'd fallen in love, but the girl didn't want me. Instead, she wanted a boring, emotionless prick, who happened to be a rich doctor and the predicted love of her fucking life. Anger choked me, and the more I thought of it, the more I wanted to put my fist through the damn wall.

Whatever.

I did wish her happiness, even if I hated the asshole.

Part of me felt guilty for hating him, since I didn't technically know him, but just the fact that he thought he could have a great girl like Kendy made my face go all red-hot with fury as a seething type of resentment kept eating me up.

I rubbed my brow, feeling a massive headache coming on. Fuck my fucking life. I stalked toward the fridge and reached for my cold beverage of choice then staggered to the couch and turned on the television.

My hands wrapped around the cold beer bottle as I stared at the TV screen, seeing nothing. Good. That's how I wanted to feel. Maybe mindless TV would help. At least until I was butt ass drunk and passed the hell out.

MY ASS HURT, and I shifted on the couch. Shit. I tipped my head back and drank my fourth beer. My stomach growled for the tenth time, but I'd decided an hour ago I'd get drunk faster if I didn't eat. The last time I'd eaten was lunch. Still, I needed to numb this dull pang in the center of my chest. It'd only been a few days, and I was sick and tired of being in pain. Being in love fucking hurt. Someone should put that on a billboard, instead of the cheesy shit they always advertised.

I turned up the volume of the TV, raising it to full blast. The bass echoed what the announcer was saying, shaking the coffee table in front of me.

When the door opened, Trey walked through with his work out bag slung over his shoulder. One look at my sorry ass and he dropped the grey backpack on the floor, strolled to the fridge, and grabbed a beer.

I didn't even offer a hello as my gaze flipped back to

the TV. If he even said her name, I'd mention Katelynn to shut him up. I couldn't talk about her. Not now. It was too fresh.

The couch cushion indented beside me, and he rested his beer on the coffee table. "Wanna talk about it?"

"Nope." I reached for my fifth beer and pounded it back. The alcohol should've warmed me up, but the cold, dull pain was still very present in the center of my chest.

When I thought of Stiff and Kendy on their date, I couldn't deal. Picturing his hands on her had my arms tensing and the veins in my forearms bulging. I gripped the beer bottle in a tight vise, having a sudden urge to break the glass just to feel physical pain. That would be less excruciating than this unbearable ache. But then I pictured cleaning it up and thought better of it.

Always the responsible one. Yep, that was me. Maybe that was why Kendy didn't want me. Nice guys finished last, after all.

Trey snatched the remote beside me and lowered the volume. From my periphery, I could feel him burning a hole in the side of my face. When I paid him no attention, he reclined against the cushions as we both pretended to watch TV.

"I don't know if I can handle seeing your sister."

I closed my eyes and let out a jagged sigh. He never mentioned my sister. This was his way of forcing me to open up.

"I made her hot cocoa," I muttered, trying to change the subject, or maybe I was just rambling now, " . . . left my stupid mug there."

He frowned, probably wondering where this was headed and what a damn drink had to do with anything.

I sighed again, not wanting to explain, and then

I found the words spewing out anyway. "Hot cocoa reminds her of home, and I thought maybe . . . I could be her home in New York."

I shook my head and felt the anger rising again, my face getting hot. "I'm so fucking stupid. I was going to win over a girl with hot chocolate." I kicked the coffee table in front of me, causing the empty beer bottles to tip over. "Why couldn't I just fucking follow the rules? I had it good. What guy falls for the 'no strings' girl?" Unable to keep my OCD in check, even drunk, I reached for the empty bottles and set them upright. "I fucked everything up."

I let my head fall as I rubbed one hand from the base of my neck to the top of my head. "I fell hard for this one, Trey. Harder than I've ever fallen for anyone."

He placed one hand on my shoulder, but didn't say anything. He was just being a good friend.

I glanced up at him, my shoulders slumping. "Get me fucked up. I want to get so messed up that I forget her, everything about her."

I wondered where she was now. With Stiff. I pictured his hands on her, on the base of her neck, kissing the birthmark on her inner thigh.

Fuck!

I hopped up from the couch and started to pace. "I can't deal, man. Every time I picture him touching her, I go ballistic. I want to barge in on their date and stake my claim. She should be mine right now." My voice trailed off as I gripped the ends of my hair. "Dude, let's get wasted. Beer is not going to do it for me."

Trey didn't need to hear any more. He stood and clasped my shoulder with one hand, nodding with understanding. "I'm your man. Let's go forget."

KENDY

THE SCENT OF spices filtered through the room as I sat at the table for two at one of the most upscale restaurants in all of Manhattan. When we'd walked into the fancy Italian restaurant, there had been a line outside the door. Sarah had told me it took months to get a reservation at Italia Restaurant. Normally, I'd be ecstatic to dine at such an upscale restaurant. This place was frequented by the A-listers, for heaven's sake! But not tonight.

James was sitting across from me in black pants and a navy blue button down. His pants were too tight for his ass, but it was like he'd worn them on purpose to showcase his assets. In all the fantasies I'd had about us, I imagined that would've had some sort of effect on me, but I felt nothing.

James continued to talk, but I didn't hear a word he was saying.

The only thing that echoed in my mind was Brian's disappointed face and his harsh words before he'd left. My stomach churned and my heart ached with the same pang that surfaced every time I thought about him.

My hair was done up in a half ponytail. I'd spent an hour making each individual curl stand out. I couldn't believe I'd spent all that time on my hair for this date, for a guy I felt absolutely nothing for.

James laughed, breaking me from my thoughts, and I fake giggled along with him. He could've said he'd pooped in his pants. I had no idea, and honestly, I didn't care, which wasn't fair to him, yet I couldn't break my mood.

The waiter, a taller guy about my age, showed up to take our order. He was looking dapper in his black and white waiter tux, matching all other servers in this fine establishment. "Ma'am, would you like to look over the wine list?"

As I opened the menu, I scanned the posh list written in curlicue. I was startled when James began to order for us. "We would like to order a bottle of Cabernet Sauvignon." He regarded me as though he knew what I wanted then winked.

I smiled, thinking I wanted white wine instead of red tonight, but hey, he asked me on this date, so I was going to go with this.

Still, Brian would've known my wine of choice. Plus, he wouldn't have assumed I wanted red.

Shoving that thought away, I sat straighter. I didn't need to be depressed tonight. I was beginning my life, starting something new. At least, that's what I kept telling myself to justify this date.

The waiter recited the specials of the day and placed the menu down in front of us before leaving us to look over our options. I knew when James had decided on his meal because he closed his menu then started rambling again about work and how much they loved him there. I glanced at his untouched water as he prattled on about other hospitals vying for his attention and wanting him to make a switch.

James was a hand talker. He was giving me whiplash with all the gestures. I had noticed this mannerism in him, but I hadn't realized how over the top it was until tonight.

"I love Manhattan, don't you?" he asked, like he had finally realized he was on a date and should include me in the conversation.

"Yeah," I said, no enthusiasm in my voice. I'd never felt more out of place since I'd moved to New York.

Unfazed by my lack of interest, he just continued on, prattling about his undergrad at Purdue and his residency at UCLA. All I did was smile and nod, sensing a headache coming on. All this crap he was talking about, I already knew, since I'd stalked him at the hospital.

Funny enough, I was glad he didn't engage me in the conversation. It would've taken too much energy on my part.

When the waiter returned, he uncorked the bottle, poured our glasses of wine and set the bottle inside the ice filled bucket. As soon as the deep-colored liquid hit my glass, I grabbed it, almost splashing it on my little black dress. I tipped the glass back and stared at my menu, deciding the salmon special sounded divine. What never failed me was my love for food. My stomach was ready to get my eat on. Although the pastas looked delicious, my heart was set on fish.

"Are you guys ready to order?" The waiter angled in my direction. "Ladies first."

I smiled at him and placed my menu on the table, my stomach already grumbling for the salmon with capers over a bed of vegetables. "I'll take the fish."

After James placed his order for a medium steak, he turned my way.

I forced a smile for both of our benefits. "It's good I'm not on a diet because I'm planning to have dessert after this," I said lightly. I had to get some pleasure from tonight especially since I wasn't going to get any pleasure from him. I knew he wouldn't be going home with me.

"A woman with an appetite. I like it." He offered an

easy smile, though it did nothing to my pulse.

"Thanks," I said, my usual sassy comeback not there.

This date had turned from awkward to plain old weird. Our conversation was stilted, and if I had to rate this date compared to the history of all my dates, I'd rate this top of the list of dry-as-dust boring.

"So, you meeting a ton of people here?" he asked.

"Yeah. I mean, a fair amount. Work keeps me busy, and I've met a couple friends who I hang out with outside of work." Too bad I could count the people I'd really grown attached to on one hand. And now that Brian had left, those friends could now be counted on one finger. Sighing, I looked toward the couple next to us, tired of small talk and feeling sorry for myself.

I was grateful when the waiter interrupted our awkward moment, setting a loaf of bread, parmesan cheese, and olive oil in front of us.

"Enjoy," he said, leaving us alone to our world of weirdness.

I forced my sullen mood to the side, telling myself again that I had decided to go on this date. I'd agreed to have dinner with him. Why couldn't I give him a fair chance?

The psychic had predicted it was him. She said I'd meet him at work, and he'd give me the moon. We'd complete each other, just like in fairy tales.

She'd predicted my life's timeline, spitting it out as the cards laid in front of me. So far, everything had gone as planned. This was the missing piece. He was my missing piece.

He continued to talk about the charitable associations he was affiliated with, which piqued my interest. It seemed as though he devoted a lot of his time at St. Jude's

Hospital, which was very admirable. But after the waiter dropped our dinner off, James started blabbering about how he was such an asset to the hospital, and I started to lose interest. Bored again, I poked my fork through my salmon. His voice was beginning to grate on me.

Looking at his brown eyes, which matched his dark hair, I wondered what our future would hold. Would it always be like this? Him talking about himself and me biting my tongue, which was so unlike me?

"So tell me about your parents," I said, interrupting him mid-sentence.

His eyebrows pulled together, like he was confused. My question was simple enough. At least, I thought so.

"We're estranged," he replied.

A soft gasp escaped me as my eyes widened. Estranged? Why?

Great. Now my babies would only have my mom as grandma.

"Both parents?" I asked, hoping maybe it was just one.

"Yeah." He looked uncomfortable, but I needed to know his background, so I pressed on.

"What happened?"

He shook his head. "Doesn't matter. I'd rather not talk about it. They've been trying to reach out, but I've been way too busy. Plus, we were never that close."

I lifted an eyebrow, trying to read any sadness in his eyes. I saw none. Suddenly, any hope of this date panning out crashed, burned, and died. It was over. A man who didn't appreciate his own parents was a deal breaker. Done.

He continued to talk about himself again, but I tuned him out, not breaking my sullen daze until he asked about

Brian.

"Was that guy I saw you with the other night your boyfriend?" His tone turned lightly suspicious.

I flinched, not sure how to answer. No one had ever asked me to explain my relationship with Brian, even though it had been brief.

"No," I answered and, when that one word left my mouth, the pang in the center of my chest resurfaced.

I wasn't about to divulge how we had been doing the friends with benefits thing, but it had become so much more toward the end. More than I ever imagined it could be.

Well, whatever it had been when we'd started, it was nothing now. We weren't even on talking terms.

"That's good." He looked relieved as he grabbed my hand. "I've had my eye on you for a while."

Oh really? I wanted to ask, but I bit down on my tongue before my smartass mouth started flying off. I wondered if he'd noticed me before he'd left with the girl at the bar. I wondered if he'd noticed me the first time or second time when he'd left with someone else.

"Have you ever had a long term relationship before?" I sassed. "It doesn't seem like you're ready for anything serious."

I hadn't even fazed him. "I'm looking for something serious, but haven't found the right woman yet." His words sounded memorized, and I wondered how many women he'd used this one-liner on. More importantly, how many women had fallen for it?

"But you know, maybe I'm looking at her," he said with a cheesy wink.

I blinked, unable to form words or even give him a reaction. As I stared at him, it hit me, the reality of my life.

How strong I'd thought I was, yet so very afraid. How I had been living according to what had not even happened yet. And staring into James eyes, I knew we could never be. Ever. Not in a million years. Not even when the stars aligned.

If we ended up together, I'd still see Brian as the man, the one who got away. Because Brian owned my heart. There was no way anyone else could have me, because he owned me, had captured my heart in a matter of weeks.

I came to the realization there was reality and there was fantasy. And wanting a life with Dr. Hot Pants—though I didn't think he was so hot, now that I was getting to know him—had been a total fantasy. I'd become so obsessed with the psychic's predictions that I'd been blind to the truth.

And the truth was that I was madly and undeniably in love with someone else—Brian.

I scrunched my eyebrows together and tilted my head, wondering why on earth I'd ever thought I could feel anything for James. I needed to learn from my past, know that I would never let someone else control my life. I needed to live in the present and face my feelings.

As a plan formulated in my mind, a foreign sensation surfaced—hope. I found I suddenly had hope for the future, real promise for the first time in a very long time.

I only hoped that future included Brian.

AT THE END of dinner, we stepped outside into the humid night. A smile ruffled my mouth as I finally realized what I needed to do.

"Are you sure you don't want to stop by my place

for late-night drinks?" His face turned hopeful as he displayed a cheesy grin.

"Yeah, I'm sorry. It's been a long day," I replied politely, though inside I was screaming for freedom from this date so I could forge ahead with my plan.

His face turned sour, but he nodded.

I told him I would take a cab home, making an excuse about being really tired, though I was anything but. My insides were itching to get to the man I was in love with.

James reached for a hug, and I complied. I was glad he didn't try for a goodnight kiss because I would've turned around, and the rejection wouldn't have been cute.

"I had a great night, Kendall."

"Me too." Though James wasn't the guy for me, I wished him the best.

After our weak embrace, we parted ways, and then I glanced at my watch, the dial almost as large as my fist.

Shit. It was ten-thirty. Was it too late to stop by?

Who cares?

The adrenaline spike had me hopping on my toes.

I knew where I needed to be, so I didn't hesitate. I lifted my hand as I waited for a cab, restless and eager. In the back of my mind, fear tried to grab me again, but I shoved it away. I couldn't let fear control me any longer. I'd made the biggest mistake by letting Brian walk away, and I prayed it was not too late to fix it.

THE CAB STOPPED in front of his condo, and my insides surged with energy. An insane grin was fixated on my face as my heart raced in my chest, knowing he was so close and within my reach.

I repeated what I was going to say in my head. I intended to apologize, tell him I had made a mistake, the biggest mistake of my life. I would tell him I regretted everything I had said a couple days ago, and then confess I loved him over and over.

I pictured the scene unfolding like in the movies—me crying, him holding me, us kissing, and then us finally together as a couple, proclaiming our love for each other.

I pressed the up button on the elevator, and I wrung my hands, my heart pitter-pattering so hard in my chest I was worried it would explode. An urge to flee washed over me. It was the same fear I was so familiar with, trying to terrorize me and alter my decision, but I closed my eyes and inhaled a long, calming breath to push all negative thoughts out of my head as the door pinged open.

When I stepped onto his floor, I heard boisterous laughter coming from down the hall. When I turned the corner, I staggered to a halt. Peeking over, I saw Brian and Trey, his roommate, as well as two strange girls congregated in front of the boys' door. There was a blonde hanging all over Brian, and I bit back the bile that crept up my throat. I didn't understand why she was literally hanging on him, when he already looked unsteady. Trey was equally preoccupied with the model-looking brunette blatantly making out with him.

Brian struggled to keep upright, using the frame of the door to keep himself from toppling over.

Was he drunk?

Yes. After a few seconds of watching him, I could clearly see he and Trey were both very much intoxicated, as were their female companions. Where had these girls come from? And how much had Brian had to drink? He couldn't even keep his head up.

The long-legged woman with the shortest skirt pressed herself against Brian's body and kissed his neck. I flinched, as though I'd been hit, a heavy nausea hitting my stomach.

Brian laughed at something she said, and I straightened, ready to stake my claim on him because he belonged to me.

I stepped out from my hiding spot, but they didn't see me as I approached. I narrowed my eyes at the witch as her hands moved up and down the front of Brian's shirt. He was so wasted he probably wouldn't remember her name in the morning. When she went up on tiptoes to kiss him, I'd had enough.

"Brian," I said, stalking toward them.

The expression on his face flipped like a deck of cards—surprise, adoration, and then he hardened and went back to ignoring me.

My stomach dropped to the floor, disappointment flooding my insides. Had I expected anything less? I'd been a total bitch and broken his heart, chewed it up, and spit it out. I didn't deserve to be in his presence, yet here I was.

The blonde eyed me, but she looked away when Brian gave his attention back to her.

Trey immediately disentangled himself from his girl and advanced toward me. "Get out," he commanded.

I clenched my teeth, ignored Trey, and focused on Brian. "We need to talk." I gave the girl a *back away* look, but she rolled her eyes and just inched closer to Brian's side, running her hands along his arms.

I gave her a onceover. She looked weak, too thin, but flaunting it with her little-to-nothing clothing as though thin was in. I could totally take her and her skinny stick figure out.

I came closer, now only a few feet between us. I needed to work for this, and begging was not out of the question. I would fight for him because I was the reason we weren't together. It was my fault. "Please," I said, begging him with my eyes.

His jaw tightened. His eyes were dilated, which told me he'd had too much to drink, but he didn't look away, which gave me a tiny tinge of hope.

My voice quivered as I spoke. "I'm sorry," I said, laying a hand on my racing heart. I didn't care I was allowing them all to see my vulnerability. I didn't care that I looked like a total dumbass. I focused all my attention on him.

"I'm so, so sorry. I just want to talk." I was on the verge of tears. I knew I'd hurt him, and I'd do anything to make it right, to make us right again.

I took a deep breath and just said the words, the ones I should've said the other day, but was too chickenshit and stuck on that last damn prediction to do it. "I love . . . I love you." It wasn't the ideal place to tell him, but he needed to know. And I wasn't ashamed to say it because it was the absolute truth.

For a brief moment, he saw me, and I soaked it in, giving myself hope. But then Trey stepped between us.

He glared at me with burning eyes as his temper flared. "What is your fucking problem? He's had a taste of you; now he's ready to move the fuck on to Brandy over here." He nodded to the blonde still pawing *my* man.

"Brenda," the blonde corrected him.

"Yeah, whatever," Trey muttered with a wave of his hand. "How was your date with the doctor dude? He didn't fulfill your dreams, so you're back here for a real man?"

"That's not it," I insisted, peering over Trey's shoulder to get a glimpse of Brian, but Trey moved to block my view. "Have you ever wished something to be true so badly that you couldn't see anything else? I made a mistake," I confessed, my insides breaking. I needed him to believe me and realize how much I regretted ever turning him away.

"Get out of here," Trey seethed. "He's done with you. You had your chance, and you fucking blew it. Leave."

I tried to move around Trey, but he blocked my view of Brian. I decided to say it anyway. "I'm sorry. For ever hurting you. For ever thinking that anyone could be better for me than you. For thinking that someone else was it . . . when you were standing right in front of me the whole time." I didn't realize I was crying until I felt my cheeks wet from my tears.

When Trey finally moved a little, Brian was looking at me, but his eyes were unreadable. He turned away, as though he couldn't bear to see me cry, and then he uttered the words that shattered me and crushed the hope I had felt just moments ago. "Just go, Kendy." Then he stepped inside his apartment, not bothering to look back as Brenda followed after him.

The color drained from my face as my lungs constricted, making it difficult to breathe, difficult to stand. I fell back against the wall, my legs turning to jelly.

There was no sympathy in Trey's eyes as he followed Brian inside, followed by his girl. When the door shut behind him, both hands flew to my chest as more hot tears coursed down my face. An ache so painful jabbed at my heart.

How could I have been so stupid to let my fears

consume me to the point of pushing Brian away? Now my worst fear had come true. It was too late. I was too late.

I LAY IN bed for hours, a crying, slobbering mess. I'd ruined things, and there was no one to blame but myself. As the light of dawn began to shine over my purple comforter, I pulled the covers closer to my chin, wiping my tears onto the blanket.

I couldn't stop picturing Brian with that girl. It hurt so badly to think of him being with anyone else but me, even though I'd basically thrown him away.

Now I was alone with my pain.

An unbearable ache in the center of my chest spread throughout my limbs. This ache maintained through the evening, only intensifying with every memory of our time spent together. I shut my eyes tightly, but the images of both of them together became more vivid. Bile rose from my stomach to the top of my throat. I felt like hurling last night's dinner all over my bed, but I chewed on my bottom lip and prayed for sleep to come. Maybe sleep would help.

Everything the psychic had said was playing in my head—from my father to my career to moving to New York. From my mother's engagement, and finally to her prediction of my dream guy, the guy who was supposed to mend my broken heart, give me hope about love, life, and my future.

I shook my head, knowing full well that James wasn't it. I should've known all along. I don't know why I hadn't seen it. Maybe before Brian it would've worked out, but now nothing would ever compare to him. No one else could ever come close.

I didn't get it. Maybe Beth was right. Maybe my future had changed.

My mind was a jumbled mess. It was like trying to decipher computer code. All I knew was that I loved Brian. I knew it in my core, the type of love that left you breathless and you wanted it to last forever. The type of love that made my heart race and my palms sweat like I was a teenaged girl. The type of love where he was all that occupied my mind, when I was at work, when I was at home, or wherever I was, and all I craved was his company.

After the sun rose, I gave up on sleep and shifted off the bed. One thing Kendy didn't do was fall down and quit.

I needed to see him, fight for him, fight for our forever. I needed to try again, but not in front of people I didn't know, and not when Brian was half-ass wasted.

But I *was* going to fight for him, just like he'd fought for me.

BRIAN

FOUR TYLENOLS LATER, I still had a major headache. It pounded painfully as I tied up the garbage bag and carried it down the stairs and out into the fresh outdoors. After seeing Kendy last night, I couldn't stomach sleeping with Brenda, even though Kendy had most likely been with Stiff.

Still, I knew having sex with her wouldn't cure the ache, so what was the point? Brenda ended up knocked out on my bed, and I slept on the couch. This morning, I had to wake her up and usher her out so I could really sleep soundly. But sleep never came.

The warm air outside hit my bare chest, and I squinted at the sun above me. The light was intensifying my headache, making my hangover even worse. I trudged over to the dumpster as the stench filtered through my nose, already making my stomach churn. Lifting the lid, I tossed the black garbage bag inside. When I turned around, I had to do a double take.

Kendy?

I was imagining things, probably still half asleep. There was no way she was standing right in front of me, looking like an angel who had fallen from Heaven.

The sunlight shone directly on her, mimicking a halo, but when she spoke and her angelic voice washed over me, I knew I was not dreaming.

KENDY

"HI," I SAID, twisting my hands anxiously in front of me. When I saw his lickable, chiseled abs, my mind flickered to Brenda and him together, and the unbearable pain that he'd been with her resurfaced.

"What're you doing here?" There was bite behind his voice, more now than last night.

"I wanted to talk. Without the audience," I said softly, but loud enough for him to hear.

Every ounce of me wanted to rush toward him, wrap my arms around his middle, and kiss him, start anew today. I'd never wanted anything as badly as I did in that moment.

"Kendy, there's nothing to talk about." His tone was hard, the tightness in his cold stare evident. "You've said all you needed to say." He moved past me, and I took a deep breath, gathering all the courage within me because if he walked away, this would be it for us. The end.

My heart stammered in my chest at an uncontrollably quick pace. "I love you. I love you. I'm so, so, so sorry." My voice leaked such emotion that he stopped mid-step. But he didn't turn around. I wrung my hands together, trying to keep my fingers from trembling further.

Warmth spread behind my eyes, an indication that I'd cry at any moment as the magnitude of how much I needed him hit me. "I didn't sleep with James. Throughout the whole date, I only thought of you." I threw everything out there, all at once, hoping it would make a difference and praying he'd forgive me. Anything to win him back, to make him love me again.

Please say you still love me . . .

Because I'm utterly and irrevocably in love with you.

BRIAN

I TRIED NOT to let what she was saying affect me, but it did. I released a sigh of relief. I didn't know if I could've handled it if she'd slept with him. I couldn't even think about another man touching her without my muscles tensing and imagining beating the douche to a bloody pulp.

I needed to see her face, just so I could drink her in, but I hesitated. I wasn't sure what this meant, but I was tired of putting everything out there for her and getting shut down.

I wanted to turn around but I was so fucking tired of getting hurt over and over again.

KENDY

"I WROTE YOU a poem." His back was still to me, but I kept on. I hated that I couldn't read his face or his reaction. My hands shook as I reached in my purse and pulled out any crumpled piece of paper. I was grasping at straws here, using my last life line as I remembered what he'd said when we were drunk and playing 'I Never'.

Once he stepped away from me, I'd lose him. This was my last chance.

I closed my eyes and inhaled a long, calming breath as my hands began to sweat. "Roses are red. Violets are blue . . . I made a mistake. I love you." I gulped hard, wrinkling the receipt in my tight grip.

I said it with such conviction, such sincerity that, even though the poem was stupid and I had just pulled it out of my ass, he had to know it was sincere.

I held my breath and didn't move a muscle. It seemed as though the silence stretched on forever.

I waited.

And waited.

And waited.

Please, Brian. I need you. Give me a sign that you need me, too.

This time, I didn't want a psychic to tell me anything. I just wanted Brian's reaction, just him. He was all that

299

mattered now. I didn't need anyone else telling me how my life was going to go. I wasn't going to put my faith in someone else's prediction in my future. I already knew how I wanted it to be. And I wanted him.

Just when my heart was about to plummet to the dirty ground, he turned. So slowly, it was almost too painful to take in. But when I saw his face, his blue eyes meeting mine, I released a thankful sigh.

"I'm tired of getting hurt," he said, his jaw tight and his eyes cautious.

"I'm tired of not moving on," I said softly. He was speaking of his past, and I was speaking of mine, too, because that's just what it was, our pasts, not our future.

The tension in his stance lessened as our eyes locked. And as silence built between us, the congestion of the Manhattan noise surrounded us in the empty alley.

I broke the silence. "I'm not going to hurt you anymore, not if I can help it."

We didn't make a move toward each other. I was afraid if I approached him, he'd reject me. My heart was on my sleeve. One more move and it would fall to the ground and shatter.

He stood there for a moment, assessing me. "I want all in," he said. "It's all or nothing with me. I don't share."

I nodded. "All in," I said it with conviction as a glimmer of hope bloomed in my chest. I was still worried that he might change his mind, though, and I contemplated what to say next.

But then I had a brilliant idea. Instead of speaking, I took action. I retreated backward toward the fire escape by the dumpster, and Brian lifted an eyebrow as I pulled the worn steel ladder to the ground. With shaky hands, I took a step up the rungs, and then another. I was a few feet up when I looked back down at him.

I suddenly felt woozy.

Don't look, don't look. Okay. Deep breath.

"What're you doing?" A flash of humor crossed his face. It was the most positive reaction I'd received from him since I'd kicked him out of my apartment, so I welcomed it, feeling lighter already.

"I'm scared," I admitted, taking another step up the ladder and gripping the iron tightly. My white knuckles were a stark contrast against the black flaking iron, rusted from age. "Before you, it was only Cole." I took another shaky step as Brian made his way toward me. I sensed he was afraid my crazy ass might fall and break a leg. If I was being honest, I was more than a little frightened, but I needed to prove a point. "It was a reckless kind of love, twisted. I didn't have control, and I hate feeling out of control. But . . . that's how I feel when I'm with you."

Another step. I was more than three feet from the ground now, and when I registered how far up I was, I hugged the stairs toward me and closed my eyes.

Don't look!

"Are you okay up there?" he asked, worry heavy in his tone.

"Y-yeah. It's just that . . ." I opened my eyes and peered down at him and only him. If I looked past him or below him, I might pass out completely. "After that night, I vowed to always be in control of every relationship I was ever in. With you, I feel like I'm on some crazy roller coaster ride that takes me higher and higher. I'm afraid of that final dip that brings us to the end. You scare me, Brian," I said, the honesty seeping out of my mouth.

A sheen of sweat formed at my brow as anxiety built in me as I noted my distance from the ground. "But I've come to realize I'd rather be on some crazy ride with you than some lazy river with Stiff."

At his tiny smile, I continued, "I wanted to believe that psychic because she told me I would heal. It was the easier route to believe in those predictions than to take control of my own life. But I don't care anymore because I can't stand another day without you." I proceeded up the stairs again, trying my hardest to ignore the ladder shaking around me. When I started to lose my footing, though, I let out a small scream.

Brian's eyes widened. "Kendy, get down," he commanded. He gripped the bottom of the ladder, keeping it steady.

"I'm just letting you know. I'm ready to fall." I shook my head because I made no sense. This was such a stupid idea. *Stupid, stupid!* I took another deep breath. "I've already fallen in love with you, but this is my crazy way of saying . . . I'm ready to enjoy the rush of falling. Letting go of control because that's what love is." My eyes locked with his as I gripped the back of the ladder, facing him. My heart stammered against the cage of my chest. "The question is . . . am I too late? Or are you ready to catch me?"

I held my breath, not looking at the ground, and once again only focusing on his beautiful face.

His smile was blinding, seriously the most magnificent thing I'd ever seen.

And I knew—he was saying yes.

"I was ready to catch you on that very first day," he said, his eyes shining up at me.

I let go of the ladder and balanced on my feet. "I trust you. You're going to catch me. I know." I met his eyes, unwavering and knowing that I could trust this man with my life. But when my gaze flickered to the concrete below me and I realized how high I was, I gripped the ladder again with my clammy hands. "Remember . . . catch me. Because if I bust my eye open and need stitches, James is going to have to mend me up. Do you really want that?"

He let out a boyish, carefree laugh, the one that made my insides tingle. "That'll never, ever happen."

And then I fell.

And he caught me.

And I would've thought it would be like in the movies where I fall and land smoothly in his arms.

But no, not in my story.

I fell in the most unbelievable, awkward position, my elbow jabbing him in the shoulder. He almost dropped me, catching me by one leg as my other leg hit the ground.

Once I could catch my breath, we both laughed, and then he set me on the ground and lifted me again. But this time, it was just like we were on our honeymoon, his arms firmly under my knees.

I wrapped my arms around his neck and grinned. "You caught me," I said breathlessly.

His face turned serious, sweet, and tender, along with his voice. "Was there ever any doubt?"

I peered up at the sky, pretending to think deeply. "Well, I was a little witch to you the other day."

He leaned into me, our foreheads almost touching. "Baby, there's no way in hell I was going to let Stiff work on you . . . not when you're mine."

His. That I was. Forever and ever, if he let me.

I touched his forehead with mine and closed the gap between us.

He kissed my nose and whispered, "The course of true love never did run smooth."

"Shakespeare." I recognized the quote on the coaster he had on his table, the night we'd played 'I never'.

He nodded as a flash of humor crossed his face. "Now, let me see that poem you wrote me."

A blush crept up my cheeks. "Uh . . ."

The teasing amusement was back in his eyes as he let out a carefree laugh.

Busted.

When he pulled back, he asked, "Are you hurt?"

"What?"

"Because I'm about to make you feel a whole lot better." The glint in his eye sent shivers down my spine.

I was smiling so big my cheeks hurt. "Oh, I'm hurt all right." I was picturing the 'better,' and my insides leapt with anticipation. Then our lips connected in the most soul-crushing, body-warming kiss from my 'it' man.

Epilogue

SIX MONTHS LATER

KENDY

THE SMELL OF grease filtered through the air as I bounced on my stool at the Chinese restaurant and waited for Brian to bring us our meals.

"Chicken fried rice for the princess," he said as he placed my food in front of me and sat down opposite me.

When he handed me chopsticks, I glanced at my watch. "Are you going to be late for work?"

He tore through the red paper, opening his chopstick packet, and shook his head. "It's fine. I don't bend the rules often."

Of course not. One of Brian's best qualities was that he was responsible and took his job seriously. Who would have guessed that I would settle down with the good boy? But as I took in his handsome face, I knew I wouldn't have it any other way.

As we both chowed down, my phone rang, and Beth's cheesy face popped right up.

"Hi, girlfriend," I answered.

Brian continued to eat as I chatted with Beth. Ever since I'd told her that we'd made it official, she called daily to get the deets. She was more than excited for me, ecstatic I had finally picked myself a good one.

"You busy?"

"Kind of." I lowered my voice to a sexy tone. "We're just having lunch. Brian had his dessert earlier."

"It's the middle of the day!" she protested, incredulous.

"Please . . ." Sarcasm was heavy in my tone. "Don't tell me you and Kenty Poo don't do the nasty in the middle of the day."

"We're at work," she said primly.

"Your point?" I laughed, knowing they were most likely at it like rabbits being the newlyweds they were.

Brian cocked an eyebrow, and I knew I was being a tad bit rude talking to Beth on his lunch break.

"Let me call you later. I want to spend time with my man before he has to go back to work."

I hung up and Brian lifted an inquiring eyebrow. "Do you tell her everything?"

I smiled sweetly at him. "Of course not. If I did, she'd know she made the wrong choice and want you back."

He shook his head, amused, and picked at my fried rice, grabbing a piece of chicken with his chopstick. "Does it bother you that we had a brief history?" He cocked his head, his face thoughtful. "Because it shouldn't. The reason Beth and I didn't happen was because *we* were supposed to. And maybe if Beth and my paths didn't cross, *ours* wouldn't have. I don't like to think that's even a possibility."

My eyebrows pulled together as I looked down at my food, getting emotional at the thought. I didn't want to think of us not being together, either.

It wasn't like I was insecure about our relationship. Brian had never given me a reason to feel like I wasn't enough for him. Still, I couldn't help but sigh inwardly with relief that I was it for him and that he had no regrets.

I set my chopsticks down and rested my hand on his forearm. "I don't care that you shared spit with my best friend because you and I have shared more important bodily liquids, and I've already told her that."

Mouth still full of food, Brian coughed, choking back laughter while pounding on his chest. He picked up his water to wash his food down. "Baby, you're crazy sometimes."

"As if you didn't know that already," I joked, laughing along with him.

"Oh, I did." He inched in closer, his eyes twinkling with mischief. "And that's one of the reasons why I love you. That, and you have the Power of the—"

"Hey," I said, slapping his shoulder.

"—of a princess," he finished, silencing me with his lips.

My insides swooned.

I'm his princess.

He focused at the overhead clock against the wall. "I need to get back, but I need me one of those." He pointed to the table next to us.

I looked at the pastry the couple was chowing down on. It was round with a light reddish center.

"I'll be back." He stood, placed the order at the counter, and then came back to our table. "I have to go, but I'll see you tonight." He kissed me on the lips, long and lingering, but not long enough for me. "They'll bring out some of those Chinese cakes I got for you. Save me one for tonight. I love you," he said, smiling at me.

My stomach dropped with disappointment. I wasn't ready for him to leave. I stuck out my lower lip in a full-on Kendy pout. "Can't you play hookie, just for to-day?" Somewhere along the way, I had turned into one of those girlfriends who wanted to hang on her boyfriend all day and night long. And I wasn't a damn bit ashamed or self-conscious about it.

He never seemed bothered by it, either. His mouth curved up in a beaming smile. "If I don't go to work, how can I afford that Tiffany ring you want?"

Tiffany ring?

Tiffany ring!

My heart stammered in my chest. For a moment, I thought I'd heard him wrong, but his smile widened. I blinked and tried to keep my face even, but I was failing miserably as a humongous grin swept up my face. So big it made my cheeks hurt.

I pushed my finger into my cheek where a dimple would be if I had one. "Okay," I said, bringing my shoulders to my ears, playing shy.

"I love you," he said again. "And I really have to go."

My heart swelled to double its size. "I love you, too," I said softly, while the couple next to us observed our display of affection.

As he walked away, I sighed, realizing we had turned into 'that' couple. The one that made out in public, was overly touchy, and way, way too affectionate. We'd turned into the couple that disregarded what everyone thought. The corny duo that would eventually wear matching out-fits and walk with our hands tucked into the back pockets of each other's jeans.

Oh well. I didn't care. I felt utterly complete.

The cute little Asian woman placed a white paper bag in front of me. "This is for you?"

I smiled up at her and gave her my receipt. "Yes,

thank you."

"Two moon cakes," she confirmed.

The paper bag crinkled within my grasp, and as a sudden clarity hit me, I blinked and kept blinking, my mouth dropping open.

She was about to turn away when I reached for her arm. "What did you say?"

She frowned, slowly extracting her arm. "Moon cakes. That's what you ordered, right?" At my utter silence, she said, "Is something wrong? Do you want to change your order?"

The ringing in my ears intensified. *Holy shit.* "What're these?" I asked again, needing her to say it just one more time.

She still seemed confused, so I pulled them out of the bag and pointed to the pastry, which was still warm between my fingertips. "This?"

"Moon Cakes." She was now looking at me like I was crazy and she might call the cops if I didn't leave soon.

I stepped back, in a daze, and gave her a nod. She took that as her permission to skitter away.

Moon cakes . . .

Holy crap, had Brian planned this?

I reached for my purse and rushed out the door. He was probably close to the subway, but I raced back down the route we'd taken to get to the train. The farther I ran, I started to doubt my ability to catch up to him in my heels, and I was a tiny bit afraid that my skirt was going to fly up and people would see my hoo-ha.

I dashed faster down the street, knowing full well that it could be a lost cause, but I just couldn't stop. The white bag swished against my hip, probably giving the moon cakes whiplash.

And then I saw him.

"Brian!" I yelled. When he didn't hear me, I yelled his name about ten more times. Well, more like screeched his name. People were glaring at me like I was a crazy person, which I was fully aware of.

My chest heaved from my unplanned workout. I needed to make an effort to work out more. Sure, I could be the Energizer Bunny in bed, but running was not my thing.

When I saw him stop by the light, I slowed to a fast jog. "Brian!" I yelled louder as a woman in a suit flipped toward me and stared me down. I threw her my 'bitch' look when Brian finally glanced back at me.

Thank God!

His eyebrows pulled together, and he forged through the crowd to get to me. Without explaining, I charged toward him in a full on sprint, and we crashed together. After a few seconds, he pulled me to the side, away from the oncoming traffic. I doubled over, needing a moment to catch my breath.

When I was better, his gentle hands framed my shoulders, his eyes searching my face. "What's wrong?"

"One second," I said, raising a finger, worried I might barf up all my food. Nope, false alarm. But then a blush crept up my cheeks at how overly dramatic I'd just been. I was starting to feel silly, yelling his name down the street like he was in danger or something.

He pulled me closer. "What's the matter?" he asked again. "Did something happen? Are you okay?"

I went up on my tiptoes and kissed his lips to calm him. "No . . . I just . . ." I stuttered, feeling my blush deepen. And then I lifted the white bag. "I got your cakes," I said sheepishly.

He blinked at the bag, confused, then his gaze returned to me. "Baby, are you okay?"

"Yes," I said. I reached into the bag and offered him one. The normally round pastry was flattened from my run.

"Kendy . . ." He still looked worried.

"I'm sorry," I said. "Please don't be mad. I just wanted to give you a cake."

His face softened and he shook his head then he reached for the bag, taking the cake from me. "Thanks, Princess. But I really have to get back to work."

My eyes raked in his handsome face, the sun beating down on him, which only made the blue in his eyes more evident. Such emotion flooded me as I realized where we had started and where we were now.

All that time before, I had been living my life, following the prediction, almost forcing it to come true. And just when I had stopped allowing those predictions to control my life, they came true anyway. It was funny how the world worked.

"I'll walk you to the train," I said, feeling a fluttering in my stomach and a lightness in my heart. The prediction had come true after all, and with the right man—my man, my chosen man.

He nodded and placed the cake back in the white paper bag, careful not to get his hands dirty. Smiling, he locked our fingers together and led us down the block.

"Do you know what they call those cake things?" I asked casually, watching his reaction.

He frowned. "Chinese cake with light reddish filling?"

I dropped my gaze and smiled to myself.

He didn't know. And because he didn't know, it just increased my love for my man, if that was even remotely possible. But a small part of me wondered if he had bought me the cakes to prove a point.

Should I tell him? Not tell him?

I peered up at him through my lashes and decided it didn't matter. He didn't believe in horoscopes or psychics. That was my thing, and it wouldn't change anything anyway. I wasn't letting predictions rule my life. I made my own choices now. To hell with the predictions! He was sure of us without 'all that hocus pocus,' as he would call it.

At the entrance to the subway, I went up on my tiptoes and placed a light kiss on his mouth. "I love you, I love you, I love you," I said as I pecked him sweetly, feeling his smile against my lips.

When he reached to give me my moon cake, I took a bite, but then placed it back in the bag for him to take to work. Because in a way, my way I guess, I wanted to give him the moon right back.

At his questioning glance, I smiled slyly. "I'm watching my calories."

He rolled his eyes then snaked an arm around my waist and bent me backward to really kiss me. "I'll see you tonight, Princess."

"See you tonight," I said seductively.

Then I watched his sexy self take the stairs to the subway, and I sighed. Though I was running my life now, it was still pretty damn cool.

The man had given me the moon.

In the form of food.

And it couldn't have been more perfect.

Newsletter

If you enjoyed this story, please sign up for my newsletter. My newsletter subscribers are the first to know about my upcoming releases and always have a chance to win an advanced copy of my book before it goes live.

Also, you just never know when some of these characters will stop by.

You can sign up at *www.miakayla.blogspot.com*.

Thank You!

Thank you so much for taking the time to read and review The Scheme. Reviews for an author are so important so please leave an honest review on Goodreads and the site where you purchased your copy.

Let's keep in touch! Here's where I'll be hanging out:

www.facebook.com/authormiakayla
www.twitter.com/authormiakayla
www.instagram.com/author_miakayla/
www.goodreads.com/author/show/7382805.Mia_Kayla

And read an excerpt of my novel
Marry Me for Money on the next page

Marry Me for Money

Prologue

THE WOMAN WAS beautiful. She looked like a supermodel ready to walk the runway. The blackest of black eyelashes swept upward, accenting the depths of her emerald eyes. Curls of mahogany sat on top of her head while the apple of her cheeks were highlighted with a slight pink as if the sun had kissed her.

I should have been excited. I should have been anxious.

But as my heartbeat thrashed in my ears, all I felt was dread.

I sat on the stool, staring at the girl in the mirror. I wondered who this girl was. I wondered where the old girl had gone and how I could get her back. The problem was I couldn't. The lie was so deep, the charade so long that there was nowhere else to go, but to move forward.

It was an out-of-body experience as the chaos of the

circus around me was happening. I hardly noticed the woman in front of me as she swished her little brush of pink gloss on my pouty lips.

Everybody was getting ready for the big day.

My big day.

Four photographers were scattered around the room, catching every moment and every detail from the shoes to the invitation to the flowers.

Orchids.

Orchids didn't give off a scent like every other flower. Too much water would drown them. Not enough sunlight would kill them. They were useless and high maintenance.

So, when the florist had asked me what kind of flowers I would like for my bouquet, I'd said, "Orchids."

It was the flower I despised the most. It wasn't because of its lack of beauty or its uselessness, but I didn't want anything that I would pick for my real day.

The photographers moved to the king-sized bed, and they snapped pictures of the regal designer wedding gown. This was another thing I never would have picked for myself. I remembered my last fitting. I had barely squeezed into the strapless couture dress. I would never choose a dress that I couldn't walk, dance, or eat in. I hated it, and that was the reason I'd picked it.

My stomach growled from starvation. I had no appetite the night before, and today Kendy, my maid of honor, wouldn't allow me to eat. It was so unlike her. I guessed it was for my benefit because I could barely fit into my dress. Either way, my stomach was eating itself because it had nothing else to feed off of.

The time went by slowly as if it were dragging on purpose to punish me for living the biggest lie of my life.

Everyone always said their wedding day had flown by. This day was killing me, killing me softly and slowly.

All I wanted was for it to be over, but the day had just begun.

I took a deep breath and closed my eyes. *If I can only get through this day . . . this one day . . .*

I just needed to get through today.

Pick up your copy of Marry Me for Money today!

Acknowledgments

MY BOOK IS done done done. This is my third book out and what I've realized is that no matter what I do, which different paths I take or how I change my process, writing a book never gets easier. And after this third book, I realize that maybe it never will. I will still whine to my writing buddies, cry when no one is looking and edit my manuscript over and over until I can't see straight anymore.

But at the end of the day it's worth it to me and to my readers.

My process is long and heart wrenching. Even when I'm done editing, I look at my manuscript and think it's utter crap, but I've created characters I absolutely love and I hope I did their story justice.

When they said it takes an army, they weren't kidding! Without further ado, I want to thank the following people for helping me make this manuscript shine.

To Michelle Lynn-thank you so much for reading Brian at the very beginning. I look up to you as an author and am so blessed that you are my friend through this crazy ride.

Angela-my developmental editor-aka the Character Whisperer. Thank you so much for calming me during my freak-out moments, helping me cut out repetition from my manuscript and making me dig deep with these characters. Your advice and friendship throughout this whole process has been amazing. Thank you! Thank you! Thank you!

Megan—my awesome copy editor!! I heart you like no other. You are my writer from another mother. Does that even make sense? Who cares! Thank you so very much for helping me make Brian and Kendy the best they could be. You are the bestest from the restest and I know we will have a long lasting editor/writer relationship until the end of time.

Becky, Kayla and your team from Hottree editing—you guys rock! Thanks for your patience at my forever lateness and helping me make this manuscript shine bright through your super power proofreading and beta services. You guys offer a service like no other and I'll be singing your praises for years.

To my awesome cover designer—Sommer Stein—I love my covers! That is all. And you're pretty great yourself.

To my patient formatter—Christine, thanks so much for accommodating my lateness and for your talented work. I absolutely love my interior designs and formatting of all my books.

And to my beautiful betas from Hot Tree and beyond—thank you for help, your time and your friendship. Know that I'm forever and ever grateful for all your honest feedback. Melanie, Kristi Lynn, Jennifer Holter, Amy Konczyk, Zsuzsi Teleki, Ashley Jasper, Sarah Clune, Karrie Puskas, Alyssa O'Brien, Brandon Lingao, Kristy Deboer and Roxi Madar —I can't thank you enough.

To Jennifer Holster, my personal awesome assistant, thank you for your help in all my craziness. You helped me get organized when I was going through a very difficult time and I appreciate you.

To my blog tour hosts! Mary from Love Between the Sheets—thank you for all my help with the blitz. You guys are so professional and prompt. I enjoyed working with you and plan to again in the future.

Sarah mother effing Reads—look how far your blog and company has come. Thank you for helping me with my tour, pimping me out on a daily basis, being my sunshine on a gloomy day and for just being you.

To my blogger friends—Short and Sassy Book Blurbs, Between the Spine, Reading in Sarah's Corner, Obsessed with Romance and Southern Vixens Book Obsession and many more that I've missed. Thank you for posting, pimping and for loving the characters I have created and the books that I write. I appreciate you guys so much.

To my readers—there is no me without you! Thank you for taking the time out of your day to escape into this story. I write purely to entertain so if this story made you laugh, cry or even mad at times, I completed my task. No words can describe how grateful I am that I have space on your Kindle, Nook or bookshelf. I'm truly honored.

To Happily Forever

www.ingramcontent.com/pod-product-compliance
Lightning Source LLC
Chambersburg PA
CBHW030021180626
46810CB00001B/143